The Emperor Reversed

Jane Barrie

Before you embark on a journey of revenge, dig two graves.

Confucius

An eye for an eye makes the whole world blind.

Mohandas Gandhi

A man that studieth revenge keeps his own wounds green.

Francis Bacon

Living well is the best revenge.

George Herbert

Part One

Archie

1

I suppose all men are encouraged to think they're superheroes or, at least, they play at being superheroes, try the cloak on for size. Cleaning out the gutters isn't exactly saving Gotham City, but I'm not afraid of heights and it's a necessary annual job, so I usually start it as the last leaves fall. I'm most of the way round when I spot the slipped slate, in the centre just under the weathervane, and I think I'll hop up and take a look, see if I can wedge it back before it slides off completely. As I lever myself off the top rung of the ladder, it crosses my mind that my boots haven't got the best grip for this kind of cusp-of-winter soggy surface. I manage a few steps towards the offending tile, it's maybe seven or eight courses up, when my foot slips and I lurch backwards; I keep my balance though. Just. I jerk back, like a tightrope walker, arms shooting out to stabilise me. 'I've been on this roof hundreds of times,' I think, 'it's no big deal.' Then my other foot slides an inch, then another, quickly, and that's it.

In moments I'm falling backwards and shouting, my hands scrabbling the air. My shoulder catches a flimsy far branch from the silver birch by the back door, but it doesn't slow me down. I smash onto the ground, favouring my left side, shoulder and hip almost together, then thigh, knee. I try, and fail, to save my head. It bounces on the sandstone flags and I blackout.

'Don't touch him.' Karen's voice sounds far away. I feel like I'm holding my breath but then I realise it's the pain which has a grip of me. Terrible, teeth-clenching pain. It's hard to breathe. I try to locate it, the full flat blade of my shoulder and chest, an awful clamping hold at the side of my rib cage. It's hard to open my eyes with it drilling up into my head and down my neck. I wish I was still unconscious.

A light is shining in my eyes and my arm is being tugged. A mask clamps over my face. Oxygen, or gas and air, I can't tell. I drift back into unconsciousness. There are voices. Noises. The pain is smothering me though, overwhelming me, a heavy blanket suffocating me in a body I no longer recognise.

'Dad, you're going in a helicopter, they're taking you soon, very soon.' I sense Joseph's face close to mine, his usually deep, quiet voice, high and loud with tension. Then there's a rigid collar tilting my chin up, hands steadying my skull and more, much more, slicing pain.

'Morphine,' I say but I don't know if the word has left my mouth and many hands lift me and I float into a dream about my boys, Joseph and Edward. We are on holiday, swimming in a calm and brilliantly blue sea. They are boys again and we lie back, outstretched, cradled by the water. I watch their tiny toes floating, tender pinkish outcrops of miniature islands. I smile and close my eyes against the dazzling sun as the ocean laps against me. It is a perfect, peaceful moment. Eventually, I open my eyes and tread water. I scan the sea. My sons are nowhere to be seen and it is getting dark and cold, very cold, and there are waves where the water was calm. In a panic, I dive down over and over into the black water, hunting, reaching out, desperate to find my boys. I know my exhaustion and the cold mean I have to give up the search, so I decide to swim back to the shore, but the beach is nowhere; I am in the middle of the ocean, entirely alone, adrift with the building tides and stronger waves buffeting and bludgeoning me. Then there is darkness.

'I think he can hear us.' It's Joseph again.

'Yes, his eyes flickered. Dad? Dad! Are you awake? We're here. Joseph and me. We're right here,' and Edward, I think, squeezes my hand.

The room is bright, and I squint against it. The bed is high and I'm looking into Edward's face. Unshaven. Tired.

'Finally! Back at last Sleeping Beauty.' He looks away, smiling across the bed, 'Call the nurse Joe,' and there's movement but it's too hard to turn my head to follow the sound.

'Be right back, Dad,' I hear Joseph's voice leaving the room.

I lick my lips. They're dry. My mouth is dry. Or odd in some way. I swallow. 'Where's Mum?' I croak. It's too hard to keep my eyes open. Must be the drugs I think as I drift away and I never hear the reply or if I do, I can't remember what it was.

It's low artificial lighting when I wake again. It must be night. There's a nurse; she's holding my hand. After a moment, she lays it back on the bed and then she's writing on my chart. She's older. In her fifties, close to my age, maybe more. 'Hi,' she says, looking into my face.

I try a smile, a tiny nod.

'You want a sip of water? Some ice chips?' she asks.

I smile again.

She places the tip of a straw in my mouth, and I suck. The water is tepid but good. A few meagre mouthfuls are enough.

'My boys?' I rasp.

'Asleep on the chairs over there,' and I see they are curled and hunched under thin blankets in two easy chairs by the window.

I nod again. As I'm slipping back into sleep, I think I must be hurt pretty badly if I'm in my own room.

Joseph has a breakfast tray. He leans over the bed towards me. 'Do you think you could eat something Dad? I'll have to feed you. Is that okay? There's a little cup of porridge.' To be honest I'm not hungry but I feel less groggy and I'm willing to give it a go.

'What day is it, Joseph?' I'm hopeful I'll stay awake for the answer this time.

'Saturday, Dad. You've been in here nearly a week. There's been two surgeries. You've had a lot of drugs.' Joseph is busying himself with the breakfast.

My arm is in a sling, strapped up across my torso. My chest feels tight, like taking a lungful of air is an impossibility.

'What did I do?' I have morphine on a driver. I press a button when the pain gets too intense, and I get a shot through my IV. A nurse explained it about a half hour ago, maybe not that long, it's hard to tell. I assume the boys, or the staff have been administering it so far. Or maybe they've told me, and I've been managing it myself. My head is muddled, stuffed with fuzz, I feel like I need to give it a good shake. Instinctively, I touch my unstrapped hand to it, and it is bandaged. So, there's a head injury to contend with too.

Joseph is offering a teaspoon of porridge. 'You want some?' He doesn't sound convinced that it's a great idea.

'How bad is my head?' I ask, 'Was that the surgery?'

'Could we let the doctors explain, Dad? I don't want to get things wrong. Is that okay? They'll be here any minute for rounds.'

'Sure. I might as well try the porridge then.' My voice sounds weak and strange to me, slow and hesitant. Joseph is pleased by this reply and feeds me a spoonful. It is terrible though. Sticky and cool, like tacky glue. I refuse the rest.

Edward appears, mobile in hand, 'Dad, you look better! Did you eat? Just been updating Mum.'

'Where is your mother?' I ask again. I can't remember when I last saw her.

'She's at home with Georgie,' Edward pulls a chair up, 'How's the pain Dad? You know you've smashed your shoulder, right?'

'I thought we'd wait for the doctors to go through everything,' Joseph jumps in quickly.

'Has Georgie been in?' I ask.

'Not yet,' Edward has started on the porridge. That boy will eat anything. 'Mum thinks a hospital isn't a great place for a nine-year-old. She's done you a picture though,' and he reaches to the bedside table and there's a big Get Well Soon Daddy drawing with the farmhouse and a sun and the car and the garden.

I smile.

I've sent the boys down to the café. I need some time to process the information the doctors gave me. Not just a broken shoulder and a head injury. No. Much worse. I've broken my back. Fractured my T4 and T5 vertebrae, shearing the spinal cord and the chances of me walking again are realistically none. It's waist down so my arms are okay, so yippee do. I have also fractured three ribs and one of them punctured a lung and another my spleen. They had to remove my spleen and reinflate my lung. Miraculously, my skull is in one piece, just a deep lesion, and no bleeds on the brain. I had internal bleeding from a fractured pelvis hence the two surgeries – marathons to deal with the spleen and pelvis and my spine. They tell me I am lucky to be alive. I don't, at this point, feel that lucky. I could have done with Karen being there when they broke the news. It was hard on the boys.

I look at the shape of my feet under the blanket at the end of the bed. I had a sense that I couldn't feel them, but I didn't want to say the words to the boys. I didn't want to alarm them. If Karen had been there, I'd have told her straight away, made her get some answers. It feels like my body just sort of ends around the bottom of my midriff. I'm like the magician's assistant sawn in half except, of course, I'm still attached. For all intents and purposes though, my legs could be being spun around in a shiny box at the opposite side of the room; they are no longer a part of me.

I have seen TV dramas where paraplegics will themselves to walk again. It begins with a tiny movement of the toe, usually the big one. When I look out of the window and think about my big toe, it could be anywhere. There is absolutely no sensation, no neural pathway fizzing and sparking, nothing that is going to make that piece of meat on the end of my redundant foot move. I believe the doctors when they say it is extremely unlikely I will ever walk again.

As they voiced those words Joseph's eyes filled with tears; he's always been the soft one. Edward looked furious though, kept asking questions which the doctors patiently dealt with, but his underlying message was that they were

11

wrong, they must have made a mistake, the diagnosis was duff. They put him straight and it was implied this had already happened in the days they were waiting for me to wake up properly. Joseph kept trying to soothe him, calm him down but, part of me was with Edward. I wanted everything checked. I wanted them to be sure. Edward, however, was not inhabiting my body; he was not experiencing the absence, the lack, the nothing that was now my legs, my backside, my feet. I could see these body parts, but they were like holograms, insubstantial and disconnected from me.

'I just don't get it. Dad's strong, he runs marathons for God's sake. He doesn't deserve this,' and I thought he might cry which Edward rarely ever does. The doctors didn't stay much longer.

I'd always kept myself in shape, but team sports didn't really interest me. Running was the constant for me. After we moved to the countryside, I cranked it up a gear, the roads were quieter and I could run in the hills, timing myself and keeping a record of distance and improvements. I noticed the change in my body; I was leaner, stronger. Hell, I thought I could conquer the world. Karen suggested I start the marathon training and, at first, I didn't think I'd manage it, but I gave it some thought and plumped for a half marathon.

There was a kid in Joseph's class with some drastic illness or other, and they were fund-raising, and I thought I'll do it for him. I decided on the Great North Run because I'd heard of it. Just over thirteen miles. Karen and the boys went out some nights, knocking on doors in the village looking for sponsors and I drew up a training schedule. It was good to be working towards something and, to be honest, all the running was a little addictive. We all drove over for the race and the feeling of accomplishment crossing that line was intoxicating.

I've lost count of the number of runs I've completed now over the years. It's a big part of family life. I'm pretty much always in training and I've been lucky, so far, and not had many injuries, nothing that's stopped me running for long.

Fourteen years and I've raised a fortune. There was talk I was going to get an MBE, but I don't do it for that. I just like to run.

I guess that's all over now though.

At my request, Joseph brings in a photograph of Georgie to put on my nightstand. I can understand Karen's point of view, I'm still hooked up to machines; there's the bag for the catheter and I have a lot of bruising on one side of my face though the swelling isn't so bad now. I still haven't seen Karen, though Ted told me she was here when I was unconscious in the early days.

They're making arrangements to move me to a specialist rehab spinal unit. It will be even harder for everyone to visit then, it's even further away, especially as I'm the only one in the family who drives.

I get that it's hard for Karen to leave Georgie. When we moved up north, we all had to make sacrifices to secure the house and the land we'd both dreamed of and talked about; we were a bit more remote than was convenient.

'Are you sure about this, Archie?' Karen was standing on the top field, looking back down to the rundown farmhouse in the valley, the sunlight skidding over the dark slate roof as it flashed from behind scudding grey clouds. I could hardly hear her the wind was so strong; the proud metal cockerel on the weathervane on the roof was whirring and spinning. Edward and Joseph were tearing around, thin sticks wavering in clutched, gloved hands, bodies stretching and voices wild at the unexpected freedom of the open ground. There wasn't another house in sight and my heart was thudding. This was a world away from the cramped terrace of the city suburb we were currently housed in and which was a stretch to afford on two teachers' salaries. Yet this beautiful property we could easily afford.

'Where's the nearest shop?' Karen was smiling and looking up at the hills behind her. She looked magnificent, her coat blew open and the wind flattened her shirt against the curve of her breast.

I went to her, put my arm tight round her waist and cupped the fullness and warmth of that gorgeous bosom.

'Who cares about the shops? No one will be able to interrupt us here,' I said and kissed her hard and, for a moment, I wished the boys would run away and play somewhere else so I could tip her down onto the grass and drag off her jeans and we could make love, naked in this ragged, beautiful countryside.

It was a freezing wind though. We laughed as we corralled the boys and headed back down to have another walk back through and around the farmhouse.

A little over two months later, we were unpacking boxes and painting walls, and I was coaxing the central heating into action and calling this unloved place home.

The reality is, there's a twice daily bus service, revolving around a 9 to 5 working day to our nearest town, which is a good ten-minute walk from the house. Because I could drive us to work, Karen never learnt, and the kids were bussed to school too when they didn't come with us. And later, for one reason and another, the boys have never taken to driving either.

So, my sons are coming into the hospital turn and turn about now. Most days. And Karen is staying at home with Georgie, our youngest. Once I'm in rehab, it will be a lot more difficult for them to visit me. It won't just be a simple bus ride away. No. I think they'll have to get a train as well.

I get a visit from the head, Angie. It's odd talking to your boss in your pyjamas. She brings an extravagant fruit basket and a card signed by the staff. The physio has already told me I'm going to have to watch everything I eat from now on; another bonus of life in a wheelchair. Not that I've really done much proper physio. Yet.

Angie perches on the chair next to the bed, she looks anxious but is trying to smile. 'The whole staff are in shock, as are the kids. How are you coping, Archie?' I'm hoping she won't cry. Usually, she's stone cold in just about every situation.

'I've been better,' I smile, 'The drugs help,' and I wink at her. She relaxes a little.

'If there's anything we can do, you just let us know. Not that there probably is anything. The important thing is for you to concentrate on getting better.' And she smiles brightly.

'Just don't give work a thought. We've reassigned your responsibilities between the SLT, and your classes are being covered within the department at the moment.' One of the advantages of being on the Senior Leadership Team is contact time is at a minimum. I co-teach a couple of sixth form classes with the Head of Faculty, Hafiza. In truth she takes the brunt and, as it's maths, there's not much to think about in terms of lesson planning. 'We're interviewing for a supply teacher next week.' To her credit, Angie meets my eye while she says this. We are acknowledging, at the least, a long-term absence here but I know we are also both thinking of the school's three floors and lack of lifts. My office is particularly small and in one of the older buildings, with three small, concrete steps leading down to it. At some point there is going to have be a frank discussion. There's not much hope for a deputy head in a wheelchair is my thinking.

Angie moves on to less precarious chit chat of other trivia, her dog's continued wilful destruction of the fancy solar lights she'd bought for her flower beds and how one of the catering staff has had a baby; it's premature and in the same hospital here. Angie is pondering a visit there too. I begin to wish she would leave; I don't even know who she's talking about. I realise with a horrible thud in my chest I'm unlikely to work again. Tiredness washes over me. I can't help but shut my eyes. When I open them later, the chair is empty.

Karen and I got our posts at Ridge High together, more or less. Two teachers in the south in the nineties with rising interest rates and escalating house prices and you're struggling financially, but in the north, it's a different matter. I was keeping an eye on the *TES* and the jobs were a good fit for both of us, slightly better for me, I admit. Karen was head of department in her old school, and she dropped back down to straight classroom teacher when we made the move but not for long, only for a few years. And it was worth it. Ridge High was small, rural and a dream compared to where we were in the south. We'd both been threatened physically, Karen with a knife, by the toe rags who roamed the corridors, muscles tight with pent up aggression and mouths full of the foul frustration they faced on a daily basis; we had to get out. At Ridge High the class sizes were manageable, attainment was on the up and the deprivation didn't feel overwhelming. It was a school I'd be happy to put my kids through.

'There's not much access to live theatre,' Karen was anxious having had both the West End, the National and Stratford within relatively easy reach before.

'You can always get to Manchester or Newcastle,' I suggested, 'And I bet the ticket prices aren't as expensive.'

As it was, as the boys became older and family was more important, her trips dwindled so it didn't matter where we were. She let others run more of the extra-curricular bits and pieces and stayed at home enjoying bathing the children and reading them their bed-time stories. Her colleagues told her having children would change her incredibly conscientious attitude to teaching but she didn't believe them, until it happened.

'How are the chickens doing?' I ask Joseph. He looks a bit sheepish.

'I didn't get them all in a few nights back, so we lost a few. Sorry, Dad. In fact, I'm not sure who was supposed to shut them up, me or Teddy. Anyway. Sorry.'

'You need a proper rota. You have to be organised. You can't let that sort of thing happen. I've been thinking about the vegetables as well. Has Mum pulled up the last of the veg? There're still carrots in there and runner beans. I don't know if we've had a frost yet, it's hard to tell in here, but they need picking. And I earthed up some potatoes to store in the ground. I think you'd be as well digging them up and storing them in the barn. It was just an experiment but without me there to monitor it, I'd feel happier if you'd just get them out and into sacks along with the rest.'

'Okay, Dad. I don't think Mum's been outside much. Teddy's been doing some decorating and she's been ... re-arranging things for you coming home.' Joseph is maintaining the air of someone who has news he'd rather not impart.

'Decorating?' I say, 'Where has he been decorating? Everything was fine. I don't understand. What's Mum re-arranging?'

'He's painted the dining room, freshened it up,' he says, 'Mum says that's to be your bedroom. Downstairs. Because of ... you know.'

I am puzzled. 'We'll never fit a double bed in there. It's far too narrow. I don't think that's any kind of solution,' I say. The dining room faces north; it's at the front of the house. We hardly use it. It's a gloomy room.

'No. No you're right ... Mum says you're entitled to a hospital bed, and a hoist. She's looked into it. To get you out quicker I think,' he gabbles, 'Do you want a cup of tea, Dad? Think I'll nip down and get one.'

I shake my head and he is thankfully gone before he can see the tear trickle down my cheek.

Karen and I talked about *The Good Life* a lot when we were first dating. I spotted her on the first day of term. The crusty old head always made every new member of staff stand up in the first staff meeting of the academic year and introduce themselves. She was low down the list of new recruits, only been teaching a year I think, but she was gorgeous; a broad, strong jaw and wide mouth that flashed a confident smile, fresh and optimistic. I fancied her straight away. I was a very young head of department then, just promoted. I make no bones about being ambitious and driven; it's just who I am. But when I saw Karen, I tried to swoop on her in the staff room at break and get chatting. Unfortunately, she was being clucked around by the other hags in her department and I didn't get a chance until I saw her chucking her bag into her boot at the end of the day. I jogged over. I didn't mind her knowing I was interested.

'So how was it?' I said. She was smaller than I had thought up close, sharp, bright eyes and thick, dark hair. I thought how well she would tuck into the crook of my arm. I looked at her mouth and imagined spooning ice-cream into it. She was captivating.

'Exhausting but good. I like it. It's where I want to be,' and she gave a short, determined nod of approval at the building.

I laughed. 'You look a bit like Felicity Kendal when you do that,' I said.

'Who?' she replied.

'From *The Good Life*. You know, the sit com, he gives up his stuffy job and they go self-sufficient. Dig up their garden in suburbia while everyone else endures the rat race.' Her mouth squidged up at one side and she shook her head, not getting the reference.

Once we started sleeping together, we watched re-runs of *The Good Life*, and she loved it. Tom and Barbara Good together against the world, getting by, relying on no-one except each other and we chatted to each other about having chickens, pigs, sheep and growing our own vegetables. Living our own good life. I held onto that dream.

When Karen appears at the hospital door, I notice the grey in her hair. Normally she keeps on top of it but coarse, curling, silver threads are clearly visible even from a distance. She's not wearing any make-up and there's a stain on the washed-out sweatshirt she's wearing. I can't remember what she had on the last time I saw her. She looks tired now. Older.

As she sits down, I try to smile. I want her to stay as long as possible. I want everything to go well so she'll come again so I determine to say nothing about the mark on her top. 'How have you been?' I say, 'How's Georgie?' and I smile again.

Karen unzips the holdall she's lifted onto her lap. 'I brought clean pyjamas. And more cordial. Joe said you were maybe up to reading something, so I brought a few of your magazines.' She busies herself unpacking things into my nightstand and stuffing my dirty pyjamas into a plastic bag to take home. She avoids looking at me as if I am an elderly relative squirreled away in a nursing home and she is enduring a dutiful visit. Her shoulders are high, her face a slight sneer, as if she's holding her breath. Do I smell? I've been in here so long I can't tell. Shame washes over me and I feel horribly unmanned. Incapable.

'It's nice to see you,' I try again.

She manages to look at me.

I speak quietly, 'Look, I'm sorry, I didn't mean for it to happen. I realise this is … life-changing for all of us.'

'You're not kidding,' she glares at me now, openly hostile.

'I didn't,' but she cuts me off before I can say anymore.

'What the hell were you doing up there anyway? You were supposed to do the gutters, not get up on the roof. I saw you climb up, you know. It was reckless, bloody reckless.'

'Karen,' I want to defend myself, but I know she's right. She doesn't usually swear but I suppose Georgie isn't around to hear it.

'You're always up on there. And for no good reason. It was bound to happen sooner or later. You're lucky you're not dead.'

'That's what you think.' Even to myself I sound petulant, and she scoffs as if I am being ridiculous.

'I want to sell the house,' and she folds her arms and sits back in the chair, chin jutting, daring me to disagree. 'It's completely impractical for us to live there anymore. After this. I can't drive. There's talk that they're going to cut the bus service. I don't see how we can stay. I'm going to get the house valued.'

I turn my head away from her. I can't believe what she's saying. For days and days, I've been desperate to see her, now I just want her to go.

It was a bit of a whirlwind romance I suppose. I'd had a few girlfriends. One of them pretty serious, until I found out she was shagging her boss. After that I decided to concentrate on work and having some fun. After all I was young, fairly good-looking, solvent, so what was to stop me. Work was good, relatively easy; I liked dealing with parents, knew the right things to say to smooth things over between

19

colleagues and I understood meetings were a means to an end, so promotion was straightforward. I could see the path I wanted to take.

But Karen was something else. She was a creative and the kids loved her. Let's face it, everyone loved her. She burst into every room talking or laughing, her bright, clashing colours wardrobe matching the energy shooting from her every pore. She was so goddam eager about everything. Signed up to do every cross-curricular activity she could, extra duties, volunteered to help with the special needs kids at lunch-times. It was exhausting. The more weathered members of staff peered over their glasses as she scribbled her name on yet another list and lifted a wry eyebrow. It wouldn't be long before she understood the reality of her teaching workload was their unspoken comment. 'Let's see what she's like at the end of the year,' someone muttered with a sly chuckle.

At one point I overheard her Head of Department mooting that Karen might have undiagnosed ADHD or perhaps she was bi-polar, having seen her out running before school in the morning. 'Energy makes energy, Terry, and she's young. Really young!' was the reply from the deputy head who was gloating over the appointment she'd championed.

That was what she was like to be with out of school too. It was, well, manic. We did so much. Karen could get up for a Body Pump class at six on a Saturday morning, do the weekly shop on the way back, then fantastic sex and a shower all done by ten; into town for a free art exhibition or book signing, then late lunch, usually with live music and a heady catch up with friends followed by maybe an afternoon stroll around a park or market; then home to do a bit of cleaning of home and body before we'd be off out again with her family or more friends, pub or a club or the cinema or the theatre, and then home for more fantastic sex. And Sundays were the same, except there was some organised and efficient preparation for school in there, usually early in the morning. So many friends to keep up with, so many cultural events she tracked, so many books she read. It was a marvel to behold. Karen lived every second of her life; there was not a moment wasted.

Every few months, sometimes longer, she'd crash and cancel everything and sleep for perhaps eighteen hours straight or more. I'd go in and perch on the bed and she'd have barely moved. She looked like a Hollywood star from the fifties when she was asleep. Her fabulous jaw so strong and proud and the lashy crescents of her eyelids so tightly shut. Her face was smooth and calm and beautiful. I could watch her sleep all day. But then she'd wake and be up and at it and the whole whirlwind would start again.

I have to admit, I spun her a bit of a line at the beginning. I implied that I was a highly social animal too, whereas in reality my life was sedentary by comparison. Christ, it was glacial. Her social life was so full I just slotted into it and was happy to tag along to events a maths nerd would never even have considered. 'So, what do you think of this?' she had asked me as we stood in front of one particularly difficult piece of modern art. The artist had used wax crayons to create what looked to me like scribbles. I was pretty sure every kid in our school could do better, but I didn't want to appear stupid; I had barely visited an art gallery before I knew Karen.

'I'm not really sure. I think I've seen this sort of thing before,' I had stalled hoping she would jump in and give me her opinion.

'Really? You have? Do go on,' I could hear the tease in her voice, and she had edged closer, putting her hand on my bum, never taking her eyes from the chaotic scrawl on the wall in front of us.

'Yes. Didn't he do some *haute couture* as well?' I mused.

Karen looked at me quizzically.

'For royalty of some sort?' I persisted.

'I don't think so. Maybe some sculpture but not …' she leant over to peer at the thick, tasteful card next to the canvas.

'Yes,' I said, 'Clothes … for an emperor… Just as stunning as this picture.' She had turned back from the card, flashing that wonderful smile, delighted at my wittiness, which I confess had even taken me by surprise.

'Archie! This is worth thousands! Hundreds of thousands. You can't say that!'

I snatched hold of her hand and dragged her close to me, 'Is it though? Some fool might pay thousands but is it worth it?'

'Keep your voice down!' she giggled, then whispered huskily in my ear, 'Let's get out of here, I want to do something less cerebral and more physical.'

And that's how I got by. Admitting, or acknowledging, my shortcomings to her. And there was so much desire from her for me. She was so physical I couldn't believe my luck. This bright, gorgeous girl who was wrapping her arms around my neck as soon as we shut the front door, who stripped off her T shirt with an extravagant stretch and reached for my zip the minute she'd completed her marking; who changed the bed sheets and yelled for me to get up there while they still smelt fresh and was curled up and naked, waiting on top of the crisp linen by the time I'd taken the stairs three at a time. It was a glorious phase, and I wanted this prize forever. I felt all those difficult days of guessing a girlfriend's mood, or negotiating for sex with presents or compliments, or time with her boring friends was behind me. I wanted this. With Karen. Always.

I proposed at the end of the Christmas holidays. We'd been together just under three months. When she said yes, I felt like I could conquer the world and I made her these promises. 'I'll take care of you. We'll always be together. I don't want us to be apart. Ever.'

As I lie here, I think about all that early sex and I think of my flaccid dick, an embarrassing mound of sheet and blanket, useless, hopeless. There's been a bit of discussion which I found frankly, repulsive. A waxy faced, sweating young woman, a counsellor of some sort I think, assured me I would be able to have a 'fulfilling' sex life again. My wife and I would have to find new ways to 'pleasure' each other. I wanted to hurl the bed pan, which was sitting on my nightstand, at her. How dare she talk to me about my sex life? She was young enough to be a past pupil. Why did I have to talk to her? Couldn't they have sent a man?

In the end she left, and I made a formal complaint, but it didn't make me feel any better. The way Karen had looked at me, I didn't hold much hope for any kind of pleasure, physical or otherwise.

2

By the time I'm ready to leave the rehab unit, I've made up my mind that everything is going to be better. It's been a difficult few months not helped by my fellow inmates. I have had to suffer the complications of staying on a shared ward. Five fellow bed mates. Hard to face each other when we've all been kept awake by the barely muffled sobs from Harry, the teenager, who's now a chest down quadriplegic after he came off his motorbike two days after passing his test. Also problematic when one of us shits ourselves, a fairly regular occurrence. We four paraplegics on the ward are supposed to be mastering independent personal care but it's not straightforward. Waiting for the staff to help with the fallout is the worst. The smell is terrible. A physical manifestation of our deepest shame. One day Rick (late thirties, experienced climber who took a chance) got so pissed off waiting, he roared and screamed and made a terrible mess with his sheets and pillows. We all pressed our buttons and tried to calm him down. They had to sedate him in the end.

As I imagined, visitors have been sparse. The unit is further from home and so it's understandable and I've got through it. The farmhouse is ready for me so the boys tell me, and Joseph and Edward are coming to pick me up and I cannot wait. I woke up at five this morning. I thought I imagined a bit of light outside. We're nearly at the clocks going forward. Almost spring. And that was my goal. Get home for the better weather. And I've made it. Christmas was a drug-addled fog and Valentine's Day was a write-off. I'm not missing Easter.

I was in the chair ready for Joseph and Edward far too early, but I couldn't help it. I've been waiting and waiting, and the minutes have sluggishly crept by. I keep telling myself not to look at the clock. In fact, I've composed a letter in my head to the NHS Trust telling them to remove all ward clocks; they're instruments of torture for the patients, constant reminders of how slowly the time passes. Plus, they serve as concrete evidence that your visitors are desperate to get away, all those furtive glances every minute or so and the briefest look of disappointment that they've to weather another half an hour before visiting time comes to a blessed end. I hate that clock.

Now I know I'm getting out, everything about the place is crawling under my skin from the soft squeak of the nurses' shoes on the easy-to-clean floors to the antiseptic smell hiding something unpleasant and sharp underneath it. Bill, in the bed opposite, (late sixties, knocked over by a drunk driver on a pedestrian crossing) is muttering again about how the tables aren't big enough to play clock patience on. He adjusts his softened pack for the umpteenth time. As he's played variations of solitaire continually since his admission four weeks ago, you'd think this wouldn't be newsworthy. I want to bellow at him as he tuts and fusses over the cards and minutely adjusts the table as if this will miraculously make it bigger. I can feel my breathing speed up and I grip tightly onto the rim of the chair in an attempt to control myself. I'd like to say something rational to him, but I can only picture myself snatching the cards from him or, worse, hurting him.

'Dad! You're all ready to go!' Edward bounds into the room; he smells of the outside which cuts through the stale, heavy warmth of the ward. I want to run and hug him. I guess that's out of the question.

'Did you manage the train okay?' I say. Joseph is already head down and filling the empty holdall he has brought, plundering my nightstand like a thief eager to exit the scene of the crime.

'No problem,' Edward is grinning, 'And the taxi is waiting. We saw the driver on the way in.'

It's an expense to travel all the way home by taxi but I can be rolled in and secured this way. We can work on modifying the car, if necessary, at a later date or the wider logistics of me as passenger not driver. For today, if I can get home quicker, an exorbitant fare is a price I'm willing to pay. Sod the expense.

A few of the nurses offer, 'Good lucks,' and 'Take cares,' but turn back quickly to their charts and conversations, and Edward pushes me at quite a lick down the corridor. Joseph trots ahead to the lift and we come to an abrupt stop. As I lurch forward, Joseph dives down to push me back upright in the chair.

'Bloody hell, Teddy, take it easy,' Joseph hisses, 'You okay Dad?'

'Yep fine, just pleased there was no on-coming traffic.' I make my tone light-hearted and both boys laugh a little, but my heart is thudding, and I feel vulnerable and nervous. 'I do have a seatbelt Joseph, but maybe take it a bit more slowly, eh, Edward?' I say, 'You don't want to break my neck as well.'

And then somehow, we're all in a taxi that is more of a minibus, and I'm finally out of hospital and the road becomes quiet and I see the countryside beginning and at last I can breathe. As we get closer to home though I feel nerves starting. How will Karen be with me? We've barely talked since the accident. I've seen her a handful of times. I want to go home but I feel like it's the first day of school and I'm the new boy; I know the boys have got my back, but this is fresh territory, and I don't know how to navigate it. Instead of seeing Karen as my partner, my wife, on my side even, I have to win her over again. I'm back to square one, at the bottom of the snake, in jail and not passing Go and she is the only one who matters. As the hills bloom and blossom and roll outside, I put the dark thoughts out of my head. It has to be okay. I'm alive and I have to make the best of it.

Georgie races out of the house as the taxi pulls up. I can picture her sitting up on the kitchen window seat, peering down the lane like an expectant puppy, her favoured post for any expected visitors. Her copious, black hair is a cloud around her, and she is smiling and yelping and wrapping her arms round my neck despite her brothers' protestations. 'Let him breathe, Georgie,' Edward remonstrates but she can't let go and neither can I. She has grown. I am sure of it.

'I want to sit on your lap,' she demands into my neck and in moments she has climbed into the chair. I let out a brief laugh, but I want to howl as I can't feel the weight of my daughter's compact little body on my legs. There's no sense of her warmth or solidity. Nothing apart from her arms around me and her chest against mine. It's half a life in my lap.

'Looks like rain. We'd better get in,' Joseph says.

The boys manage the chair across the uneven path, and I see the ugly ramp that now covers the charmingly worn stone steps leading up to the front door. Joseph nips ahead and opens the door wide, 'Ta da!' he tries but the light is off, and the hallway is gloomy.

On the day we bought the farmhouse, I'd carried all three of them over the threshold, Karen first, scooping her up, despite her protestations, then heading back for the boys, carrying one under each arm and landing them all in a heap in a welcoming entrance that at that time seemed so full of promise.

Today it's width and depth, 'Big enough for a Christmas tree,' we'd decided on first viewing, are diminished by the bulky chair, my bags, and my adult sons. I am filled with crushing disappointment.

'Let's go and get some tea,' and Edward lifts Georgie off as Joseph takes charge and we head up the hall that runs the length of the house. I note how close the wheels are to the wall. If I'm pushing myself, I'll have to watch my knuckles and elbows.

There's another ramp into the kitchen; it's long and shallow to accommodate the three steps down. The dresser, a bargain find at one of the local sale rooms, that stood against the wall has gone. No room now there's a ramp. No room now there's a cripple in the house.

'Georgie, go and get Mum,' Edward says lightly as he fills the kettle.

'Do I have to?' Georgie whines, 'I think she's in the top field. She said there's a fence needs mending. I'll have to put my wellies on.'

The rain sounds like handfuls of wet sand battering on the window.

'She can't be out in this, surely?' Joseph says.

'I'll give her a shout,' Edward leaps up the ramp and disappears.

'I made you a card,' Georgie hands me a glittering "Welcome Home Daddy" card. I wince as I see that she has drawn me in a chair. Difficult for a nine-year-old, the legs are splayed and sticking out like a rigid lifeless doll and the wheels are enormous. The rest of them are standing, smiling. The sun is shining. I grin and lean over to give her a kiss.

'It's lovely, darling, thank you,' I fix the smile on my face and breathe hard because I want to cry. Really cry.

The back door slams. 'I'm soaked. Just going to jump in the shower,' Karen shouts and I wonder how many more avoidance tactics she can employ before she has to face me.

Later, as we're sitting round the kitchen table, everything feels a little more normal. I have got over the shock of the removal of my beloved oak captain's chair. There's just an empty space for me to be pushed into and I realise with a jolt I'm not going to experience different seats ever again. I don't even really feel like I'm in this chair, just sort of hovering; it's hard to explain. But the captain's chair is gone, and a void remains. However, we don't talk about any of this. We avoid The Void. Probably better that way.

At the table, once we're all sitting together, drinking tea, eating biscuits, Georgie has a sticker book out, I think for a moment maybe it will be alright. Or maybe if there are moments like this, it will be bearable. Manageable.

I still have to see the bedroom though. The layout of the farmhouse is kitchen across the bottom end, the full width of the house with a utility and pantry off it. The light is fantastic in there, you get sun all day. When it's not raining. We eat in here. It's warm. Probably the warmest room in the house. There's a wood burner, an ancient one that we keep lit most of the winter. I like to make a pot of coffee and keep it hot on there. We've a couple of old armchairs next to it. Joseph reads there too. That boy's head is never out of a book. Drives me mad. At the front, facing the drive, is the dining room, now the bedroom, and a downstairs loo, plus a boot room and at the back a large and sunny living room with doors out onto the garden. The garden doors could do with replacing though, they're draughty in winter; it's a wonderful room on a summer evening however with the doors open and the warm evening air drifting in. We've a small study too at the back of the house; a handy room which Karen and I share. It's a wonderful house; I love it and I have to be thankful that there hasn't been any more talk of selling it. However difficult it is for me to manage here, stay we must. This is where we are meant to be. Forever.

Karen is taking her time with the shower. Edward jokes that maybe she's having a bath and has fallen asleep. I notice that there are other changes in the kitchen. It is uncluttered. Different. I can't quite pinpoint what it is but I'm still on quite a lot of medication for the pain so not at my sharpest.

'I think I could do with a lie down,' I say eventually, 'We might as well have a go at the hoist and all that gubbins before I get overtired. What do you think?'

The boys jump up and rush around clearing the cups and plates and then we're off back down the hall and I'm too dispirited to try to propel myself even though that was my intent. To be as independent as I could be from the outset; after all I am still the master of the house.

'Let's show you this first, Dad,' Edward says, and he opens the door to the downstairs loo. I feel another slump in my gut as I note the wood panelling that I'd lovingly restored, stripped and waxed has been ripped out; the whole room is tiled white and is now an efficient and accessible wet room. The fixtures and fittings are basic. I assume Karen wanted to keep costs down. I hope this doesn't imply a short-term fix, an interim stop gap before a move.

'I'll just go in boys, if you don't mind. This is great.' And they wheel me in and close the door and I put my chilly hands over my face and try not to sob. I manage to get it together enough to catheterize myself to empty my bladder though I know it takes a long time and the boys are hovering outside like expectant fathers. As I cover myself up again, I'm not sure I can face the bedroom but there's no point putting it off.

It's much worse than I'd imagined. The north facing room has been painted a stark, icy white all over. The thick wool carpet is gone, and an unpleasantly practical vinyl of some sort laid down instead. I turn my head from it as I imagine that I now have to be considered in terms of leakages and spills and uncontrolled bodily functions that must be dealt with efficiently and with as little fuss as possible. There is a hospital bed, and I don't know why I need one, and a hoist hanging, waiting, more practical torturer's wheelhouse than sex dungeon. By the window is a small table and chair as if two people could sit and eat. Am I to live in here? A sizeable television is on the wall, perfectly placed for viewing from the bed and, to my horror, another *Sky* box. She wants me confined in here. Captive. Restrained. An invalid, a cripple. Shut away, excluded from my family.

I say nothing.

'Let's have a go with the hoist, Dad. It's pretty high tech,' Joseph says.

'Yeah,' Edward adds, 'We've both had a go. We think you'll be able to do it yourself once you're stronger, which means you'll have proper independence.'

The hoist is better than the ones in the hospital. They fumble around a little as they get the sling under my arms and secured trying, unsuccessfully, to be careful of my still not fully mobile shoulder. 'It's dead simple to use,' Edward waves the remote in front of my face as I am pulled up out of the chair like an ungainly sack of potatoes and hang like a sad puppet while Georgie applauds. I reach to grab the bar above the bed, and it steadies me as I swing over. The boys lift my legs onto the bed and pat them for no good reason; they engage the side safety rails. I refuse a blanket and don't want the curtains drawn though the downpour outside is smudging any view I may have seen. They all tiptoe out as if I am an obedient child on the brink of slumber.

I stare at the rain cascading down the glass.

I wake and I don't know when I fell asleep. I wake and it is dark outside. I don't understand how this is possible. I've tipped sideways. I'm very cold; teeth-chatteringly cold. I am used to the constant, hot-house, ambient temperature of the hospital and my clothes are relatively light for the farmhouse. My first thought is to jump out of bed and warm up by moving. This happens to me quite a lot, especially on waking. I forget that I can't walk, can't drive, can't run, can't piss and shit the way I used to. Which brings me to another urgent matter I'm pretty sure I need to deal with.

Looking around the room, there's no clock. I have no idea what time it is. Why is there no clock? They know I don't wear a wristwatch and I can't reach my mobile so why haven't they put a clock in here? It's the most important detail. As I am thinking all these things, I am trying to prop myself up with my stronger arm and reach for a blanket which Joseph offered and then put just out of reach at the end of the bed. I want to commit murder, I am so cold.

'Edward! Joseph?' I call, but, surprisingly, my voice is weak. I don't have the force behind it that I used to despite years of strong, projected barks across schoolyards, dining rooms and classrooms when and where necessary. I clear my throat and try again, 'Edward! Georgie? Joseph!' It's pathetic the volume I manage, and the door is closed, and the walls are stone and thick. Looking around there's nothing within my reach that I can even throw at the door to attract attention. Where the hell are they? Is it the middle of the night? Have I slept that long? Why aren't I hungry? I shout again, 'Karen! Karen! KAAARRREEEEN!!!' I collapse back against the pillows with the effort, hoping I'm not going to cry.

Thumping footsteps batter down the stairs and the door bursts open. 'For goodness sake, what on earth is the matter?' Karen is fully clothed, so not the middle of the night then, and flushed with anger.

'I couldn't get anyone to come,' I say. I sound meek, pathetic. 'I'm cold,' I add.

'I see,' she says, staring at me from the threshold, her hand still on the door. 'Wait there,' and she disappears.

'No fucking choice,' I mutter.

A moment later, Joseph and Edward arrive followed closely by Georgie and there's blankets and a hot water bottle and then a trip to the loo, followed by a hot drink, and a fan heater while the radiator warms up and they show me the baby monitor they bought which they forgot to turn on and Georgie sets up a puzzle she's playing with at the table and Edward turns on the football and Joseph brings me toast and I relax and they're all here.

Except Karen.

We had decided in the hospital I was going to have carers. Karen refused point blank to take it on and, though Joseph

30

said he'd do it, Karen wouldn't let him. 'He has his own life to lead,' she said. This means that a stranger will be coming in every morning and every evening to get me up and put me to bed. They will deal with my daily shower, until I can manage it myself, and help with the hygiene aspects of my catheter and so on.

I try to think of her as a nurse. She has a uniform after all, it's a tight fit though creasing and squashing her, making her look uncomfortable rather than professional, and it could do with a wash. Her hair is untidy, but her face is friendly, at least at the start. Her name is Amber. She keeps up a constant stream of chat. I imagine that is her coping mechanism. It's not proper engagement, it's a verbal barrier. She never actually looks at me. I can't get a word in as she manhandles me out of my clothes and into my pyjamas having stood, hands on solid hips, as I brushed my teeth, nudging the chair forward an inch or two as I miss the basin with my spit, and it dribbles like bird shit into my lap. She dabs it away barely pausing for breath in her monologue about her cats and their refusal to crap in their litter trays unless they were in her living room. I am trying to indicate I don't want to hear any of this, but she knows we have cats so thinks I'll be fascinated. 'I wouldn't mind so much but my hubby says the scrabbling and scraping in the litter ruins the tension if you're watching something like *Line of Duty*. You know, because you can't help looking to see what they're up to. Even though you know, you know. I just turn up the telly if I see one of them heading over to them. Doesn't bother me, like.'

As she tucks the duvet into the rails, (she strikes me as a person who likes some sense of order) I pray that the person they send in the morning has either taken a vow of silence or likes dogs. We have been warned we could see up to fifteen different people in the course of the month. Not much chance to build a relationship then, or even a routine. The sooner I get to grips with things myself the better. She stands and looks at me for a moment in silence, a little smile on her face. For a second, I think she may be going to kiss my forehead or sing me a lullaby, but she just picks up her lumpy bag, slings it over her meaty forearm and says, 'Night then, see you again,' and she's gone.

It is nine o' clock.

The later they come, the more you pay. Or the harder it is to staff. Fair enough really. Who wants to be doing all this on a Friday night for minimum wage because I'm sure that's what they get?

There's a knock and Georgie appears, book in hand. 'Mum says you can read to me here if I go straight to sleep afterwards. That okay?'

'Absolutely,' I say, and she climbs on the bed and gets in with me and we start *Pollyanna* which I've never read before. It is Karen's childhood copy, battered and creased, dog-eared, well-loved. I am however finding Pollyanna a bit wearing with her Glad game; I mean her life is awful, an orphan, a rotten aunt, what has she to be so cheery about all the time? She grows on me the more we read however, which is, I suppose, the point. Georgie sits up and looks at me, 'I knew you'd like this Daddy,' she says, 'Later in the book, Pollyanna has an accident too and she can't walk like you either.' She's smiling.

'Oh,' I say.

'Yes, but in the end, she tries really hard, and she learns to walk again,' and there's that Pollyanna optimism in Georgie's eyes, as if she's unlocked a big secret for me.

'Right,' I say, 'Good for her,' and I close the book. 'You know, Georgie. I'm tired now. Are you? I think I want to go to sleep. It's been a busy day.'

'Okay, Dad,' she says and climbs off the bed, pulling up the rail after her as Joseph showed her earlier in the afternoon. 'We'll read more tomorrow, shall we?' she grins with the same energy that Karen had in the early days. I almost feel an ache in my chest from missing that so much.

'Can you turn out your light?' Georgie is at the door.

'Yep,' I nod.

'Okay, night, night then,' and I hear her running softly up the stairs.

I lie and think about Pollyanna. I wish I could re-write my story so it has a happy ending.

I've always had a tendency to insomnia. The running helped with that, most of the time. Now I'm hardly moving I've slipped back into bad habits of napping through the day and glaring at the ceiling in the small hours while sleep refuses to come. In the rehab unit, it wasn't so bad. I could always get a tablet when I got desperate and there was always activity - it was a waking night; people were at work around you after all.

Here in the farmhouse, it's another matter. I revelled in the fact that we'd left behind the omnipresent sepia of the streetlights when we'd left the city. I loved how dark it was. We could step out of the back door and see the stars on a clear night, and the fells were giant sleeping monsters when the moon was full. No light pollution here. It was a joy. Now I want to ask for a nightlight like a timid child. My room is so dark in the small hours. Nothing comes through my window, and I can barely make out the shapes around me. I have to admit the darkness becomes more terrifying to me every night. So, I keep my eyes closed and I keep coming back to Karen and I have begun to obsess about whether I am losing her. Rationally I know it's impossible for me to hear her phone ping with messages through the ceiling, but I'm sure I can.

My mind goes back to how I wanted her, how much I pursued her, and I know she's had interest over the years, attention. From men. And women. And now I'm stuck in this bed, or the chair, and those admirers must be clamouring at her door. Over the years I've watched at staff meetings the way her stillness, her poise, her concentration just demands the gaze of others. As a deputy I've always sat, flanking Angie, at the front and you can observe the little interactions and exchanges as the meetings progress. Karen no longer effervesces like she did in her youth but she's still completely captivating.

A few years ago, we were having some in-service training on safeguarding and Karen took out a lipstick. It was a sort of burnt orange. Dark but still vivid. Our chairs were horseshoed around a projector screen for the obligatory *PowerPoint* presentation. It was after lunch, a good lunch before funding was cut to the bone, making everyone relaxed and a little dozy. Karen's chair was fairly near the front, close to the screen; she always wanted a good view wherever we went. She was gazing up at the screen and, almost unconsciously, took the lipstick from her pocket barely even looking at it. As she dragged the tip to and fro across her bottom lip, my breath quickened and I glanced around, calculating most of the male staff had their eyes on her. She took her time putting it on. Never took her eyes from the screen. Later, she said the men watching were bored, or their eyes were naturally drawn to the movement. She had no idea how she looked; a rich black, roll neck jumper and that thick mane of hair demanding to be plied and pulled, glistening attentive eyes and her chin tilted up the better to display her broad mouth. I could barely concentrate the rest of the afternoon and was pushing her up the stairs the moment we got home, dragging the jumper up over her head before we'd even closed the bedroom door. I admit part of the turn on that day was I knew Karen was desirable to others and yet she was mine. She was my wife, and she was coming home with me, lipstick and all. God, I sound like a caveman but that was how primal I felt around her sometimes. That was the strength of feeling, Karen brought out in me.

And now I'm lying in bed tortured by who is trying to storm the castle now they know the drawbridge is down and the moat is empty.

When we were first together, I pretended to be cool about Karen's previous boyfriends but in my head, I hated them all. If they ever came up in conversation, I belittled them in a jokey way; I was terrified she'd go back to them at first.

On our way back from the pub, in those initial few months together, she told me about having sex in some park with a guy she picked up at a party. The way she told it, they were heading back to her place, but they couldn't wait so they nipped into this park and just did it, up against a tree. Some dog walker had wolf whistled once they'd finished, catching on to what had been going on and Karen had flashed her boob at him. That got the party guy going and they'd gone at it again. It all sounded quite sordid and uncomfortable, and, at one point, I was worried she was going to say the dog owner joined in while Fido sat and watched, panting and tongue lolling at his master's exuberant frolicking but, thankfully, that's not the way the story went. We laughed about the whole thing, and I marvelled at, and delighted in her sexual freedom but now, well now, she is not past sex, not by a long way, and how can I convince her I am worth bothering with if she can't even bear to be in the same room as me?

If only I could sleep maybe it wouldn't seem so bleak. I resolve to try to talk to her properly in the morning. We have to sort something out; things can't go on like this.

'Mum's gone down to Manchester for the day. She said she needed a few things at the agricultural suppliers on the way and then she wanted to pick a few things up in the centre. She's taken Georgie.' Edward is clearing away the breakfast dishes. They must have left before the carer even arrived. It smacks of subterfuge, creeping out of the house, not telling me of her plans; it's unheard of.

A thought strikes me.

'How is she getting there?' I say.

'Didn't she tell you?' Edward turns from the sink towards me, 'She passed her test a while ago. January? Or maybe February? Took a crash course.'

I am amazed.

'Then why didn't she pick me up from the rehab unit?' I speak carefully, quietly.

'Think she thought the taxi would be easier for the ... you know, your chair.' Edward has his back to me.

'Yes, I suppose that's reasonable.' And it is. But I can't help myself even though this isn't Edward's question to answer. 'But if she's been driving since February, why didn't she come over to the unit?'

'Oh, she did. She drove us over quite a lot. Or picked us up. Just always had other stuff to do. There's been a lot on Dad, and she's been at work.'

'So, she came over with Georgie too?'

'Yes, sometimes. Now, what do you fancy for lunch? Think I might make some butternut squash soup. That's filling but not too high in calories. What do you think?' And he starts to forage in the fridge for ingredients. My sons haven't managed to get themselves meaningful employment yet, but they know their way round a kitchen.

'Yes, whatever, fine.' In the distance, I watch the chickens picking their way around their coop, scratching and pecking at the barren earth they've turned to dust with all their scraping and jabbing. There's barely a blade of grass growing in their

35

pen. We'll have to relocate them. Strike that. The boys will have to relocate them. I shake my head at the thought of a wife who can drive miles to a specialist spinal unit and not step in to lay eyes on her paraplegic husband.

The second time she came to visit me in the hospital, I asked her why she didn't come in the helicopter with me. Someone had told me there would have been room; she could have come if she'd wanted to.

'You weren't going to die,' she said matter-of-factly, 'they told me that on the ground so I didn't see the point. I thought I should stay with Georgie.'

If it had been Karen on the stretcher, I'd never have let her out of my sight.

3

My parents told me when I was ten that I was adopted. I had no idea. Not a clue. I knew they were older than my friends' mums and dads. They didn't mix easily; kept themselves to themselves. My house was quiet whereas there were always women chatting in the kitchen of Mikey's house or sitting on chairs in the garden. In the summer, Dads congregated around the gaping maw of car bonnets or even a lawnmower. There was chat. But not with my parents. They were private people. Shy, perhaps. Or bewildered by the wider world. Mum had a brother who lived a long way away; we hardly saw him. Dad was an only child. Their own parents were crinkly and frail when I was a small boy and died long before I left school. Family occasions were restrained, reserved. Christmas ran to a sherry trifle and a box of jellied fruits but little more, almost deliberately rejecting the excess which surrounded us. Though I was always given the latest fad of a toy as I was loved.

I knew that my mother adored me. She would do anything for me, trotted round the house after me, told me I was the best at everything, smiled and smiled into my face while Dad dug his veg patch at the bottom of the garden or tinkered away on the car in the garage. Mum would play cards with me, or *Kerplunk* or *Buckeroo* or anything I wanted to tempt me to stay in with her rather than tear off out with my mates. She baked and baked rows of sweet, crunchy biscuits and countless steaming puddings and anything and everything I liked. Dad never got his favourites; it was all up to me as soon as I could talk. I remember saying, 'I'd rather have something hot,' when she presented me with quiche and salads one day. She scooped up my plate, and in no time was clattering pans and happily frying up bacon and eggs. As I got older, we'd chat over breakfast about what I'd like for tea.

There was a good deal of security in having a beautifully pressed uniform laid out for me every morning. My school bag packed with every book carefully backed. Mum sat watching me complete my homework, jumping up to fetch me squash or a snack should I tire. She delighted in my company and when I look at some of the kids in our school today who come to school hungry, dirty with barely a kind word spoken to them, I occasionally think of my mum and the hours she devoted to me.

It was all a lie of course. I felt lied to. I don't think I've ever got over the shock of being told she wasn't my mother. We both had the same colouring, reddish hair, blue eyes. People remarked on it. 'Of course, you're more like your mother, Archie,' they said and neither of my parents said anything. They let me believe there was a genetic relationship, a connection, a bond. My dad was a maths teacher, and I was good at maths too – that's where I got it from. No. Apparently not. It was all coincidence. Dad and I enjoying working through my maths homework over the years was just a meeting of similar minds; we were strangers really, thrown together by the universe.

When they told me I was adopted, I thought they were going to tell me someone had died. They sat me down at the dining room table just after my tenth birthday. My mum had tears in her eyes. She started with, 'Archie, we want you to know that we love you very, very much,' and that made my tummy feel funny like she was saying something nice but there was bad news ahead. The sun was in my eyes, and I remember the room was hot. My friends were waiting for me. We were going to take our bikes down to the river. I was hoping this wasn't going to take too long.

'When you were born things were difficult,' Dad said.

This was confusing. I'd only heard lovely stories of me as a baby. In fact, I'd only ever heard how delightful I was.

'Sometimes people have babies, and they can't look after them,' Mum said, 'And sometimes people want to have babies, but their bodies can't manage it. Do you understand, Archie?' A tear dropped onto the table. The table was Mum's pride and

38

joy, she polished it with beeswax, and it smelled a bit like the church.

'We were unlucky because we couldn't have babies ourselves,' said Dad, 'but a very, very kind lady, your mother, gave you to us. She couldn't look after you, so we adopted you. You were her son but then we adopted you when you were a tiny baby, and you became our son. As soon as we saw you, we loved you like you were our own and we wanted to keep you forever and so we adopted you, and you are our son. But there was another lady who was your mother when you were born. She loved you. She gave you your name. But she couldn't look after you. So, she asked us to instead because she knew we would love you with all our hearts and keep you safe and give you everything you needed. Do you understand Archie?'

There was a scabby little girl in the class below me called Melanie Hewitt. She was adopted. She didn't have many friends. I knew what it meant.

'Why are you telling me now?' I said quietly.

'We think you're old enough to understand about it now,' Dad said. Mum was snuffling into a hankie. The rims of her eyes had gone pink. She looked like a rabbit. One of those startled, blinking, white ones that magicians pull out of hats. She wasn't looking at me.

'Are you going to give me back?' I stared at Dad who recoiled. Mum gave a little shriek.

'I told you we shouldn't have said anything!' she wailed at Dad, 'No, Archie, no, I love you, you're my little boy,' and she rushed over and gripped me tight round the shoulders. Her perfume smelt sweet and sickly, and her hair looked brittle and dry, close up, like it had no colour. Fake almost. For the first time I did not feel comforted by my mother. I wanted to escape.

So, I did.

'I'm going out to play,' I said, and I wriggled off the chair and away.

Me and my pals tore off on our bikes down to the river; the sun was hot on our bare backs as we paddled in the shallow, glinting water with our trousers clumsily rolled up to our knees.

I told my friends the news.

Raymond Fisher laughed. 'You'll have to marry Melanie Hewitt,' he said, jabbing a pudgy finger at me, 'You're a match made in heaven.' The others laughed and Ray swaggered a little with pride at his retort. Fat, freckly, Ray was an easy target for a lot of our jokes so I couldn't blame his haste to get the first dig in.

I leapt across to him in three quick strides and, with the horrible realisation of a triumph turning sour, he turned to try to get away, but I was fast. I shoved his back hard, palms flat, wrists locked. He lurched forward and splayed into the water. I jabbed my knees onto his back and locked my hands onto his writhing head, forcing his face into the fast-running flow. I held him there until the others knocked me off him and he surfaced, coughing and crying.

Grabbing my stuff, I biked home barefoot, the sharp grips of the pedals biting into the bare soles of my feet. My rage made me push down harder. As I hurled my bike onto the driveway, I saw smears of blood on the dull metal. Tears of shame at my action and anger at my parents, made my abandoned bike swim and shake before me. I wiped them away. Instead of going into the house, I skulked down to the bottom of the garden and hunkered down behind Dad's shed until much, much later hunger drove me in to face a mother I never felt about in the same way again.

Over the next few weeks and months, one or other of them would try to talk to me about the 'precious task' they'd been given or how 'being adopted meant I was even more special.' I refused to speak about it, and I don't think they ever understood how much of a shock it was for to me to hear 'it' for the first time, out of the blue, like that.

I'm looking at photos of Joseph as a baby on my phone. Edward uploaded them from old photo albums for his twenty-first, I think. Karen and I both look so young. Well, we were young, I suppose. Moments after he was born, I held him for the first time, a tiny, twisting and shifting bundle so light in my hands, and I saw he had my nose, long and straight, a bit odd on a baby, a bit too grown up. It was unmistakeable. I cried. 'He's the first family I've ever had,' I said to Karen and the midwife came and stood next to me and put her arm round me.

'Definitely Daddy's boy,' she said smiling at my son and handing me a tissue for my tears.

I never wanted to let him go. I mean, I loved Karen but the feelings I felt for that boy at that moment were astonishing. And later, it could have been months later, Karen said how awful it must have been for my mum and dad never to have been able to have kids of their own.

'She had countless miscarriages you know, your mum,' she said, 'she told me before she died. She wanted to tell you, but I know it was hard for you to talk about it all. They tried for years until the doctors told her she had to stop.'

It's not up to you to do the right thing as a child though. It's the adults who are supposed to have the answers.

I find tears are yet again on my cheeks. A regular occurrence at the moment. I know that I am dwelling on the past and finding it hard to imagine a future. Joseph suggested antidepressants but I'm still taking painkillers and, until I'm clear of those, I don't want to be downing anything else.

I just have to pull myself together.

Karen has told me over the years that I have abandonment issues because I was adopted and that perhaps I should look into finding my real mother and father.

'I don't want another set of parents,' I always say, 'I had enough problems with the ones I had. Why would I want more?' Karen makes a face I can't understand when I say this. I know it's a bit of a throwaway comment, but my real mother made a decision not to know me and I have to respect that.

Karen might be right about the abandonment though.

I don't want her to abandon me.

I text Edward and Joseph and put in a polite request for a snack. I can't be bothered to go to the kitchen and the fruit bowl that permanently sits in my room looks dull. I want something to wake my mouth up. Actually, I want one of my mother's biscuits, warm from the oven, baked just for me.

I first thought Karen was having an affair with Martin about six months after he started working at Ridge High, which must be about ten years ago now. I was on the interview panel and so was she, as Head of Department. In my opinion, it was going to be hard for her to be objective about someone she did her PGCE training with and when he applied, I argued for him not to be shortlisted.

I'd already stalked him on *Facebook*. There were lots of photos of him when he was younger, all high cheek bones and floppy hair, a budding actor. Then his teaching, lots of trips, productions, adulation. And he'd taught abroad, international schools in Vietnam and Beijing. I fucking hated him.

Unfortunately, his references were excellent, so no one backed me not to interview, but it was a main scale post, so it was a bit odd for him to be applying for this. He was Head of Faculty in his current school in Newcastle.

'I'm looking for a change of pace,' he grinned, 'To be honest, the more managerial the role, the more it takes you away from the teaching and that's what I love. As you know I've already published one book and that's what I'm interested in doing, really exploring drama in education, writing more, exploring more, and Ridge High is the perfect environment to do it.' Angie and Neela, our Chair of Governors beamed.

'So, we're going to be your petri dish, are we?' I said, 'I would have thought the pupils and their learning outcomes should be your focus.' I smiled warmly.

'Oh absolutely. Don't get me wrong,' he raised his hands in mock apology, 'What I mean is that with Karen's agreement…'

'Mrs Blackthorne,' I interjected.

He just about managed to stop himself rolling his eyes, 'Sorry, sure, yes, with Mrs Blackthorne's agreement, I'm going to be trialling new and innovative teaching methods and ideas to get the best results for Ridge High students. I want to build on my considerable experience so I can pass that on to others. I'm hoping to foster my links with Newcastle University, I've already made several contacts, and possibly Durham too. I want to move drama in education back to where it should be after years in the wilderness.'

'That sounds amazing, Martin,' Karen leant forward in her seat, 'What sort of things have you in mind?'

'I'm really interested in Boal, as all practitioners are obviously, but Boal as a tool for change, and particularly how young people can be made to see that they can action change in their own lives. I'd like to do some key work on Invisible

Theatre building on looking at local issues and trying to inject a passion and immediacy into the local community through young people's work. I know that might sound like a pipe dream, but it's worked in much more disenfranchised areas than we find ourselves in. And, in order to focus on this important work, this vital work, I don't want any additional responsibilities within the school. I'm not saying I won't do my fair share, because I absolutely will, but I think this could be great for the students and the school.'

And then he and Karen went back and forth in more detail about bloody Boal, whoever he is, and the Theatre of the Oppressed, until I thought I was going to explode.

Angie was beaming, 'I must say it's really inspiring to hear two subject specialists have such an in-depth conversation with such passion. Now let's move on to some specific problem-solving questions which I don't think are going to be much of an issue for you Martin.'

They all laughed.

There were six candidates, and we went through the pretence of discussing each candidate, but it was a *fait accompli*. The job was his as soon as he loped out of the door. Karen had wanted to invite him round for dinner after the interview, but I said it would be awkward if he didn't get the job. In the end, he had to get back for work anyway, so they went off for a quick drink. Karen insisted on getting a cab home. I tried not to ask too many questions, but she was in a very good mood when she got back and couldn't stop talking about what an asset he was going to be to the department.

In the September, a few days into term I found him showing round pictures of him and Karen on the PGCE in the staff room at lunchtime. I arrived to do my usual 'get them to reg on time' to find Karen was sitting too close to him, bare legs crossed and angled towards him, their knees touching. She was hooting with laughter. Carol, Head of Business, passed me the phone. The pair of them, Karen and Martin, were in the centre of a small group in what looked like a grimy pub or club. Their faces were practically touching. Karen's eyes were wild with the night's excitement, her cheeks flushed, mouth open and smiling and Martin's arm was slung around her shoulder. He looked like he was saying, 'You,' to the camera, the shape of his mouth making his cheekbones even more dramatic and giving his mouth a seductive, girlish pout. His eyes were half-closed, partly obscured by the thick mop of hair falling forward. They looked like a rock duo. They looked beautiful.

'Seems like these two have had a bit of fun in the past, eh, Archie?' Carol said.

'Indeed, it does,' I smiled, 'But then haven't we all?' I winked at her, 'Bell's about to go everyone. Action stations.' And I handed Martin back the phone and pretended to check the duty board with an air of calm worthy of an award. I put my hand up to a name and saw my fingers trembling. I clenched my fist and headed back to my office as slowly as I could manage.

At first Karen denied there was anything going on, but I'd seen so many affairs in school along the way. The beetling over to each other's classrooms at any opportunity for no plausible reason; the same last two cars in the staff car park every day; the first two cars in the car park in the morning; always sitting next to each other at lunch and during staff meetings. Then swapping duties to do them together and signing up for the same trips and arriving late to parents' evenings because you've been to the pub, or something more sordid, rather than have the sandwiches in the canteen with everyone else. If I were to have an affair, I would avoid my lover at all costs during working hours; that way no one would suspect a thing.

He used to drop her at the end of our lane, and she'd walk the last bit home. If I stood up on the top field I could see his car, a flashy MG that made the heads turn at school. Our boys were older, around seventeen and fifteen, I think. Joseph was definitely thinking about university applications because I took them both to an Open Day one Saturday. Karen was supposed to come too but she was unexpectedly ill which was very unlike her. Unbearable period pains she said. 'It must be my age. I can't sit in the car for hours and then walk round a campus. We'll have to re-book.' Looking at her pasty skin, I agreed she was in no fit state; even her lips were pale, almost bluish. I hate to re-arrange plans though and I didn't want to disappoint the boys.

'We'll just make the best of it. The best thing you could do is go for a brisk walk up the fell. Exercise is the most effective reliever for stomach cramps,' I told her, and the boys and I muddled some supplies into a backpack and had a day being steered through big and small glass and metal buildings of differing levels of bleakness with slogans shouting at us intermittently in neon colours on breeze block walls at the edge of a city by a cheery boy who I suspected of being a nerdy Christian type but Joseph quite liked, while I spent the whole day calculating whether Karen's period was due and if she was telling a lie. While I was watching the boys eat thin burgers and soft fries and sip chemical cola, I was working out whether she was with Martin.

I trawled over the week's conversations; had she said where Martin was going to be this weekend? He featured almost non-stop in her day-to-day chit-chat, so I had a good idea of his broad social calendar – a trip planned to Iceland for half-term to see the Northern Lights, going to Kendal for new climbing boots, visiting his mother who had had a fall, off to the dentist for a replacement filling, a jaunt to York to meet up with friends travelling over from Vietnam in their school holidays etc etc. God, it was usually never-ending but this week I could remember nothing. In fact, her silence about Martin's comings and goings seemed remarkable when I looked back. Suspicious even.

The boys were busy with a hands-on experiment in one of the many chemistry labs. I stepped out into the corridor and phoned Karen. No reply. I phoned again.

'Hello?' she sounded groggy.

'Were you asleep?'

'Yes. I was asleep.'

'I thought you were going for a walk?'

'Yes, you did but I didn't. I hardly slept last night. I'm trying to catch up. I'd only just managed to get off.'

'Oh, right,' I felt bad. Then I remembered she was a drama teacher. This could all be a performance. 'What's the weather like there?' This made no sense. I had no way of knowing what the weather was like and what did it prove anyway? I was an idiot.

'Goodbye Archie,' she said evenly.

'Goodbye Karen,' and I finished the call and went back to pick up the boys.

'I quite liked the tour guide, but I don't think that place is for me,' Joseph said as Edward napped in the back on the way home.

'Okay,' I said.

'I think I want to actually be in a city, not in the middle of nowhere,' he sounded fairly determined.

'Are you saying you've been there, done that?' My tone was relaxed.

'Kinda. Yeah,' he said.

'Okay then,' I said, 'So today wasn't wasted.'

'No,' he said, rummaging for crisps in his rucksack.

'You'll miss the country once you're away from it though,' I said, 'You've never really known anything else. City life is hard.'

'Yeah. S'pose so,' he said cheerfully as he crunched on a mouthful of crisps.

Karen was dressed and looked better when we got home. The smell of chicken pie filled the kitchen.

'I'll just get changed,' I said and nipped upstairs. In our bathroom I counted the number of *Tampax* in the box under the sink.

The following evening, I asked her how her tummy was. 'Much better,' she said, 'but still a little sore. Tender you know.'

I'd just counted the *Tampax* again; she hadn't used any.

That's when I knew.

Because I can't get upstairs, I can't check her phone. Martin's long gone. On closer analysis his employment history belied the ability to really stick at anything. He had justified all the two and three year posts as career progressions but I'd say it was a short attention span, or he just couldn't hack the job. He could talk a good game though. Had everyone fooled. Especially Karen. But not me.

So, who is it this time?

I don't want to check her phone though so in some ways I'm relieved that all I can do is sit here and stare at the paper. Edward has decided it's a good idea to get the weekend papers delivered to give me something physical to read rather than just look at another screen. Never really got the hang of books, though perhaps now that will change. Even the paper seems pointless though. Words, words, words. Strangers' opinions on matters that have little to do with me. Do I care about new ways to cook kale or the top ten vegan holiday destinations or about some artist who saved a load of homosexuals from the Nazi death camps? I can't even bring myself to care about the cost-of-living crisis or Putin's latest abominations or even that old chestnut, climate change. I sound like a grumpy old man who's lost touch. I swipe the paper onto the floor and think that maybe I do need something to lift me. Next week Harrison's coming from the next village to fit a ramp on the French doors in the living room. I'll be able to get myself out onto the terrace at least. That will be a little tiny bit of freedom and I'll be able to feel the sun of my face and see the fells and the sky.

'Lunch, Dad.' Edward comes in with a tray. The past few days we've been eating in here rather than the kitchen. My world is shrinking and shrinking even inside the farmhouse. He busies himself setting out plates of salad and glasses of water. I note he has a large pork pie. I have a small one. My calories are being carefully counted and so is my roughage intake. I don't want to get fat. Or constipated. For the first time in my life, I have a paunch. My stomach muscles have slackened remarkably quickly, my previously toned, taut and tanned legs have dwindled to pallid, useless sticks.

Edward tucks in. I'm pretty sure he'll have another pie in the kitchen after this plateful.

'I think I need to start exercising properly,' I say.

He looks up, confused.

'In fact, can you wait for lunch? Would you take me out to the garage? Could you manage that?'

'Absolutely.' Edward's thrilled at whatever little plan I'm cooking up and we wrestle me into another couple of layers against the chill in the spring air and he pushes me down the ramp over the uneven path towards the separate double garage that's at the edge of the drive. It's a bit of an effort.

'We'll need to work this out Edward. I can't get across here myself. Could we lay a concrete path? Self-levelling? Something quite straightforward – maybe around the edge so it wouldn't look too out of place?' I say 'we', but I mean

Edward and Joseph; my days of renovation and home improvement are over.

'That sounds like a great idea, Dad.' He's unlocked the garage doors but there's something wrong, I can sense he's worried. Maybe he thinks the exercise idea is a non-starter.

'Open them up Edward. I'm thinking we can re-arrange things and set up something that's a cross between the physio at the Unit and a kind of home gym with a few free weights, a pull-down bar, that sort of thing.' For the first time in months, I actually feel a spark of enthusiasm. I want to reassure him that we can do this, together.

'Look, Dad,' Edward starts.

'Just open them up,' I insist.

The first one is the expected, organised storage I left behind; tools, bikes, boxes of junk we should have gone through but haven't got round to. I think we'll easily be able to move much of this up into the eaves or even up into the attic and re-purpose this side into a gym. I keep my second car in the other garage so I don't really need to see that though I suppose it will be nice to see the old girl while I'm here. We don't park the day-to-day car in the garage. It just sits by the crab apple. I know there's an argument for parking in a garage overnight but it's a faff to open the door and if it looks like a hard frost, one of us just hurls an old blanket across the windscreen if we remember. We live in a very low crime rate area so no worries there really. My pride and joy is kept in the garage though.

When we bought the house, the double garage was a bonus, as were the scattering of other outbuildings. It was built later than the farmhouse, and in better nick. Watertight so clean and dry.

And I'd always wanted a classic car. A proper collector's item. When I sold Mum and Dad's house after Mum died, I thought, why not? The car came up at auction and she was a beauty, a dream, perfection - a diamond blue Mercedes 280SL.

I felt like James Bond driving her back with the top down. I kept gliding my free hand across the royal blue leather, caressing it, still beautifully soft, just a little creased with age. She had been treated by her previous owner as an investment piece, so the mileage was ridiculously low and the chrome still shone with a mirror finish, barely a mark on it. There were all sorts of details that I couldn't believe, the original Becker Europa radio was still in place; not a crack or scratch on the Burr walnut of the dashboard and every single dial replete with the original factory markings. She was the most incredible find.

We were a match made in heaven. It's funny the effect your childhood has on you. How bits of it stay with you. One of my earliest teenage fantasies was Farah Fawcett-Majors. That taut body, the blonde hair and the flashing smile was pretty much every boy's wet dream when I was growing up. But I also remember Bobby Ewing driving a Merc 280SL in *Dallas*. Mum always wanted me to sit and watch it with her, and Pam Ewing was pretty gorgeous too with those great tits, so I didn't mind once in a while. I loved Bobby's car though. So sleek and powerful in the Texas sun; it was a world away from the drab life I was living. Then I saw an article in my classic car mag about Farrah driving a Merc 280SL as well. So that was it. I started searching for one and when I found her, I had to have her. Even paid a bit more than I wanted to, but she was worth it. And Farrah was her name as soon as I saw her.

The hours I've spent polishing and waxing the bodywork or tinkering away on the engine. When I first took ownership, I realised I needed to clean out the plenum chamber. I had to remove the blower motor completely, clean down the chamber, removing the surface rust before carefully treating and painting it. I managed to track down a new blower motor, case and seal and, goddam it, I fitted them all myself. The joy of that solitude, just restoring and working away. I loved everything about it, the smell of the oil, the beauty of the way the engineering worked, the problem solving. Even when I hit a wall there was nothing like tracking down a part or getting on one of the on-line forums and tapping into all that knowledge. The roar of the engine too. Nothing like it. Fantastic.

Edward lifts the second door, and the garage is empty. Completely empty. My car is gone.

'What's going on? Who's moved Farrah?' Edward is looking straight at me, but I know there's bad news coming. 'Your mother's not insured to drive her,' I say, 'I'm the only one on the policy. Where is she?' I cover my eyes with my hands. 'Oh hell. You two didn't take her out, did you? You didn't ...' I can hardly bear to say the words, 'You didn't crash her, did you?' Picturing that magnificent feat of engineering as twisted metal is almost too much for me.

Edward springs over to me. 'No Dad, no,' he crouches down next to me as if I am the child and he the parent who must soothe the youngster in the face of another tragedy, 'Mum sold it,' he says quietly.

'Sold Farrah?' I say in quiet disbelief.

'Yeah. When you were in hospital. To pay for all the modifications. The wet room and that.' He gestures over towards the hideous ramp as if it is an embarrassing relative, we have to acknowledge but must try to ignore.

'Sold my car. But,' I'm doing some calculations, 'she must have been worth... What did she get for her?'

Edward brightens, 'Oh good money, I think. About thirty grand.'

'Thirty grand!' I explode, 'She was worth double that!' I've been home for weeks and my car has been sold for months and no-one has told me. I am no longer being treated as an equal; I am an appendix in this family.

'It's just that, well, Mum knew you wouldn't be able to drive it and she had to find the money so you could come home.'

The one thing I had for myself was gone. The only thing I had for myself. I barely drive her anyway; the mileage is so limited on the insurance. I could still have tinkered away on the engine, started her up, fine- tuned her, polished and waxed her; hell, all I wanted to do was preserve her, and now she is gone. I am both bereft and livid.

'Take me back inside, Edward,' I say turning my head from the gaping empty chasm before me. I can't bear it any longer.

I get myself onto my bed dismissing Edward rather more gruffly than I'd have liked; I'm managing the hoist and bar more or less on my own now. I lie there like a rag doll, my stomach growling with hunger, awash with self-pity, hoping Karen will leave me. How could she be so heartless? And why hadn't she told me? Yet again, I am filled with panic for the future. How can I survive a life so devoid of love and meaning? I decide to start hoarding my painkillers in case everything gets too difficult. I have so little agency I need to think ahead while I still have access to strong medication.

4

'**Y**ou need to stop treating the children like your slaves.' Karen is lecturing me.

'I don't. They do stuff for me. Most of the time I don't even ask,' my voice sounds like a whine. I am pleading with her to believe me.

'Well then you need to accept it but then ask them to stop. Point out that you are more than capable of doing things yourself,' she persists.

'Huh,' I say.

'You are.' She's right back at me, 'You're just doing them at a different height, that's all. We've changed things around in the kitchen. Most of the stuff is easily within your reach. You should be as independent as possible, Archie.'

'Okay.' I sound sulky.

'Don't you want to be independent?' She sounds like a mother talking to a reluctant toddler. 'Don't you want to show the doctor/dentist/torturer what a brave boy you can be?'

'Of course I do,' I say crossly.

'Good,' and she turns on her heels to leave.

'Except that it's hardly independence, is it?' I say.

She exhales loudly with her back to me and faces me, folding her arms in complete exasperation. 'What do you mean?' she allows.

'Look at me, Karen. Think about what my life is,' I say.

'That's hardly my fault.' Her eyes flare.

'And it's hardly my fault the children still want to be a part of my life.' What the hell, she's desperate to leave the room anyway.

'You should think about getting a job. There's nothing wrong with your mind.' Her chin juts up again. She's taking me on.

'As far as I'm aware I'm still on sick leave. I still have a contract.' I feel a fizz of rage pulsing behind my sternum.

'Officially, yes, but we both know you can't go back no matter what occupational health say. Think about it? How can you even lead an assembly? You can't get on stage. And how can you get to the maths block? The majority of the classrooms are upstairs, Two flights of stairs.' I think she's enjoying this. 'There's only one accessible toilet for God's sake, in the DT block. You couldn't even get into the Head's office because of the narrowness of the corridors. I've thought about it. Angie's asked me about it. Unofficially. It's a non-starter, Archie. The best thing you can do is get online and start thinking about some homeworking posts. Give your brain something to do.'

I shake my head at her. 'Anything else?' I say, 'Any other little bombshells you'd like to drop. You beggar belief, Karen. Since the fall, you've ripped out the heart of this house, sold my car without my permission which I'm pretty sure is illegal, and now I hear, you've effectively resigned on my behalf, without a word to me. You're a piece of work Karen, you really are.'

'Oh, hell's teeth, stop being so dramatic, Archie, I haven't got time for this.' She looks everywhere but at me.

'No, you never have. You can walk away though can't you? You can leave. Step out into your other life. Without me. But I can't. I'm stuck in this,' and I rattle the wheels. 'Be independent you say! Making myself a sandwich and getting out into the garden under my own steam is hardly a full and satisfying life, is it? For your information, I'm already doing the Access courses online,' I lie, 'I'm already thinking about the future, updating my skills, though I thought it would still be within Ridge High somehow. I don't know what else you want, Karen. I can't do anything right anymore.' I'm aware how bitter and snipey my tone is.

Karen rolls her eyes. 'Oh, Archie, give it a rest? I just said stop treating the kids like slaves, I didn't need a whole life history. And I don't need to hear you whining. I've got to get to work.'

I hear her rev the car excessively before she zooms up off the lane. Let's hope she doesn't have an accident on the way to work or where would that leave us?

For years we've talked about selling the house, well, Karen's brought it up and I've rejected it. I understand that it's not been ideal for her but for me it has been everything I have worked for, everything I have longed for. I always felt peaceful here, safe, king of my castle, I suppose. For Karen she found the winters particularly a grind, the bleaker, shorter days were hard and, not driving, added to what she felt was a lack of freedom. Once spring arrived, she always perked up though and put her energy into the garden, the animals, outdoor activities with the children.

Lately, I have to admit that now I am spending so much time in the house I am wondering whether this is really where our future lies.

I find myself thinking that if we were in a town, I could get myself to a coffee shop or to a library. I could even perhaps learn to love window shopping. I think that in a town, I would like to have a room with a view of people passing. I would like to feel as if I was part of life, even though I'd be largely just observing it. At the moment I'm bloody Rapunzel in a tower in the middle of nowhere. As I sit and stare out of the kitchen window at the dull green fells; they don't call to me like they used to when I could fling open the back door and race up them, lungs full of the chill air, heart feeling lean and strong. No, at the moment, I find them misshapen and oppressive, great, lifeless, lumps thrown down like clay on a potter's wheel to serve as barricades; I want to sweep them aside so I can see what's beyond. At the moment they feel insurmountable and unfriendly, and I resent them.

Perhaps this will pass. Perhaps this is a phase. I'm not sure it is though.

And I'm not sure how to bring up with Karen that I'm having a change of heart and that perhaps a move would be the best thing for all of us.

As I'm looking out of the window, a car pulls up.

I'm not expecting anyone.

The morning carer has been and gone.

I lean further towards the window seat to get a better view. My heart sinks as one of the neighbours, Jan, springs from the car.

Jan Townsend is ostensibly as friend of Karen's, in that their paths have crossed at village functions. Jan's moody girls have sullenly progressed through Ridge High and are now, no doubt sulking their way through universities, though I don't recall which, despite Jan having yelled it into my face at every opportunity. I think, from memory, she's very proud of at least one of them. Hell, I can't even remember their names. I'm not even sure how many there are. I'll let her do the talking. She barely pauses for breath as it is.

I watch her check her appearance in a little mirror, puff her rigid, dark hair and deftly apply lipstick to her thin mouth. Perhaps she's come to ask a favour, maybe she's heard Karen wants to sell the house and she's looking for a good price. Her husband, can't remember his name either, has property. No, that's wrong, it's all coming back to me, she does. Lots of property. One of the reasons the girls were so sulky was because they were sent to the local comp instead of some grand independent with expensive uniforms and a hush hush drug problem. Jan could have afforded it. Easily.

I watch her slam the car door shut and head straight for the front door. She doesn't bother to knock. 'Hello? Archie? You here? It's Jan?' I am affronted by the sing-song bellowing. Just because my legs don't work, doesn't mean to say she can just barge in.

'Archie?' I can hear her opening my bedroom door. Bloody hell! The nerve.

'In the kitchen!' I shout crossly.

She clumps up the hallway, 'I thought I'd catch you on my way over to town. It's been ages since I saw you and I've been meaning to pop in. Just had so much on. You know what it's like. Busy, busy, busy. Shall I put the kettle on? Oh, you're a good colour, aren't you? You look great! Really good! Tea or coffee?' I shrug a whatever to her. 'No signs of any … I mean apart from the obvious … I mean no *scarring*, visible that is, which is pretty incredible given the list of your injuries. Really, it's a miracle you survived. You're lucky to be alive. But I'm glad there's no *scarring* because you always were a handsome chap, Archie. I'd see you running past my house, had a great view from my kitchen window you know, and I'd think, look at the legs on that, especially in the summer when you'd had a bit of sun. Made my day. In fact, I went through a bit of a phase of planning my day around your running. Ha! Imagine that? Well, I can tell you that now, can't I? Here we go, a nice cuppa. Just what the doctor ordered, eh? Now, I wonder if I can find you a biccy.'

Jan sits opposite me, eyes bright and expectant and sips her tea, then has a physical look through the biscuit tin, swirling them as if they need a stir around. I'm pretty sure they're all the same. I make a mental note to throw them all out once she's left. I hope that won't be too far away.

'So, what have you been doing with yourself?' she starts again, mid dip of her biscuit, 'Tell me everything.'

'Really?' I say.

'Yes!' she shrieks as if I've been on a round the world trip or just met the person who's found a cure for cancer.

'Mainly, Jan, I sit in this chair and look out of the window. I eat and piss and shit and then I sleep. Sometimes I need to wear an adult nappy, sometimes I don't. Strangers come to the house and undress me and tuck me into bed like I am a toddler. I have to watch every morsel that I eat so I can manage to heave my body weight around by my arms and not my legs. I haven't left the house since I came home from the hospital and my wife is barely talking to me. I am one of this year's paraplegic statistics. No. I tell a lie, I'm not even that. I am last year's paraplegic statistic. So yes, there you go, as you said, I'm lucky to be alive.'

I feel a bit bad about the bit about Karen but what the hell. This is how I'm feeling today; it's hard to see a good side.

Jan looks at me for a moment. Then the sides of her mouth pull down in an exaggerated clownish sad face. 'Oh dear, Mr Droopy Drawers, we are feeling sorry for ourselves, aren't we?' she mocks.

'Are we, Jan?' I say, 'You seem fairly chipper.' I wish she would leave. Her lipstick is horribly vivid, and I can smell her sour breath, she's talking so loudly.

'Come on, Archie, it can't be that bad? Karen said you were down in the dumps, but you do sound a little, well, self-indulgent. I mean you've got the boys at your beck and call and with all the technology there is these days, this could just be a temporary setback. You could be walking again in five years.' She smiles manically at me.

'Karen said I was down in the dumps?' I say.

'Well, not in so many words. She implied it.'

'When? When did she imply it?' I lean across the table at her.

'We were both at that new wine bar that's opened in town. You know where the Italian was that closed down a while back. It's now a wine bar. All very chic. Industrial pipes everywhere and stripped wooden floors. I think that look is a bit passé if you check out *Insta* but anyway the locals seem to like it. Karen was there with some of the teachers from school. I recognised a few of them obviously.'

'Which teachers? Who was there? When was this?' I try not to sound too desperate for information. In my head I'm working out when Karen has been out but it's hard to keep track as sometimes I nap in the evening if my pain's bad and I'm not always sure if she's in the house or not.

Jan is rummaging in her bag. 'I can't remember their names, but why don't you have a look at the photos? I've got them on *Insta*. Hang on.' She starts to scroll through her phone and then she hands me it and there is Karen looking flushed and joyous surrounded by a group of five or six beaming faces. I swipe along and the next is Karen and the irritating Business Studies teacher, Carol, chinking vast, quarter-filled wine glasses, then Carol and the back of someone's head, and then I'm looking at Karen grinning at a guy who is beaming in the camera. Her arm is on his shoulder, hand relaxed, nearly touching his brilliant white, T-shirted chest. He looks smug. The cat that got the cream. It's Charlie. The latest addition to the English department. Charlie fucking Linton. I knew he was an appointment I was going to regret with his even teeth and pop culture references that went right over my head. I thought he would have been too young for Karen but apparently not. I've never liked him.

I hand the phone back to Jan and resist the urge to smash the biscuit tin onto the floor. 'Yes, the usual crowd,' I say calmly, 'Was it a late night?'

'I'll say. They had to kick us out,' Jan screeches, 'That lot was particularly lively, shall we say. At one point there was talk of dancing on the tables. Lots of good booze there to draw in the punters.' She looks down fondly at her phone and sighs.

Her attention snaps back to me, 'Anyway, Mr Grumpy Guts, enough of that, now what are we going to do about your terrible mood, eh?'

I realise I am glaring at her.

'What do you suggest Jan? Bionic legs? Turning back time?' I snarl.

'What about a hand or two of rummy? Have you got a pack of cards?' she chirrups.

Jan leaves shortly after that. I cannot help my blunt riposte to her suggestion. As she speeds off up the drive, no doubt already texting or talking to anyone and everyone she can think of about her terrible treatment at the hands of the cripple who used to be such a 'good guy', I turn my attention back to Charlie Linton.

I can only remember Karen making vaguely scornful remarks about him. I got the idea she thought he was fairly shallow and too chummy with the pupils. He missed deadlines, turned up late for duties, that sort of thing. English and Drama share the same office and therefore the same chat at breaks. How did I not pick up on him as a threat? I thought he was going out with one of the younger Art teachers at first, and then for a while, I thought he was gay. He did have quite flamboyant dress sense. Then I saw him watching a group of the sixth form girls far too closely. There was no mistaking his interest there.

I do remember wandering in on a lunchtime poetry group he was running. This was just after he'd started back in late September. I was doing a bit of patrolling and prowling, the bread and butter of a deputy head. The noise from the classroom was what drew me in. We're lucky to have quite a few extra-curricular activities at Ridge High. Most staff keep their non-contact time as we have a permanent cover supervisor. Angie is always banging on about the staff being 'the school' and keeping them on board 'no matter what'. I'd say over half run some sort of club or activity and about ninety per cent see kids in some form out of lessons to offer subject help or enrichment. It's impressive.

The noise levels coming from Charlie Linton's classroom were not what we usually expect, however. Remarkably, no one inside really noticed when I pushed open the door on what appeared to be absolute chaos. Linton had stacked and pushed all the desks and chairs against the window wall so he, and a mass of students of all ages, could crawl around on the floor. In their midst were a large number of sugar paper sheets which had been scrawled upon and torn up into giant jagged strips. These were being ordered and pinned up at various points on the walls around the room by yet more students. Instructions and requests were being yelled by everyone.

'I need a description that could fit with the moon!'

'That line won't work there; it jumps ahead too quickly.'

'Did anyone write anything about greed?'

'We need to start again. I want to trade everything we've got!'

Finally, Linton looked up and saw me, he had a marker pen in his mouth and, grinning on all fours, looked like a moronic dog bringing his master a bone. He spat out the pen. 'Hi!' he bawled, with inappropriate familiarity I felt, 'Welcome to Poetry Stock Exchange. We're writing, buying, selling and trading to get the best final poem in twenty-five minutes.'

I like to think my refusal to crack a smile caused him to jump to his feet; the students continued to ignore me much to my annoyance; they were utterly absorbed in the task. And collaborating right across every year group. I felt a twinge as I wished we were going through an Ofsted inspection as this sort of thing always goes down really well. Then I remembered the noise.

Linton scratched his head elaborately, clearly totally chuffed with how everything was progressing, 'Sorry Mr Blackthorne, it looks chaotic, but they all know exactly what they're doing.'

Jamie Robson from Year 8, a weary little snitch prone to tears, suddenly jumped onto a chair and sounded a klaxon horn. I jumped. 'Ten minutes to close of play!' he shouted, and the fervour ramped up a notch as the teams now manically scrambled to reach their goal.

'A klaxon?' I turned to Linton.

'Too much?' he tried to charm me by flashing his impeccable white teeth at me.

'Too much,' I admonished. I felt like a curmudgeonly outsider. If Linton had not been so much the centre of everyone's enthusiasm; if his rolled-up shirt sleeves had not revealed lean, tanned forearms flecked with golden hairs; if his trousers had not hung so easily across his hips caught with an understated but clearly very expensive, soft leather belt; if I hadn't been able to see the muscles of his powerful shoulders move beneath the fine fabric of his shirt as he lunged around the floor reaching for the shards of paper and pressing them into eager hands, perhaps I would have joined in with the shared delight. Perhaps I would have leant against a desk and marvelled at the creativity he'd unlocked in these disparate youngsters. Perhaps I would have stayed to listen to them read their collaborations, pride and belonging swelling their voices.

Instead, I said, 'Get this mess cleared up in time for registration,' and turned and left slamming the door closed behind me. Annoyingly, this had no discernible effect on anyone in the classroom.

I think about the photo and the look on Karen's face. She never looks like that at me. She hasn't for years. Hell, she barely looks at me at all. So, Charlie Linton is the latest apple for the teacher. I begin to plan and think about what I have on him. Irritatingly, there are steps down into the study. When Edward gets back, I'm going to ask him to hook up my work laptop. There hasn't been any point so far but now I want to have a good look at Linton and see what I can find.

5

'You said you wanted to sell the house. I don't understand,' I am parked in the doorway of the French doors watching Karen savagely attack a potentilla in the garden. 'I don't know why you're digging that up. It's perfectly healthy,' I add for good measure.

'I don't like it,' she says, 'I never have. It has mean little flowers and dull leaves and it irritates me and it is the first thing I see when I look out of the window so I'm digging it up. I've suffered it for fourteen years. Not anymore. It's annoying,' and she plunges her fork into the soil at the base of the poor shrub and rocks it back and forth, slowly loosening its hold in the ground.

'You've been saying we're too remote here for years. What's changed?' I wish the ramp was down so I could get a bit closer to her, make her stop and pay attention to me.

Her conker brown hair has fallen over her face and, leaving the sorry potentilla for a moment, she swipes it back with a muddy hand and glares at me. 'What has changed Archie, is that I can drive now. I'm not trudging down to the bus stop or having to fit in with your day. I can, at last, suit myself.' As if to emphasise this, she stretches expansively taking in a lungful of air, eyes closed, face turned to the milky sun, almost smiling, 'We've got everything we need here, the house is adapted for your requirements, Georgie likes school, my job is going really well. Why should I move?'

'I'm trying to tell you that I'd be happier if we were in the town, Karen. You've no idea how cut off this place can be. It's like, well, it's like a prison. I've barely been out of here. I can't get down the lane, I can't get more than ten yards from the front door. I'm trapped Karen. It's not fair.' My voice peters out. I'm not even sure she's listening to me; she's manhandling the plant now, tugging and grunting, legs straddling it in a most ungainly manner.

'You could wait for the boys to do that,' I shout.

She stands up, pink-faced and sweating. 'I'm quite capable of up-rooting a small shrub,' she snaps, 'And, as to your whining about the current situation, I beg to differ, Archie. I am fully aware of how cut off this place can be; it's you who has been blissfully unaware of the fact so now you know how I've felt, don't you, Archie, all these years? While we've had to fit in with your plans, all your bloody marathons, hanging around for your SLT meetings, all those hours and hours and hours of my life wasted, waiting for you because you had the car keys, and I couldn't drive. The shoe's on the other foot now, isn't it?' Karen has abandoned the plant and is walking towards me, fork clutched in both hands like a spear, 'So, Archie, you'll just have to get used to it. I've had about twenty years here, which is more or less a life sentence, you've had a few months. Time for you to dig in mate and get used to it.'

For a moment, I am speechless. 'What's happened to you, Karen?' I say, 'I've never heard you speak like this before?'

'Don't you get it, Archie? Everything's different now.' She's holding the fork as if she might jab me in the stomach and, with the look in her eye, I have a vision of her impaling me and fishing me out of the chair, as if I am a shrimp in a prawn cocktail, and waving me like a helpless, limp flag above her head as she cackles triumphantly.

I retreat back into the living room and head for the kitchen. My hands are shaking as I lift the paper and try to focus on the words in front of me.

There's a primeval roar which makes me flinch; I gather she's unearthed the potentilla.

Edward has been away at some team-building event in the Lake District. I watch his solid back as he stirs a pot of chilli and hope these aren't going to be regular occurrences. The fact that he has a job at all is a matter of some surprise to us all; like Joseph he vaguely traipsed around some universities but when it came to it, he couldn't commit, citing too much debt and lack of any real interest in a specific subject. Karen made quite a fuss.

He's done a smattering of on-line courses and had a handful of short-term jobs, mostly tech-based and involving commuting no further than from his bed to his desk. He's smart, Edward, but lazy. Anyway, this latest job seems a bit more promising; he's had a few days in Manchester and a week's training in London. It's an American firm. All since Christmas.

His life seems to be picking up too since my accident. I found an ad for a studio flat circled in the local paper; Edward's never mentioned moving out before.

Perhaps he has a girlfriend.

'So, were there many people on this jolly?' I ask, taking a clutch of peanuts from the bowl Edward has set before me. I know I shouldn't have too many but today has been stressful. I chuck them into my mouth and crunch. I relish the salty flavour washing around my mouth and I furtively reach for another handful briefly mourning the days when I never gave a thought to what I ate or drank.

'It wasn't a jolly, Dad, we were bonding and there was problem-solving and some of the guys said the management use it to cherry pick potential movers and shakers for the future.'

'Weren't you doing the high wires through the trees? For the kids?' I take more nuts. I can't help it. They're delicious.

'It's not just for kids, Dad.' I can hear the patience in his voice, and I want to smash the bowl of peanuts against the wall. His tone implies that I am completely out of touch with the world. 'Yes, part of it was that, but we did it as a team and we had tasks within it, like one of us was blind-folded, one of us had a hand tied behind their back, one wasn't allowed to speak. You know that kind of thing. And we had to carry all these different items with us. And collect things on the way. So, we had to work as a team to get through the course. It was great. We had this natural leader on our team, Sohaib, he was brilliant, really calm and easy-going but he had all these cool ways to get us through the problems.' Edward is chopping salad and I can hear the smile in his voice.

'I'd have thought you'd be the natural leader, Edward,' I say, and I see his shoulders stiffen a little. He turns and faces me, smiling tightly.

'Not really Dad, not much experience, think that's your gig, isn't it?' and he turns back to the stove, 'This is just about ready. I'll go and shout Georgie. Do you want to set the table?' and he bounds out of the kitchen leaving me to wheel my way over to the cutlery drawer.

I set out places for the four of us, leaving a fork for Karen on the side. She rarely eats with us. There is always something unmissable on the TV or she has some reading to catch up on and she'll eat in the study, or she's feeling wiped, and she'll take it upstairs. Sometimes I eat in my room so she can eat with the kids. I know it's me she's avoiding, though of course, she won't come clean and say it. Instead, we keep up the pretence that there is a valid reason why we never sit down as a family of five anymore.

I wonder if she'll ever forgive me for falling off the roof.

There have been some terrible moments where Karen has been what I can only describe as cruel.

One weekend, just after the carer had left, I had the worst kind of accident, it wasn't the first time it had happened but, in this case, it was a long time until a carer was due back again. There's a good reason why it's called fouling yourself. It is repugnant. Disgusting and distressing. Neither Edward nor Joseph were home, which was unusual, practically unheard of in fact, and Georgie had been at a sleepover. Karen and I were, for once, home alone. How many times over the years had I longed for us to have the house to ourselves? Child free, hours alone. Time to re-visit those long-gone days of our early romance where time stretched ahead of us, and all our thoughts were for each other.

I sat in my own shit, the fresh stench unbearable and an absolute assault to the senses. It's not like a baby's nappy, though those can be fairly rank on occasion. No, this is on a whole other level. Thankfully, I couldn't actually feel it, but I was prickling with embarrassment and yelling for Karen as well as phoning her. In between my shouts I could hear her bloody phone tiddly-dee-deeing upstairs and yet she wasn't answering. I was reluctant to wheel into the hallway, knowing any movement was going to make the whole unthinkable situation in my pants a hell of a lot worse. I kept up the phoning and the shouting, the smell becoming intolerable.

Finally, Karen came thumping down the stairs hell for leather, and burst into the room. 'What the bloody hell is it now? You're more demanding than a toddler!' Her face contorted, 'Jesus! What is that smell?'

'I'm sorry. I've … look, I didn't realise I needed to …' To my shame, I felt my face flush as my wife looked at me with utter revulsion.

'You're joking?' she spat at me, crossing her arms aggressively. 'I'm not changing you, Archie. I refuse to do it. You'll have to manage yourself.'

'I can't Karen. How can I? I need to shower. I can't do that. It's not safe.' I sounded pathetic.

She stared at me.

'Can you phone a carer?' I begged.

Karen let out a hard sharp laugh. 'It's difficult enough getting them here on a regular basis, so there's no chance we can call and one of them will rock up in the next half an hour. This is just great, Archie. Christ, the smell is unbelievable. I'm going to have to open a window.' She strode over and pulled up the window letting in a blast of cold air.

'When are the boys back?' Joseph had helped out showering me on more than one occasion.

'I don't know!' Karen sounded exasperated, 'I don't know their every move! They're grown men Archie, in case you haven't noticed. They have their own lives to live now.'

'Does everything you say need to be so … hurtful. I'm just trying to think of a way out of this situation. I can't talk to you anymore. It's like you're a different person. Have a heart, Karen. I'm sitting here in my own filth and there's nothing I can do about it. Have a little … compassion, can't you?' I felt tears hot in my eyes.

'You don't need to remind me about your filth, it stinks! I don't know what to do about this, Archie. I guess you're going to have to figure it out,' and with that she stepped out and shut the door.

I sat there, because there was fuck all else I could do, and then I wheeled myself into the wet room. We had a bar over the chair in the shower for me to grip. I'd never tried any of this on my own before. Somehow, I got myself onto it and pushed my trousers, then my pants down my useless legs, one-handed, the other hand steadying myself between the bar and the chair rail. It took an agonizingly long time, and I ended up with shit smeared all down my legs and over my hands. Several times I retched but managed not to actually vomit. There was little I could actually do about the soiled laundry. I was just happy I had managed to push it far enough away from the chair so, once this hell was over, I wouldn't be trapped in there with the cloth tangling in my wheels or foot plates.

I turned on the shower and washed myself as well as I could, staying in the hot water as long as possible. The room wasn't overly warm and though grappling with my clothes had worked up a sweat, that moisture, evaporating quickly, had added to a drop in my body temperature.

There was only one small hand towel in the bathroom; my bath towel had gone into the wash that morning after the carer had helped with my shower. I knew it was going to be dangerous to be wet and try to move around and I'd sprayed as much of the chair as I could safely reach with the shower to clean it off as well. I sat and sat letting everything get as dry as possible before I tried to move back into the chair. The towel was heavy and damp, but I still wiped it over the frame and seat, hoping it might make a difference.

I was naked, cold, tired and defeated. It was barely ten o' clock and I just wanted to be back in my bed. Gripping the bar with one hand and my chair with the other, I attempted the lift across. I didn't make it. My arms weren't on my side. Wrestling off my trousers had obviously been more of an effort than I thought. I tried again and luckily crashed into the chair, though there was a heart thudding tilt as the uncontrolled force of my full body weight hit home. Luckily, the chair righted itself rather than tipping right over. I was winded and pretty sure there would be a bruise where I'd caught my side as I thudded across, but I was back in.

Looking down at my groin and legs as I got ready to wheel myself to the bedroom, I noticed how spindly I'd become. Obviously, I'd never sat unclothed in the chair before. My legs used to be strong, powerful, all lean muscle. They could carry me for miles. Now, in a few short months, they'd wasted away to little more than bone.

A wave of grief washed over me, and I looked up at the arctic white practical ceiling. I could have been in a care facility. There was nothing in here to tell me I was in my home. The shower head was dripping, echoing bleakly in the sterile room. My crumpled trousers were leaking a gingery rivulet into the steel drain. I felt a sob catch in my chest and, for a few moments, I shut my eyes against it all.

As I pushed open my bedroom door, a blast of cold air assaulted me. The draft from the window must have blown the door shut and the room was now freezing. I couldn't reach to close it and, anyway, I hadn't the strength to pull down the sash window.

Exhausted, I managed to haul myself into bed and pull up the duvet and some of my blankets after a fashion. They weren't enough but they were better than nothing. I didn't bother phoning Karen; I knew she would ignore me. Falling into a dreamless sleep, I thought about my cache of painkillers and wondered whether this was a sign that I should just get on and take them.

It was much later when Edward woke me, dressed me, fed me. He eventually told me Karen had gone out, and I'm sure I caught the disapproval in his tone when he reported this. He wanted to phone the GP, kept talking about hypothermia. Said I wasn't making sense. We never spoke about the mess in the shower. He would just have dealt with it. It's hard to understand why Karen behaved like that but I suppose she must have had her reasons.

There're the little things as well that just show a lack of consideration for my situation; the remote control for my TV finds itself in her study which, as I may have said before is down two steps. And I think we need to order a new one anyway as the batteries need replacing all the time. Quite often I watch in the middle of the night if I can't sleep, and it's frustrating to have the remote in my hand and the screen refusing to leap into life. Karen needs to think about the batteries she's getting. Perhaps I should order some. It's happening all the time.

And then there's silly stuff that shouldn't matter but, when you have nothing else to consider, take on a greater significance I suppose. Like every packet of biscuits I have in my tin apparently gets dropped as there's never a whole one in there. Karen knows I like to dunk my biscuits in my tea, especially digestives, but I open the tin and it's like looking at a box of jigsaw pieces, or a starter pack for a mosaic. There's no nice whole ones. I'm not blaming anyone, but they need to take more care.

Karen has accused me of carelessness in the past. In fact, I think one incident may be at the root of her fury.

It was quite a few years ago when I was in the early part of my hill running phase. Looking back, it's fair to say I was a little obsessed. I was up in the fells most weekends. And some evenings. Well, every weekend really and quite a few evenings. And I'd got it into my head that I couldn't miss a practice run so, even when the weather forecast wasn't good, I was reluctant to postpone. Usually at some point from four on a Friday afternoon and around seven on a Sunday evening, the weather would allow for a run; a good couple of hours. This one particular weekend was different though. It was relentless rain and there was early fog in the mornings too, treacherous for runners. It got to around three on the Sunday and I couldn't stand it any longer. The clouds seemed a little higher and the rain was light, a drizzle really. I told Karen I was heading out.

'Don't, Archie, it'll be worse higher up.' I knew she was worried.

'I won't go up. I'll stick to the low paths,' I told her though I only said this to stop her complaining, 'I know the fells like the back of my hand, I'll be back before you know it.'

It was the end of summer and temperatures had been falling steadily and that's one of the problems with the fells. It can be a sunny day at ground level but get up high and into a bit of a cloud cover and you're looking at a drop of ten degrees minimum. Couple that with poor visibility and weak navigation skills and you can be in serious trouble.

As I headed up, my hand touched my mountain marathon pack as a reflex, waterproofs, a compass, an energy bar, a small torch, water, all in one neat package clipped around my waist. I had excellent running shoes and quality running gear too; I wasn't an amateur, and as the path stretched up and out beyond me, I was elated to be leaving the Sunday afternoon fug of the kitchen behind. My stride lengthened and soon I was moving higher, and I thought the sky looked brighter in the direction I was heading. When sunlight pushed through the violet clouds, the fells glistened, lush and plump with the recent rain. Even the stony scree under my feet was vivid and vibrant and I found myself smiling as my breath quickened and I worked my way higher.

I was making good time and toying with moving down and cutting back through the village as a bit of a compromise, but I couldn't resist pushing on further up the track. I reasoned that were only a handful of weekends left before the weather made this route permanently hazardous and, with my experience, I couldn't foresee there would be any real problem.

At the summit of the fell, I allowed myself a brief respite. Checking my pulse, I noted how quickly it was slowing as I drew in deep, powerful breaths of clean, sweet air. It was hard to ignore the gathering bruise blooming in the clouds behind me though. As I began my descent, I estimated I was at least an hour from home.

Ten minutes later, a light mist thickened into an oppressive impenetrable fog. Unpacking my waterproofs, it was eerily quiet. Surprisingly there was no wind, unusual for the fells, just persistent steady drizzle seeping into every opening, down my neck, into the pack as soon as I opened it, into my mouth as I swore when my cold hands couldn't get the zipper to work on my jacket. So much rain. Quiet rain. And the light was fading.

I decided to save the torch as long as I could and started running again, but the fog seemed to be getting thicker. I had to keep looking down to follow the path. It was hard going, and it was affecting my rhythm. In my head I was trying to work out if there was a shortcut I could take or a safer route, but it was hard to make sense of everything. My running had slowed down because I couldn't see properly and I felt out of sorts, clunky, like a wind-up toy needing the key to be turned.

With no view of the skyline or landscape, I was becoming disorientated too. I had no idea how far I'd come down, or even how long I'd been running. It could have been five minutes or fifty. Bizarrely, I couldn't place myself on the fell at all.

I didn't see the rock that I fell over. It was big so I should have. I lurched forward and fell heavily over to one side. Unluckily for me, the trip sent me off the path and I rolled down the bank, steep and away to the right. Had I fallen to the left I'd have tipped up the fell and, like as not into a gorse bush or two. But no, I plummeted down the side of the hill instead.

As I rolled, I have to say I quite enjoyed it to begin with. I remembered rolling down a hill near our house as a child with my friends. It was grassy and fairly smooth and every year we'd have a bit of a craze for doing it and then it would wear off and we'd move onto something else. It was a good slope for sledging too and rolling Easter eggs.

When we wanted to plunge down ourselves, we'd lay along the top, arms tucked in, eyes closed, legs straight, a row of little corpses, and all set off together, giggling cigars getting faster and faster as we gained momentum. Sometimes we veered off course and crashed into each other, or worse came to a premature halt. That was the pits. You felt cheated and we'd run back up and start again.

Falling off the path was quite like rolling down the hill at first, except my limbs were not controlled. I was not a neat tube, and then I began to somersault over and over, tipping this way and that, landing painfully on my coccyx, hitting my head and my knee and my elbow, skating and skidding on the sodden terrain. I wondered if I was ever going to stop. An image of a steep drop flashed into my head; there are several stony crags slabbed into the fells, popular with climbers, and my stomach lurched at the thought that I could find myself bouncing off one of these and sailing through the air to my inevitable death.

Instead, I slammed into a tree. Not a very big tree. A sturdy, wizened old hazel was my guess though I couldn't be certain. I was grateful that it had halted my descent, whatever it was, though the sudden stop was abrupt and painful.

I sat for a moment assessing my injuries and trying to think what to do next. My first thought was how cross Karen was going to be.

I knew I had a problem with my ankle. Even moving it in my trainer wasn't pleasant so I was fairly sure getting up and running was going to be problematic. I was now completely disorientated having no idea how far I'd fallen or where I was in the first place. The fog had settled into a deep sombre grey and the light was closer to the gloomy twilight of winter rather than late summer. More worrying was the temperature. It was now undeniably cold. Exposure is a serious issue for a fell runner, and I could feel, just sitting there for a few minutes, my body temperature was slipping.

Paralysed by indecision, I ate the energy bar and switched on the torch. It glared blindly into the fog, achieving no purpose whatsoever. The rain seemed to be relenting a little but that could have been my imagination or just wishful thinking. It was interesting to be completely stuck with no idea what to do next.

Heading down had to be the best move so I resolved to try to walk on my now throbbing ankle. Sharp pain shot up the inside of my leg as soon as I put any weight on it. Could I have broken it? This felt impossible. Another more positive attempt at loadbearing made me shout and I sat back down gingerly.

There was no signal on my phone as I knew there wouldn't be, another reason Karen had offered against the run, but I tried to send a text anyway.

I had no choice but to wait, or to crawl on my hands and knees which didn't seem a viable option.

It was several hours later when the Mountain Rescue Team found me. I was, by this time, having a little nap, or as they put it, 'semi-conscious'. Karen had called them and, as they strapped me onto a thin stretcher, a swarthy faced, bearded guy said, 'Today's your lucky day, lad. Your missus was frantic. What would she and the nippers have done without you, eh?' He smiled at me, all uneven tobacco-stained teeth and warm breath.

'Bloody nutter, up running in this, I was halfway through my Sunday tea! Pork and crackling with roasties in goose fat. It'll be ruined by the time we're down. It'll be dry as a witches' titty.' Another older chap glared at me as he took the other side, his face dark and disgruntled.

'It was a lovely day at home when I set off,' I managed through my chattering teeth.

'Liar,' Goose Fat Roasties replied.

'Leave him alone,' Tobacco Teeth came to my defence, 'he's not a novice. Look at those running shoes. They're top notch. Just a bit of bad luck is all, eh lad?' and he winked and me as his teammates huffed and grunted as they negotiated my weight to the Land Rover and ambulance parked surprisingly close to where my tumble had ended.

Karen graciously saved her recriminations until she was sure I was going to survive but the words 'reckless' and 'rash' were repeated as she remonstrated at my behaviour. 'What were you thinking, Archie?' she was perched on the hospital bed both hands enveloping my free hand, the other being attached to a drip to bring up my fluids. 'You can't take chances like this, not now we have the boys and Georgie, it's just thoughtless. Thank God you're okay. You've no idea, how worried we've all been. Oh, Archie,' and she cupped my face with her hand, and I thought she might cry.

'It's okay,' I had said, 'It's only a bad sprain, not broken. The weather would have lifted. I could have made it down. But it was lovely of you to send help. I'll be more careful in the future.' And when I said those words, in that moment, I meant them.

Except that I didn't always manage to be careful. I've had a few near misses. A couple of prangs in the car, some lucky escapes with a combination of power tools and forgetting the right safety equipment, usually in the rush to get a job finished or solve a problem, so I have nearly - I emphasise nearly - lost an eye for lack of safety goggles and pierced my foot when I wasn't wearing great footwear. There were lots of occasions where everything went swimmingly, but Karen tends to focus on the negative and, of course, my latest accident has been the icing on the cake. I think she thinks I deserve it. That it was, in some way, inevitable. All my mini accidents and mishaps have somehow been leading up to falling off our roof and ending up a paraplegic. It's the finale we've all been waiting for.

6

It's the early hours of the morning when I hear voices in the hall outside my room. As it's the weekend I assume it must be Edward or Joseph coming in but then I hear Karen. Giggling. She sounds drunk. In seconds I am wide awake. There is someone with her. I can hear two voices. And one of them is a man's.

There's a bit of to and fro in the hallway. I lie tense and alert, willing them to pad along the wall behind me to the kitchen.

The voices quieten to silence and then after a while I hear footsteps go upstairs.

I have been prescribed sleeping tablets and have been steadfastly refusing to take them. Addiction to prescription drugs isn't a path I want to take. Without a second thought I reach into my nightstand, unscrew the bottle and take two. I lie back, eyes tight shut, praying that they will work quickly.

I don't hear anything else.

It's after eleven the next morning when Karen appears in the kitchen with Charlie Linton in tow. As it's a Saturday, Edward has made me coffee and nipped out for a few groceries, dropping Georgie off at a friends' for the day.

'Archie, you remember Charlie,' Karen breezes in and heads to the coffee machine.

Charlie at least has the decency to blush.

'Archie, how are you?' the moron says and offers to shake my hand.

'Really?' I say, looking him straight in the eye, 'You expect me to shake your hand?'

He withdraws it and takes a timid step back, 'Sorry, I was just, I mean, yes, I suppose it's a bit formal, sorry.'

'It's not the formality Charlie,' I say, 'It's the fact that you're fucking my wife.' I know that sounds blunt, but I really can't help myself.

'Archie!' Karen turns with a mug in her hand, 'What the hell are you talking about? Charlie slept in the guest room. How bloody rude! How bloody embarrassing!'

'Oh, so you're not fucking my wife?' I say. This time he really blushes.

'Look, sorry we just had a bit of a skinful last night and Kaz said it would be okay to crash.' He runs his hand through his impressive head of hair, 'There's nothing going on, we're just mates,' he stammers out.

'Just mates? More like friends with benefits,' I look from one to the other, 'And 'Kaz' said it would be it alright, did she? Well as long as you serviced her while you were about it, that's a bonus, seeing as I'm no longer capable. Bloody decent of you Charlie, good going mate!'

'Look, sorry man, nothing happened. I don't know what you think's going on, but this isn't some kind of Madame Bovary shit or Lady Chatterley scene. We just went out and got loaded.' He turns to Karen and he's obviously very uncomfortable at being challenged and found out, 'Sorry Kaz, I don't need this on top of a hangover. Think I'll split.'

'You'll split? This isn't 1969 you fucking idiot,' I yell as he and Karen retreat out of the kitchen. I watch them talking on the drive out of the window. She looks upset and, gratifyingly, so does he. If they weren't shagging, why did he blush when he came in the kitchen? Why was he so shifty? And why did they both wake up at the same time if they were in separate rooms? No, it's far too convenient. My mind fills with images of them coiled together, glossy with sweat, upstairs in my bed. I slam my fist onto the table.

'How fucking dare you?!' Karen shouts as she storms back into the kitchen.

'Don't use that language in front of me,' I say.

'Fuck off!' she replies.

'Nice, Karen, very classy,' I am seething.

'That poor boy. What must he think? What is he going to say to people? Who the hell do you think you are saying something like that, out of the blue?' She is gripping the worktop with one hand, steadying herself.

'I'm your husband. Your husband who has had to put up with, who has had to suffer, you bringing some young man home and into her bed right under my nose.'

'Some young man? I work with the guy! I know him. He's my friend. You don't know what the fuck you're talking about. Tell me if I'd brought back Carol, would you have accused me of sleeping with her?' Her voice is shaking but I know I am in the right.

'Of course not, she's a woman,' I say holding my ground.

'I slept with women before you,' Karen spits the words at me and I know that had I known this before my accident I would have found this erotic, would have wanted all the details. Instead, it feels like a sucker punch. Now I have to worry about everyone being a potential rival. This is intolerable.

'You're just saying that to hurt me,' I counter, 'I don't believe you. But I do believe you're sleeping with Charlie Linton.'

'Christ, Archie, he's only a year or two older than Joseph. And I'm an old woman as far as he's concerned. He doesn't fancy me. Not every relationship has to be sexual. I know you find that hard to understand.' She glares past me out of the window as if she can't bear to look at me.

'Our relationship certainly isn't,' I say after a moment or two of silence, 'and I can't help but think that that's what's going to drive you away, Karen. We're not talking, we're not spending any time together, I'm worried about us.'

She slowly turns her gaze back to me. 'If you ever embarrass me like that again, I'll put you in a residential facility. Do you understand? A fucking home with a load of other invalids. That'll be it. I don't have to do this, Archie. I'm trying to keep it together, but I don't have to. Do you understand? You behave, or you're on your own.' With that she goes over to the stove and continues to make herself breakfast, frying eggs and making a chunky sandwich which she eats messily, taking great mouthfuls with relish, standing up in front of me, spilling a thin trail of vivid, yellow yolk down her top. It is disgusting. Eventually she goes leaving the kitchen hazy from the smoke from her hot frying pan and

I can feel the smell of the grease settle on my clothes. I stare at the cold coffee in the cup in front of me, trying to digest the enormity of her threat and work out what to do next.

Part Two

Karen

1

I was in the top field when I saw him put up the ladder to clean the gutters. I had been collecting eggs from the chickens and noticed there was a potential breach in the hen house, so I'd fetched a couple of tools and a bit of wood to do a make-shift repair to deter the foxes. By the time I had finished I saw Archie leaning up and peering onto the roof. I knew that within five minutes he'd be up on it. He was always up there, any opportunity.

'Please let it be this time,' I muttered to myself and one of the chickens cocked its head at me.

I watched him teeter along the bottom of the roof. There was a stagger and my heart leapt. I crossed my fingers. He regained his balance. 'Shit,' I looked down at the chicken having a little peck at my boot, 'Better luck next time, eh, Pippin?'

I jerked my head up as I heard his cry just in time to see him thud heavily onto his back by the door.

I waited, unable to believe my luck. I wanted to shout out and jump for joy. He wasn't moving. I edged further behind the hen house, hoping the boys hadn't heard him. The longer they left him, the better the chances were.

It had only been a minute, maybe less, when Joe sprang out of the door. I set off at a run. The last thing I wanted was them doing CPR. By the time I reached them, Ted was there too and Georgie was hovering by the back door. Ted was on the phone and, disappointingly, Archie was clearly alive, though there was an impressive amount of blood coming from a head wound.

'Shouldn't we try to stem that bleeding,' Joe looked up at me, pale and eyes wide, from where he was kneeling by Archie's side.

'Don't touch him,' I snapped, 'You might do more damage if he's hurt his neck,' I justified.

A first responder miraculously arrived within minutes and then an ambulance hot on her heels, and finally a helicopter which found it easy to land in the field despite my protests about scaring the animals.

'You can travel in the helicopter with him, Mrs Blackthorne,' the paramedic told me, 'He's stable. Looks very promising.'

'Is he going to die?' I asked.

'No promises but I've seen much worse, and they've pulled through,' the earnest young woman thought she was giving me good news.

I turned to Joe and Ted. 'If one or both of you want to go, that's fine. I'm staying with Georgie. She's had a terrible shock.'

'Of course, Mum,' said Joe and he hugged me and charged off to the waiting machine that would carry away the man who had held me captive for most of my adult life.

The first time Archie hit me I didn't really feel any pain, just surprise. Shock that it had happened. It was somehow a very childish attack, quite hard to take seriously though, of course, I should have. Taken it seriously, that is. I should have dumped him there and then and that would have saved this whole sorry mess, but that's been the problem all along. I have been befuddled by Archie, he has managed to confound me and muddle me and mix me up so that my decision making has been, well, non-existent. Archie has subsumed me and consumed me by degrees over the years, until I have lost sight of the Karen I was when Archie and I were first seeing each other in the fog of the Karen I have been forced to become as Archie's wife.

So yes, the first time it happened I was sitting in the bath. Knees tucked up, lots of bubbles, too hot water, a delight. It was a weekend afternoon, coming into spring. Such a potent time of year. Archie was sitting on the cane backed chair in the bathroom of my parents' Victorian house and we were chatting. I think he'd been alright up to a few minutes

84

before he hit me. And now I can't even remember what set him off because that's always the case with Archie; it can be anything or nothing. The volume of the TV, too loud or too quiet; a last-minute change in plans brought on by external circumstances, for example a kid's cancelled football match; an accidental breakage, like a dropped jar of jam; a laundry mishap such as a dyed shirt or a shrunken jumper or it can be an opinion voiced on the radio or a shirty shop assistant or a someone, anyone, whose face he just doesn't like. In short, it can be anything at all. That's the gift of having a violent husband, you never, ever, ever know what's coming next or why.

So, I was enjoying the bath and I think I may have been teasing him in the way normal couples do. I was known as fairly mouthy, assertive, opinionated, back then. Archie liked that about me. He'd told me.

But not that day. No. I said what I said, and his face suddenly set in this hard expression, and he lurched over to me and slapped me hard on the top of my arm.

It was an impressively loud smack because my arm was wet.

Like I say, I didn't feel pain, I felt shock.

'What the fuck was that for?' I said.

'Don't use that sort of language in front of me,' he replied and left the bathroom, slamming the door so loudly the glass rattled in the window.

I sat quietly waiting, shocked, for a few minutes and then got out, wrapping myself in a towel.

I'd always thought in these circumstances I'd be sure of my response. Anger, rejection, refusal to accept this, the worst type of patriarchal domination. But we were getting married in two days. My wedding dress was hanging pressed and ready on the back of my bedroom door. Guests were invited, presents bought, food had been ordered. How could I tell my mum and dad the wedding was off?

Archie was sitting on my bed. I was ready for a fight, but he looked up at me and tears smeared his face. He looked terrible.

'I don't know what came over me, Karen,' he sounded horrified, 'I think it must be nerves about the wedding. I'm so sorry. Can you ever forgive me?' and he took my hand and the tears kept coming and he didn't wipe a single one away.

I'd seen my dad cry an occasional tear but never anything like this. Dad would always whip out his handkerchief to clear any evidence that he was overcome with emotion as quickly as he could. When Archie sat on the bed, his cheeks awash, hands clutching my hand, I was overwhelmed with how emotionally open my husband-to-be was, how in touch with his feelings he must be, to be able to let me see him cry like that. I believed he would never hit me again.

What a fucking idiot I was.

I have never been what I would call a traditional battered wife. Archie has never beaten me enough that I have needed to go to A and E. He's clever like that. He also rations out the punishments so it can be months and months between one of his hidings but, of course, I'm always waiting for the next one.

No, Archie is not the traditional once a week down the pub, get pissed and knock seven shades out of her indoors; he is a planner, a strategist, a plotter. We are all part of a grand game to Archie, and we have to play by his rules, or we are made to suffer.

Archie does not physically hurt the children. If he did, I could not have stayed and, why have I stayed you are asking? Mainly, because he made it impossible to leave.

As a battered wife, you spend a lot of time fantasising about the demise of your husband. I encouraged Archie to take up fell running in the hopes that some accident might befall him, or there may be some undiagnosed genetic weakness in his heart. Even buying a fast old classic car seemed like a good idea; I hoped he might crash it but no such luck.

So they spirited Archie off in the helicopter and that evening, Georgie and I made popcorn (too messy, noisy and unhealthy for Archie) and watched a silly film together (a pointless activity as far as Archie was concerned so hardly ever allowed) and she slept in my bed (unheard of). I had changed the sheets and I cuddled up close to her neat little body and drank in the smell of her hair, and for the first time in years, I felt I could properly think. Archie wasn't in my head, wasn't threatening me verbally, physically, mentally. I felt free, I felt relaxed, and it felt completely brilliant. I slept the way you do as a child when your bedroom is beautifully clean and tidy. A virtuous sleep which looks forward to waking up to the order you've made and the chance to play in that new world you've created. I slept like I hadn't slept in years and when I woke up to my daughter's beautiful head on the pillow next to me, I realised it was very important that whatever the outcome of the accident, this was my opportunity for things to finally change. For all of us. I would be able to work out how to leave Archie once and for all.

That night Ted phoned to let me know his father was in a coma and, I freely admit, that I prayed that Archie would never come home. I willed him never to wake up. I hoped my luck had might have changed once and for all.

2

Now he's accused me of sleeping with Charlie Linton, I am thinking about poisoning Archie. What is it going to take to get rid of him? Over the years there have been many accusations. That's another charming facet of the violent husband; on the one hand you can never ever come up to scratch (lazy, fat, ugly, stupid, bovine, weak, simple, idiotic; the insults are endless) no matter how hard you try but apparently you are also completely beguiling to any and every other male on the planet.

When I met Archie, I felt properly courted. I finally understood what the word meant. Previous boyfriends had ranged from casual flings to fairly serious relationships which had entailed weekends away, birthday gifts exchanged, Valentine's Days that were romantic or not but with Archie our liaison was like a military operation. The formality of the word courtship was completely applicable.

For example, every time he picked me up to go out he brought me some token of attention; the latest CD from a band I didn't really like but I'd sung along to a track in the pub we were in; a novel from an author I'd mentioned in passing or a weighty art book from an exhibition we'd popped into the previous week; sometimes it was jewellery, earrings or bangles, even an anklet; of course there were chocolates, but expensive ones, and beautiful bouquets of exotic flowers which didn't look altogether friendly, knotted with raffia and caught in brown paper. I was fresh from my student days and my wardrobe was limited and a little shoddy. One day he turned up with a pair of boots; the exact boots I was wearing but brand new. They were red suede, stiletto heels. I looked at the new pair nestled in tissue paper in the box. Why would I buy the same boots again? My pair were scuffed and worn out. Next time I'd buy something else. Sometimes it was a bit much, but he just said he liked to treat me; he wanted me to be happy; he wanted me to have nice things.

Archie hated me to look scruffy. He produced grooming products and made me appointments at smart hair salons. He booked me in for facials and manicures before nail bars were everywhere. Before we went out, he would trail after me to the bedroom to watch me get dressed, offering an opinion that always influenced what I wore.

So, he preened and polished me, turning me into the prize he wanted, and then he began to show this obsessive jealousy if I received any male attention. I find if you smile or talk, pretty much to any man, they think they might have a chance, and before I was with Archie, I never took any of these interactions seriously. Archie however could fixate for days over the smallest interchange. I quickly learned to keep my head down and my mouth shut and to try to talk only to women. It was just easier that way.

In the early days though, I couldn't believe my luck. Here was this man who was willing to slot into my world. He was charming to my friends, attentive to my small family and he showered me with gifts and compliments. He seemed so self-assured. Even when there were times when he was assertive, I liked it. Taking a waiter to task or not putting up with shoddy goods, I saw as a strength. My father never complained about anything. I always saw him as sweet and biddable but, seeing him through Archie's eyes, I began to think of him as weak. In the beginning, there was a part of me that liked the fact that Archie was a teeny bit macho. It was refreshing. He was a man not a boy like all my previous relationships. It was a little bit thrilling.

When he proposed my mum thought it was a little soon. It was Boxing Day, and I was hungover when she cornered me about it. 'You hardly know him, Karen. Okay, get engaged if you must but wait and see. See how your job goes, love, there's no need to tie yourself down surely. You always talked about travelling and you're so young.'

'Archie wants a spring wedding Mum. We don't want to wait. What's the point? We've made the commitment to each other. His favourite flowers are daffodils. So, we're thinking, Easter.' Mum looked aghast like I'd told her we were moving to the other side of the world. If I'd been older maybe I'd have asked her why she was so concerned about me marrying him. But I didn't because Archie had been pouring the story of the wedding and our lives together into my ear since I'd said yes the day before and it was all I could hear in my brain. It was all I had room for.

'What about *your* favourite flowers, Karen?' Mum said quietly.

I don't remember what I said but I hate daffodils now. You rarely see them in bridal bouquets as well. They're just not special enough. Just one step up from a weed.

3

When I was little, I used to play at being a teacher, making tiny exercise books for my toys and a register which I carefully marked. I wrote in tiny sums with obvious mistakes and dished out detentions and told off my teddies for whispering. During the summer holidays, I could keep 'school' going for days and days. As an only child with attentive but busy parents, I created imaginative worlds at any opportunity and dived into them. As an adult, becoming a drama teacher was an easy transition.

Growing up, I loved the rhythm of the school year, the autumn term with all the learning feeling like it's built around falling leaves and then making paper chains, leading up to carol concerts and winter weather and Christmas cards with cotton wool snowmen. I loved the spring term and playground games without our winter coats, and then Easter eggs with the hint of summer just around the corner. And the final term of the year was always hot and sleepy, with sports day and the school field dried hard from the sun, and daisy chains and cartwheels and the chance of a lesson outdoors and bringing home fat bags of our schoolwork in July with all the promise of the summer break ahead of us. My friends complained about going back to school in September, but I couldn't wait, though I never told them. I wanted to be in the thrum of the classrooms, my brain busy, I wanted the fizz of the connection of my mates. My house was too quiet; I loved the company of school.

Having finished a drama degree, I decided to teach. I was never going to make it as an actor. I wanted the security of a monthly pay cheque, and I couldn't face the scrubbing around for agents and auditions. I just wanted work. And structure. I wanted a concrete life that was my own.

Tess, one of the girls I shared a house with in my third year was going to start her own touring theatre company. 'Join us, Karen. Your writing is fantastic. It'll be a blast. I've got an Arts Council grant and a motor home! We can please ourselves.'

I loved Tess. While she was telling me this, she was tie-dying an old dress in the sink. There was already an ejaculative splash of purple up the white wall. Tess had moved from her punk phase with full green Mohican in the first year of the degree, to new age hippy. She picked a shoot off some mung beans she was sprouting on the windowsill. 'I don't know how you can opt into all that authoritarian, hierarchical, patriarchal shit. I hated school.'

I smiled. 'I'm teaching drama Tess; I'm nurturing empathy and creativity and independent thought. And I loved school. Not everyone is traumatised by it. And if they are, they need people like me to talk to.' I gave her a winning smile.

'You'll hate it.' Tess was now pummelling and wringing out her knot of fabric in the basin. 'You're too talented to be wasted on a school.'

So, I set off to train as a drama teacher and Tess set off on a tour, firstly around the wilder parts of Scotland and then across into Europe in a jalopy of a tiny, converted van with a couple of other pals; a tiny, bespectacled girl, Isla, and a thin reedy guy whose name I can't remember. Somewhere in Berlin, Tess and Isla ditched the guy and found Elke instead and, I followed her progress over the next couple of years through grubby postcards and gabbled phone calls at unexpected hours until we finally caught up again the day of my wedding. But more of that later.

No, I want to talk about Martin. Martin was on my course. Confident, good-looking in a scrubbed clean kind of way and determined to be the most creative student at every task.

I need to state that I couldn't wait to get started. I wanted to be in a studio and teaching. I had pored over the GCSE and A level syllabuses over the holidays, completed all the pre-course reading, I had watched footage of Dorothy Heathcote teaching drama to primary school kids in the northeast and I already thought Jonathan Neelands was the bees' knees. I can approach a task with gusto. I have a capacity for thoroughness.

Our tutor, Sid, said he wanted us to produce a Resource Pack. A fully realised scheme of work built around a topic of our choosing which was to ultimately show all our understanding as drama teachers. As the course proceeded, Sid said, he'd guide us as to what we might include in the Pack, ideas for script writing, role on the wall, character building, and so on. We were to trial the Pack during our first and second teaching practices and then submit it as part of our assessment at the end of the second term.

I loved the whole idea and began collecting ideas immediately. This was just my bag.

Martin, however had a different tack. 'Don't you think they're just working out what they can use for their next book? I mean, get us to come up with all the ideas and then they can polish them up and hand it all over to their publishers? I'm not playing along. I'm keeping my ideas. I'll do something that fits the brief but I'm keeping my best work for me, thank you very much.'

There were only twelve of us on the course and Martin had become a natural leader. Mutters of agreement broke out amongst his disciples.

'You're probably right, Mart,' said Felix, a nervy ex-Red Coat from *Butlins* who I feared was going to have a very difficult time in the classroom, 'What do you think we should do?'

'It's not for me to say, Felix, but we know Sid's books are all on the reading list, right, and they all need to keep getting published, don't they? I'm just saying, if I've got a great original idea, I'm not handing it over to Sid is all.'

That sealed it and whenever the Resource Pack was mentioned shifty looks were exchanged amongst the group and no one wanted to discuss their progress with poor old Sid.

One morning, Sid introduced us to a game called Blood Potato; it was basically hide and seek but with your eyes closed except the designated seeker is a murderer - a blood potato. I've played this game hundreds of times over the years, kids love it, but I've never seen anyone play it like Martin.

The idea, which I always stress, is that if you are still and silent, you cannot be found. Once you are caught, you're out. So, keep still and quiet and the murderer can't catch you. As everyone has their eyes closed, as a teacher you watch the students move around the space, arms outstretched until they bump into each other. If one of them is the murderer, they whisper, 'Blood Potato' and the victim must die a brutal and agonisingly loud death. Amidst the silence that has gone before, this can be pretty terrifying, even though everyone knows it's a game. The point of the game is to understand tension; playing the game helps you understand breaking silence and stillness in performance.

When Martin played Blood Potato, it was a sight to behold. I was caught early on, which was annoying, so I was relegated to sit and observe in the paltry audience. Martin worked with a hand clamped tightly over his eyes, one arm flailing wildly in front of him. Every so often he would run full pelt into the space, heedless of what, or rather who, may have been ahead of him. Or he would jump loudly to the side and then slap an extended foot down repeatedly before hurtling off in the other direction. It was an anarchic approach. Of course, these bursts of noise and chaotic movement, would totally discombobulate the murderer who would attempt to catch the space that Martin had already vacated.

If the murderer came close, Martin would run, often colliding with a wall or others; he was completely reckless in his desire to win. He was always the last man standing against the blood potato and he would taunt and tease and eke out his shenanigans until his hunter admitted defeat.

Martin always wanted to win. I didn't like him at all. And I thought he would be a horrible teacher.

At the end of the second term, we had the session where we presented our Resource Packs. One by one Sid went through the group and received the most pedestrian of offerings, topics already covered in sessions by him, insultingly thin folders. One boy even handed in two A4 sheets stapled together. I don't even think they were double-sided. At last, he came to Martin.

'One sec,' Martin said, and he hopped up from his chair and out of the studio doors.

'I must say I'm a little disappointed,' Sid said, 'You all seemed so enthusiastic at the start, though I suppose the teaching practices get harder each year. We have to remember not to overload you. And it is hard to continue to think of new ideas especially as drama in education becomes more widespread and popular. Don't look so downhearted. I'm going to mark these as generously as I can.' At this little speech everyone certainly did look a little forlorn.

Martin then appeared through the door carrying a grey vintage battered suitcase. It was covered with old, faded luggage stickers in muted colours. He sat back in his chair, set it down at his feet, snapped open the locks and spun the case round towards Sid. 'I find paper documents a drag, Sid, so I've prepared this for you,' and he slowly lifted the lid to reveal a packed interior. There was clearly period costume of some sort and a pair of gentleman's shoes, some paperbacks and several aged official looking dossiers.

Sid gasped.

'It's an exploration of the Weimar Republic and the rise of Nazi Germany,' he chirruped, 'I've drawn on Brecht as the primary resource obviously, and there's costume as a starting point for character work, plus facsimile travel documents necessary to exit the country in 1933. I've developed some script starters too in case a practical space isn't available during some weeks, and the pack is, of course, fully differentiated.'

'Martin this looks intriguing, let's all have a closer look,' and Sid moved off his chair and knelt down on the floor in front of the suitcase his hands running over the silk-lined, russet interior. 'Beautiful,' he murmured.

Felix, sitting next to Martin and his number one fan, leant across to him and whispered, 'You fucking cunt.'

Martin smiled serenely.

When Archie showed me Martin's application form for the post at Ridge High, I was careful how I answered. For one, I'd already put him through on my shortlist. There was no reason not to; he was very well qualified, overqualified really for a main scale post, and had excellent experience. His application letter showed that he, unlike most of the other candidates, had researched the school; it was tailor made to fit what we were looking for. To reject him because I knew him as a trainee and didn't like the cut of his jib would take some explaining. I was relying on the fact that Archie favoured pretty women and loathed handsome men, and he could be charmingly persuasive as far as Angie was concerned.

'Didn't you do your PGCE here?' his mouth was set in that familiar line which meant trouble.

'Yes, he was on my course. We had different tutors though. I hardly had anything to do with him. You know what it's like.' I looked back at my computer waiting for him to pull me back, spin round the chair, maybe grab me by the hair? Or possibly he'd favour a hard slap across the face. It was always difficult to tell what he might do.

'Huh. Are you friends on *Facebook*?' I tried to regulate my breathing. Showing fear only made things worse.

'No.' This was true. I didn't like him. Why would I be his friend?

'Would you want him to get the job?' This was a difficult one to answer. Say yes and that's alarm bells for him, say no then why have I short-listed? And don't leave a pause, for God's sake, don't look like you've got something to hide.

Without a moment's hesitation I said, 'I'll probably be happy to be guided by you and Angie. You've both got more experience than me. See what the other ones are like as well, eh? Think I'll just finish this off and then I'd better start tea. That okay?'

'Yes. Yes, okay then,' and that was that crisis averted.

At the interview though, Martin was exceptional. Articulate, well-travelled, cultured, polite and generous in allowing me to talk about my modest career in comparison to his experiences all over the world. He'd seen so much theatre; been to so many countries. And he was funny. I laughed with him, and it was marvellous to relax into that, even if it was only for a few hours. There was no doubt that he was the only possibility for the job but there was also no doubt that Archie hated him. On sight. It was hard to believe Martin was the same sneaky young weasel I'd known all those years before.

He was upfront about the reasons behind his application too. As a Head of Faculty, his next move should have been to Deputy Head, but he said he loathed the meetings and the paperwork and ultimately, he wanted to write. I'd already ordered a copy of his book for the department, and it was reasonable, nothing ground-breaking, a few too many arty black and white photos of Martin in different drama spaces clearly imparting nuggets of wisdom to rapt students; he was all expressive hands, ankle-grazer trousers and bare feet and looked much younger.

When we were eating lunch with the other candidates, he dominated the conversation with plans for a second and third book, one for students, one for teachers and ran through the bare bones of the play he was editing and the play he had just started. He spoke so passionately about his artistic life, his thirst to create that had been stultified by his position in middle management, I felt a twinge of jealousy remembering the work that Tess and I had produced together in my undergrad days.

As I suspected he would, he made quite an impression in September. He arrived obscenely tanned on the first Inset day of the year, wearing flip flops and a white linen shirt over stone washed jeans. During the obligatory staff meeting, he kept his sunglasses on, and I suspected he might be napping. As he sucked scorching black coffee in the department office afterwards, he said his flight from Vietnam had only landed at six that morning. 'Been out visiting old friends. Had to make use of my last days of freedom. Exhausted though, can't deny it. Should be having a little siesta right about now. Never mind, I'll catch up tonight. Now what have we here,' and he looked over his timetable, 'Oh Karen, so many munchkins. Barely any A level. Save the best for yourself, do you?'

There it was. What I'd expected. 'No, Martin. Thought you didn't want lots of responsibility anyway with all your creativity going on out of school. The exam classes are a lot of work, and you still have your fair share as we discussed at your interview.'

He tipped his sunglasses down and peered at me over them, 'Just teasing, happy to help you wherever you need me,' and he smiled a pinched little smile, 'Now I need to make a quick call before we start the next round of misery.' As he left the office, I considered whether to be offended as Archie was leading the next session. I decided I couldn't be bothered. I decided I could be bothered to be offended by his attitude that he was here 'to help' though. I needed a doer. Not another prick in my life.

But we'll get back to Martin later.

4

I'm just swapping the batteries in Archie's remote control again. I do this every ten days or so. I have a dead pair that I put in so that it won't work. It's a teeny source of joy to me to imagine him lying awake at night with nothing to do and unable to turn the TV on.

Does that make me a terrible person?

No. He deserves it.

He deserves much worse.

When I put the Merc up for sale the guy who came to see it couldn't believe the condition lived up to the advert. 'He must be a real caring chap your husband. Look at all the love and patience that's gone into her.' I swear there were tears in his eyes. Silly old fool.

'How much did you get for her?' Ted asked me as we watched it being loaded onto the pick-up truck.

'Thirty grand,' I said knowing he'd eventually tell Archie. I'd seen sixty-seven thousand clear in my account that morning.

'Why do men call cars 'she' and 'her'?' I said, 'They're piles of metal.'

'It's affectionate,' Ted gave a wave as the truck moves off at a sedate pace.

'It's demeaning and possessive,' I said and headed back into the house.

After I've done the batteries, I give the biscuit tin a vigorous shake for good measure. Archie smacked the side of my head onto the kitchen counter in front of the boys because there wasn't a whole digestive for him to dunk.

He's never going to see a complete biscuit again if I can help it.

When Joe was born, we didn't know we were having a boy. What I've come to realise about men like Archie is that they can't keep up the pretence of normality for long so everything rushes along like a high-speed train until you are so committed you look around you and can't find a way out.

First there was the wedding, on the surface a romantic gesture of absolute commitment and then his immediate longing for a baby. 'I have no real family, no flesh and blood. I've never been in the company of anyone who looks like me, I'm alone in the world,' he said over and over. I'd have liked to have enjoyed being married a little longer but after six weeks of his campaigning over our first summer holiday together I agreed to stop taking the pill.

We got pregnant fairly quickly once the decision was made which was a bit of a shock but when Joe was born the following September, as I lay in hospital that first night and watched his little scrunched up face, I knew I was worried that he was a boy. The thought that crept into my head was, 'Is he going to grow up to be like Archie?'

At seven months pregnant, Archie walloped me again. This time, I'd over-boiled his breakfast egg. I laughed when his face clouded as he tried to unsuccessfully dip his feeble toasty soldier into the hardened yolk. He snatched up the hot egg and hurled it at me; it flew past my ear, exploding onto the wall behind me.

'Fucking hell,' I started to say, but he was on me, bunching both sides of my shirt collar in his hands, his face too close to mine. We shuffled back, quickly, like terrible ballroom dancers, my arms poker straight by my side, my eyes locked with his, until my head slammed into the wall and the egg smeared into my hair.

'I've told you not to use that language in front of me,' he spat at me and with one fist gripping my shirt at the neck, he jerked me forward and slapped me hard across the face. Twice. Forehand and backhand.

Then he let me go.

'Get that shit out of your hair. You've an appointment with the midwife later,' he hissed at me and left the kitchen.

I felt the pain that time. I didn't cry though, but my stomach tightened in a forceful, painless contraction. I breathed and waited for it to relax, knowing my body was assessing whether my uterus was still the safest place for my unborn child. There was another contraction. No pain again. I knew the adrenalin was stimulating it and that it wasn't labour. Yet. I had read every book available. I wanted to be prepared.

After ten minutes or maybe more, the tightening stopped, and I turned my attention to what had happened. I say I turned my attention. As I caressed and soothed my taut belly, I decided to buy an egg timer.

My mum and dad popped in all the time after Joe was born. They didn't live too far away and were happy to drive over whenever they had time. Dad had an immediate connection with his grandson. He was already talking about making a little wooden rocking horse and brought some preliminary drawings for me to see. He'd cradle Joe and walk and sing and coo; he couldn't get enough of him.

I guess I was in that early fug of the new-born stage, and I didn't really notice that their visits had begun to dwindle. One Sunday afternoon when Joe was coming up to three months, Mum and Dad had called in bringing mince pies as it was nearly Christmas. They'd been shopping but said it was hellish. 'We thought we'd call in on the off chance,' Mum said.

'Great, Mum, we haven't seen you for ages. Joe's really grown since the last time.' I had ushered them in, but they hadn't flung their coats over the banister as usual and put the kettle on. Something had changed.

Archie made tea and we sat rather formally, both Mum and Dad peering into Joe's cot, hoping he'd wake up for a cuddle.

'You're not in any rush, are you?' I'd said, 'He'll wake up soon.'

'Actually, I have some news,' Archie announced, 'I've found us somewhere new to live. It's another rented place, of course, but closer to work and it'll mean we can save more quickly for our own place. Shouldn't be long before we can buy now. Nearly have enough for a deposit.'

I remember looking at him in amazement. He had chosen a place in which I was going to live without me? What was wrong with him?

Dad spoke first. 'Tell us more Archie. Where is it?' His tone was bright and friendly but there was a forced edge to it, like he was a little bit scared of Archie.

'It's over the river. Near school. There's a garden. For Joseph. And three bedrooms. For when we have the next baby,' he beamed at me.

'I thought it was short term,' Mum said. She sounded furious.

'How can Mum and Dad help out with the childcare if it's so far away? It's in totally the wrong direction,' I said. Joe started grunting and snuffling in the crib.

'It's a practical solution Karen. It's a cheaper area.' Archie was talking to me like I was a retard.

'Yes, because it's horrible. If Mum and Dad can't look after Joe, we'll have to pay a fortune in childcare. We won't be able to save anything. Honestly Archie, I don't know why you didn't discuss this with me first. This is a terrible idea.' I couldn't believe it was true.

Joe was beginning to fuss properly now, and Mum stood up to pick him up; I still had half a mince pie on my plate, and I hadn't finished my tea.

'Sit down Pattie!' Archie's tone was threatening and sinister, 'The boy has to learn that not everyone will dance to his tune just because he makes the tiniest squeak.'

Mum sat back down and glanced at Dad who looked aghast.

'Don't fret Karen. There's nothing more to be said; I've signed the lease.' Archie bit into a mince pie and sat back, satisfied, in his chair.

Joe wailed and I flexed to go to pick him up. Then I remembered the stinging slap across my jaw and relented.

Dad stood up, 'Come on Pattie. We're not staying where you're spoken to like a dog and we have to listen to a defenceless baby cry for no good reason,' and they gathered their things and left, Mum clearly on the verge of tears and Dad furious.

Archie and I sat for several minutes listening to Joe's wails. 'Aren't you going to deal with him?' he said eventually and left the room, and I rushed over and snatched Joe up, feeling the milk squeezing and pouring from me as it had in our early days together.

That was the start of Archie's careful campaign of separation and isolation. Military precision and meticulous planning are the way to success for the abusive husband. Cut off all your wife's support and she can only turn to you.

5

Joe and Ted are playing cards with Georgie when I get home from school. They're all in a good mood. Ted has finished work early for once; Georgie has won most of the games they've played, and Joe says he's thinking about buying a greenhouse. This makes me laugh.

I look at my beautiful children and hope and pray that they are not too damaged by Archie. I think Georgie will be alright. He was never very interested in her but for Joe and Ted it's more complicated. I can smell something good cooking and I hang at the edge of Ted's chair and feel his warmth radiating into me as Joe deals another hand and Georgie tries to make her stuffed orangutang sit up next to her. 'I want to go first this time,' she demands, 'If you go first Tee Tee, you always win.'

'Whatever you say, George, but I'm dealing you the worst hand possible just to let you know.' Joe teases.

'Mum!' she appeals, 'Make him stop!'

'I'm kidding, it's the best hand possible. That's why you're winning.' They both have patience that stretches like a never-ending unfurling ribbon for their sister. Always have. When they were little, they didn't show each other the same kindness.

I hear the squeak of Archie's wheels in the hall.

'I'll eat in the living room,' I say and head for the back door.

'You don't have to leave on my account,' he yells after me.

'Yes, I do,' I shout, without looking back.

In the living room, I flop onto the sofa with the day's post. There are a few bills which are dull but, interestingly, there is, at last, an estimate for a garden room. The firm came to measure up weeks ago and now I have concrete figures. My plan is to have it built at the end of the lawn. There's a perfect south-westerly spot with a wonderful view. It will be insulated and warm and Archie will never be able to get there. I will make it a retreat from the house, my own space. I'm going to use the rest of the cash from the car.

'Should we all just move, Mum?' Joe and Ted and I were having one of our late-night chats after one of the gruelling days at the hospital. Ted and I had been painting all day and Joe's reports of Archie's reaction to a downstairs room didn't bode well.

'I'm hoping you're not going to be at home forever, Ted,' I added sugar to my coffee. I didn't usually but I felt like I needed the boost.

'No, sure,' Ted blustered, 'But you'll need help with Dad, and you never liked it here. Why aren't we just selling up?'

'Ted, it's not that straightforward. I'm learning to drive, once I've passed my test it'll be so much better. And now we can all be more ... independent I think we should give it a go.' The coffee was good, but my shoulders ached from the painting, and I wanted my bed.

'He might not accept being downstairs,' Joe sounded wary, 'He didn't take the news well.'

'I'm sorry you had to tell him Joe,' I reached for his hand across the table and then for Ted's, 'I'm sorry you're both having to take on so much. I just don't want to deal with him at the moment.'

'It's okay Mum,' Joe said, 'Whatever you want to do.'

That was the point. I wanted my life decisions from the moment Archie fell off the roof to be mine and mine alone.

There's an episode of The American Office where Jim buys Pam their first house. Jim and Pam are the central love interest of the show. He is tall and goofy and affable and smart and him buying the house is supposed to be romantic and amazing and thoughtful and surprising and what every woman would want. When I saw it, I wanted to smash the TV to pieces. Why did Pam wander around all eyes wide open in awe and delight? Archie did that to me, over and over, and I fucking hated it. It was selfish and controlling and manipulative and the worst kind of trickery.

I agreed to the rented shithole when Joe was tiny; I was too exhausted to put up a fight. When he came home six months later and told me he'd put an offer in on a Victorian terrace, I wasn't as surprised. Joe and I had both had terrible colds which wouldn't shift. Archie always timed these bombshells to perfection when I couldn't think straight enough to fight back. When he pushed the completed mortgage papers in front of me to sign as I breastfed Joe, I took the pen. There were too many times I chose the path of least resistance.

I quite liked the little terrace though. It was a bit closer to Mum and Dad, so they tentatively edged their way back into Joe's life and that eased the burden on me a little too.

Almost as soon as Joe was born, Archie was talking about more children. I couldn't imagine managing another baby. Joe was docile and delightful but the thought of two was terrifying. I only held Archie off until I'd just finished maternity leave, just before Joe's first birthday. When I miscarried at seven weeks the relief was enormous. I didn't feel guilty. I figured my body knew what it was doing.

Here's the thing though. Archie could not or would not tolerate illness or weakness. But I digress, we'll come back to that later.

Anyhow, the terrace was in a better area, a play park near enough and I made a few baby friends, and I thought maybe my life wouldn't be so bad.

Despite my best efforts, Ted arrived a little over two years after Joe and, with a full-time job, two kids and a sociopath for a husband, I felt like I lived in a wind tunnel, a constant battering of noise and force and resistance that I was striving to walk uphill through in order to make what little progress I could.

When, several years had passed by and I found myself standing in a bleak field in the north of England looking at a glum house with a sagging roof topped by a weathervane that refused to turn in what felt like a force nine gale, I felt only mild surprise that it had come to this.

'Where's the nearest shop?' I had argued with him, 'and how will I pick the kids up from school?' I didn't drive. There'd been no necessity in London. Here though, how was I going to manage? This time I wanted to fight before he sealed the deal.

'It's completely impractical. The heating is ancient, the windows need replacing and I bet you get snowed in in winter.'

'There's room for a vegetable garden,' Archie had replied benignly, 'like in *The Good Life*. We can be self-sufficient.'

'I fucking hate that tripe. We can buy vegetables in *Sainsburys*, why do we have to grow our own?' I was having to shout to make myself heard over the wind that was blasting down from the hills.

Archie turned to the boys who were standing a little way off, pinched and cold, talking quietly to each other. They were a little daunted by all the space, I think. 'Joseph, why don't you take Edward up into the house and see which bedroom you'd like to sleep in when we live here?' Joe obediently scooped his brother's hand in his, and I watched despondently as they disappeared into the house.

Archie grabbed my upper arm and marched me further up the field towards a little copse of long-established trees. He pushed me in front of him. I staggered further between the trunks. I knew he was hiding me from view from the house in case the children looked out of the window.

'This is what we talked about,' he snarled, coming closer to me so I stepped back into the solid trunk of a tree. 'When we were first together. This is what we've been working towards, a place of our own, some land, a decent environment to bring up the boys. We've got good jobs here and this is the sort of property that I want. I need something that gives me a bit of status. That tells people who I am. Do you understand?'

'Yes, yes, okay. I see what you mean, look I'm worried about the boys on the stairs …' I tried to move past him.

'I'm not finished. I want you to love this as much as I do. Do you understand Karen?' and he pulled me in front of him and held me, one hand locked under my chin forcing me to look at the house, the other around my waist, hugging me tight.

'Yes Archie, it's lovely,' I managed.

'I'm not sure I believe you. You'll have to do better than that,' and he pulled me in tighter to him.

'It's a perfect family home. I can see us living here forever. I want the boys to grow up here too.'

He released the grip on my chin and began to stroke my neck instead. 'Keep going,' there was another jerk, another tightening around my waist. It was horribly uncomfortable.

'I want to grow vegetables with you. I want us to be a family here. I think the house is beautiful. You are so thoughtful and clever to have found it for us.' I tried to make my voice sound believable, hoping it might be enough.

'That's better, much better,' the stroking around my neck was menacing; he was toying with me like a cat with a mouse, 'Go on.'

'We'll grow old together here and everyone will look at this house,' I faltered, repulsed because I could feel what was happening as his breath quickened and his grip tightened.

'Yes, yes,' he shook me, 'Keep going,' both hands grabbed down onto my hips now, grinding me against him.

'And everyone will look at this house and see how important you are,' my voice faded as I knew what was to come and then he pulled me back into the trees unable to wait any longer and behaved in a way that he thought was completely reasonable but was, in fact, utterly degrading with my face pushed up against the rough bark of a tree, ears straining for the sound of my sweet boys running to find their mummy who had been gone too long.

Back in London, when he told me his offer on the house had been accepted, I smiled and took the glass of champagne he offered me. When he turned his back, I tipped it down the sink. There was nothing to celebrate as far as I was concerned.

Once I knew he'd never walk again, I had the chance to sell it. I'd wanted to move from this godforsaken place before he had even dragged me over the threshold. But here's the irony. Over the years I had made the best of a bad job. I had worked hard on this sad sack of a house, and I had been rewarded in small ways; by the morning light that streams in through the kitchen window, by the joy of collecting eggs from my cheeky chickens and, most surprising of all, since the accident, there has been such an outpouring of love and support for both myself and the children that, I realise, we are truly part of the community. Or should I say, they know. I thought I'd managed to hide what our life was like, but what I have found out is that Archie Blackthorne is universally disliked. And my god, the neighbours have rallied to support us. Without saying 'We can't stand your husband,' suddenly I have found myself enveloped with smiles and encouragement and cheery waves and invitations where before there was a wary nod or a curt greeting and nothing more.

So, I will build my garden room and I will plan my revenge. I will plot in the way that Archie plotted to make my life a misery. I figure he's taken over twenty-five years from me so I'm planning to torture him for as long as it keeps me entertained.

The batteries and the broken biscuits are just me getting started.

6

I see Charlie in school on Monday, he's been trying to avoid me at every opportunity for the last fortnight I'm heading towards our department office at break, and I see him coming in the opposite direction down the corridor. He smiles and then does this weak half smile and lifts a finger like he's forgotten something; he turns sharply and heads back to his classroom.

Having made us both coffee, I head for his classroom. He is sitting at his desk, legs crossed and slumped, looking morosely out of the window.

'You can't avoid me forever, Charlie. Drink this. My husband is a twat and there's not a lot I can do about it but you're my friend and you're important to me so let's try to pretend that weekend never happened, eh?'

'I'm not avoiding you Karen,' he sounds like Eeyore and continues to look at the sky outside.

'Yes, you are,' I sound impatient, and I don't want to. I like Charlie.

'Yes, I am, you're right,' and he looks up at me and for a horrible moment I think he might be going to cry.

'It's okay, Charlie, I know you didn't need all that hassle, I understand. Drink your coffee. Who have you got next?' I perch on the side of his desk.

'Free lesson. Got some Year 8 marking to do.' He drinks his coffee.

'I'm free too,' I say.

He looks at me again. 'The thing is Karen, about Archie, it's just that,' he gets up and moves closer to me, 'I don't know how to say this but ...'

'What is it, Charlie? Honestly you don't need to worry about Archie. He's having a difficult time … adjusting that's all.'

'No, Karen,' Charlie looks at me, 'he was right.' He shakes his head.

'What do you mean he was right? We didn't sleep together Charlie.' I am confused, have I missed something?

Charlie is hanging his head in anguish. 'No, no, I know, I know we didn't, but Karen,' he looks up at me, 'I wanted to.'

I lean back.

'I've always wanted to Karen,' he continues, 'I think you're amazing, you must know that. And you're so fucking beautiful and smart. Jesus, Karen, why do you think I hang around you all the time? Why do you think I haven't got a girlfriend? I'm sorry Karen but I'm completely obsessed with you. I'm completely into you. Just like Archie said. I want to …'

'Wait, stop, what are you talking about Charlie? You can't be serious. I mean you're not even thirty, are you? I could be your mother.'

'Hardly. And you're not. And anyway, it's just a number. You don't look anything like your age Karen. You know you're hot. Jesus, half the sixth form fancy you. But I know you, Karen. I know you as a person. And I just, well, I think you're …'

'I can't listen to this Charlie. I thought we were friends. I'm really sorry if I gave you the wrong impression, I thought we were having fun. As mates.'

'Yes, we were. We were. Keep your voice down,' Charlie crosses to the door and pulls down the window blind and turns the latch.

'What are you doing?' I ask.

'Nothing. Just making sure we're not disturbed. I need to talk to you about this. It's been eating away at me for weeks. Months.'

'Okay. Well, we can talk with the blind up and the door unlocked,' I say.

He doesn't seem to hear me. He steps closer to me again and stands in front of me, over me. 'Ever since Archie's accident. I've just felt like you've wanted me to be more … available to you. Like you've wanted to spend proper time with me. All the nights out, the drinking, the talking, the dancing, God, the dancing the way you move, I mean Karen it's been a lot for me to control myself. To not make a move and there's been so many times when I thought you wanted me to, but you were like too far gone and I didn't want to, you know, misread the signals, but Karen, I think we would be good together. I mean, I think we'd be great together.'

He takes a step closer and, in one move, his arm locks in around my waist and he pulls me up towards him. He kisses me, hard, though he might describe it as passionately; the other hand goes to the back of my head, keeping the contact going. The arm around my waist moves. His hand snakes down between my buttocks, reaching and reaching. The hand on my head slithers down onto my breast, squeezing tight. He bites my lip, then inhales horribly as if he has been deprived of oxygen and pushes a flat palm onto my sternum forcing me back down sharply onto the desk. The hand that was on my arse is now wrenching up my skirt and his legs are between my knees, forcing them apart.

It has been a matter of moments and I cannot believe what is happening. Am I to be raped on a school desk at the beginning of period 3 on a Monday morning by a barely qualified English teacher with a penchant for the Beat Poets? Not if I can help it, I think.

'Get the fuck off me, you animal,' I shout, though not very loudly, and I start to fight. I thrash, knee, kick, bite, push, punch, scratch. And I scream and shout which gets louder. Finally, I land an accidental but significant head butt on his cheek bone, and he recoils just enough for me to push him away and get to the door where I burst out into the corridor and run.

Angie takes in my appearance, a missing shoe, bloodied mouth, wild eyes and panting breath.

'Do I need to ring the police?' she says, her hand reaching for the phone.

'Yes,' I say.

'So, he stayed with you on Saturday night? A fortnight ago?' The police sergeant is trussed up like a complicated parcel in her uniform. She has a ruddy face, neat hair and a large, gristly nose, good for looking into other people's business no doubt. She checks her notebook, 'The sixteenth?'

'Yes, we'd been out. A whole group of us. He stayed over. In my marital home. In the spare room.' I have already told her this. Her eyebrow twitches.

'And did he insert his penis into your vagina,' her tone is matter of fact.

'No, I've told you that already,' I try to stay calm.

'Did he penetrate your anus?'

'No!'

'Just have to go through these questions to be sure. And did he insert one or more fingers into your vagina?' She is looking at me as if she's taking a lunch order.

'There was no insertion,' I say, 'Into any orifice. He was trying to do that, but I got away. He groped me. He kissed me. He bit my lip. He ... handled the outside of my underwear, front and back. He touched my breasts. I've told you this.' I think I hate her.

'I see,' and she makes more notes and then shifts position in her seat. 'And your husband is disabled. Recently disabled?' Her pen is poised over the notebook.

'He is. An accident before Christmas. November. A fall. From the roof.' She makes a note.

I can feel anger and injustice bubbling inside me. 'What relevance is that though?' I ask.

'I'm sorry?' the sergeant looks at me with a benign smile.

'What relevance is my husband's physical condition to the sexual assault which was meted out on me this morning?' I persist.

I don't think she likes this. 'We're just trying to get the facts straight, dear, that's all.'

'But he was miles away. What has he got to do with anything? Look at my fucking face? He has nothing to do with the state of this. I'm sorry I didn't mean to swear.' I take a breath.

The sergeant rests her notebook in her lap and smiles again. 'It's just that the young lad has a different story Karen, that's all. Says you've been carrying on with him. For months. Says you like it rough. Says you've had sex at school. Multiple times. Says you're not getting any at home and that's why you've been using him.'

I think I may scream. Angie squeezes my hand, and I am so grateful that she is with me.

'I'd like to undergo a rape test,' I say, 'A doctor will be able to see that no intercourse has taken place for days. If it is possible, a doctor could see nothing has been going on for months. Charlie Linton is lying. He is a lying little shit.'

'I'll organise that then,' and she stands up and leaves.

I'd thought there was no point in a rape examination as I hadn't technically been raped but if he was going to say that he'd been having sex with me then this was a means to disprove his allegations against me.

I turn to Angie. 'Perhaps I'll just go home and forget all about it. What's the point. What purpose does it serve? She's a woman and she doesn't believe me. So much for empathy for the victim.'

'I believe you Karen, hang in there,' and she puts her arms around me and hugs and hugs.

In bed that night, I think about whether it was my fault. Had I led Charlie on? Am I the sort of woman who attracts violent men? Do I secretly crave the company of violent men? Then I thought about the framing of my behaviour and my treatment throughout the day. What had I done to provoke Charlie? How had my actions lead him to believe that I wanted sex? What had I said to encourage him? Did I usually sit on his desk? Could he see up my skirt? I mean, I had brought him coffee after all. What more of an invitation did he need?

The fundamental problem is that there has always been talk of men being unable to restrain themselves, unable to contain themselves, unable to control themselves in the face of the temptation that women offer to them. My experience of living with Archie was that he was absolutely in control of himself; he could pick and choose when to release his vile temper. He turned it on and off to suit himself, and to better serve his purposes.

Teenagers, immature idiots, also argue that they can't help themselves, in extreme cases such as fighting with each other or in petty examples such as belching or farting or swearing. When they 'lose control' in my presence, I always say to them, 'You would have enough control not to do this in front of the Head or the Queen or Beyoncé, so you can control yourself in front of me too.' That gives them something to think about. It's about respect. It's about making a choice.

It was the same with Archie and the same with Charlie. He wasn't so overpowered with lust that he had to fuck me to orgasm no matter what. He didn't lose all cognisance of what was going on. He just decided he would do it in the hopes that either he would get away with it or he hoped I might comply in some way or be too ashamed to tell anyone. Chances are he's done it before in some form or other. If he gets away with it this time, he'll probably do it again.

Archie did. Archie chose when to lose his temper. His emotions didn't rage so out of control that he rampaged up and down Tesco grabbing everything off the aisles and pushing over displays. He didn't attack men twice his size, or punch toddlers in the face. He wasn't so enraged that he completely lost his senses. No. He lost his temper at very specific times and in very specific ways. He only broke objects that were of value to me or the children; he only physically assaulted me but rarely where a bruise would be visible; he made sure the attacks were not witnessed and could not be reported and he was always in a really satisfied mood afterwards. Archie managed to maintain more or less a satisfactory working persona – there were no temper tantrums there. No. If things went badly in school, he came home and took it out on me. He made a choice. A calculated decision.

When men kill men and they're strangers, no one reports it as the victim's fault. 'He just had much bigger muscles than him, he couldn't tolerate it and just snapped', 'He didn't like the fact that he drove a better car, it was all too much for him', 'The full head of hair was a signal that things were reaching breaking point.' But I think if Archie had killed me, I would have been to blame. Somehow it would have been my fault because that's the way the death of women at the hands of their men is seen. The men are driven to it. They can't help themselves. They lose control. For a split second. And knife their wife of forty years, a hundred times.

And I was, in some small way, always waiting for that moment, waiting for Archie to kill me. I certainly thought if I tried to leave, he would hunt me down. He would never let me go. There was a side to Archie that was psychotic, totally cold. A white-hot rage burned at his core, and it terrified me. Cold emotion and a delight in venting that rage; not the best choice in a bedfellow.

7

You have to be careful if you have two sons and your husband is a psycho. With Georgie, I always felt my job was about secretly empowering her; to make sure she wasn't tricked into the same situation I found myself in. Years ago, lying in the bath considering the vast island belly that was Joe, I was convinced I was having a girl. All the way through my degree I'd leaned towards the more feminist playwrights, the female way of working, I liked the company of women, not in a particularly queer way, so it just made sense to me that I would create another woman. Also I had the feeling that with a son, my role would have to be to take away, to modify the natural privilege and sense of right to ride roughshod over others that society drenches so many men with from the get-go. I didn't necessarily want that. I didn't want to be a downer.

At that point, in my head, I was still managing to justify Archie's behaviour to myself; I was the frog in a pan of cold water on a slow burner and the temperature was tepid so there was no urgent reason to jump out.

When the boys were little, I would describe Archie to others as a 'hands-on' Dad. He did spend time with them, on his terms though. And nothing was ever straight-forward. I'm sure a lot of parents are relieved when their other half straps the kids in the back of the car and heads off to the park allowing a brief respite from the whirlwind that is child management. I hated it when Archie took the boys anywhere. And so did they. It didn't happen often. Luckily.

Thankfully, family outings were rare too. After the move up north, Archie really came into his own. He liked to begin every weekend with a list, produced after the boy's tea on a Friday evening. Early on these were handwritten, later printed out. We all had jobs to complete by Sunday night.

Archie liked us all to be kept busy. It was exhausting.

Even as small boys, he had Joe and Ted weeding and cutting grass as soon as they could manage the mower. He would make them empty every bin in the house on a weekly basis turn and turn about. They had a dishwasher rota which they completed in silence and with great care as a breakage could release, at best, a detailed lecture from Archie or, at worst, a complete meltdown. They had to keep their rooms immaculately tidy, and any books or toys accidentally left out or forgotten for whatever reason would be thrown out. He made them clean the cars, inside and out, no matter the weather. They had full waterproofs and wellies, and he would watch them with a mug of tea at the kitchen window seat, while they worked away, poised to go and inspect and find their efforts lacking.

Where we could, the boys and I helped each other. I would do as much as I could for them, retrieve the toys from the dustbin if possible and, if Archie was in a good mood, I'd try to persuade him that I *wanted* to mow the grass, weed the vegetable garden, clip the hedge, etc etc.

Archie's list of jobs was far more enjoyable; complete a three hour run times two, polish Farrah, fine tune some obscure part in Farrah, read new car magazine, research repair to barn roof, fathom out the weathervane renovation, and so on. His list was always longer than ours, which he always pointed out, but there was never much actual graft on it.

The marathon running was our only salvation. Without that I would be negotiating my way through a lengthy sentence in Holloway. He would set off and we'd give it fifteen minutes or so and we would relax. The television would go on or I'd put on loud music and we would leap and dance around the kitchen. Sometimes we'd bake with extravagant mess or, on warm days we'd run up to the top field and roll ourselves down the hill whooping and giggling with delight. The boys would take it in turns to choose a favourite game or they had the option to be on their own, often Joe's choice, to finish a book by the stove in the kitchen while Ted and I pulled out his unfinished *Lego* from under his bed and sat intently working away.

On his return, Archie had a strict routine that he would follow; cool down, shower, record his route and time in his study, then eat so he never concerned himself with us for at least half an hour. This gave us time to settle back into what we were supposed to be doing. Jobs from the list on a Saturday or homework for the boys on a Sunday. As a group, we had excuses ready if Archie ever questioned why everything took longer while he was out on his run, but usually he was too tired to ask.

When he was in training for a marathon the runs were longer and that was even better. More freedom! Well, freedom of a sort, because it was very difficult to actually leave the house.

I am sure you're wondering why an intelligent and resourceful woman like me didn't just pack up my boys and leave for good? How could I tolerate this life for twenty-eight years?

There is another side to Archie; his ability to charm and re-frame a situation to his advantage. Every situation. He isn't that bright, but he can sniff out an opportunity like an animal whose survival depends on it. He has what I would call low cunning. There's a *commedia dell'arte* stock character, a zanni or servant called Arlecchinno who is described as having the intelligence of a seven-year-old. That is Archie. He will drive every situation to his own advantage in the way that only a child can. It is totally self-serving.

Just a quick example of this to whet your appetite. I was promoted to Head of Department only two years after I started at Ridge High; Angie could see I was committed and focused and I was a teacher for the right reasons. When the deputy head post came up three years after that, she told me I should apply. I was surprised and flattered but I worked on my application and as I read through it, I realised I believed what I had written, and I had a vision for what I wanted for the school. I pored over the exam results and identified areas for improvements and came up with strategies we could implement which could yield results. I put in the work, and, by the end, I wanted the job. The day before the deadline I went to the study to print my application off to find a *Post It* note attached to the screen. It read, 'Thanks for your help with my application. Wish me luck. A.' When I checked the history he'd changed the file, re-written it, copied and pasted his work experience but stolen all my ideas.

I was livid.

I should have been more careful.

I still submitted an application, but it was half-baked and weak and I would have given Archie the job too. The most galling part was how disappointed I knew Angie was in me. It was hard to meet her eye at the end of the interview.

Low cunning you see; finding a way to serve himself at every opportunity.

And so, we come to the main reason that I couldn't leave him. I had to protect the boys. Archie had seized the chance to completely trap me forever when we first moved north.

I admit I was not happy, but I would never have killed myself. I loved my children. I don't even think I was clinically depressed. I was ill, yes, physically ill. Terrible flu. As I have said, Archie will not tolerate physical weakness of any sort. He does not have a sympathetic bone in his body.

It infuriated me that once Archie was put in charge of staff absences, I thought everyone would realise what an unfeeling robot he was, but no, with them he faked it, managing to say the right thing and not shove them into a wall if they intimated they had a headache so bad they felt they might faint.

Archie will tell anyone and everyone his boys never missed a day of school. We all shudder to remember the reality of this. Having to drag ourselves, shivering with fevers, throats raw or stomachs churning, through the torture of a school day then being made to finish a meal before finally slipping into the blissful cool and quiet of our beds for a few brief hours before being dragged out again, heads pounding and legs weak to struggle through another day.

So, as I said, I had proper flu. Archie had relented and allowed me to lie on the top of our bed while he watched the children. It was the weekend. I dosed myself up, praying I would rally so I could get back to the boys. It was quiet. I hated that. He was probably making them stand in silence somewhere as a punishment for nothing in particular. Anyway, I must have drifted off into sleep because the next moment I was being shaken awake by paramedics.

'Mrs Blackthorne? Mrs Blackthorne? Can you hear me?' A light was shone in my eyes. I tried to sit up. 'Just stay where you are until we see what's going on.' Someone was taking my blood pressure and my head was pounding.

'Yes, I came in and found these,' Archie was speaking. I looked over and he was by the door with another paramedic who was examining the paracetamol bottle. 'It was full, or as near dammit.'

I couldn't hear what the paramedic said to Archie.

'Yes, she's always been, well how can I put it … fragile, especially after our youngest was born. But I'd no idea she was feeling like this, I mean, my god,' and to my horror he started to blub, properly. He was standing in the bedroom doorway sobbing like a little boy.

Like I said, I had flu. I was not well. None of this made sense to me. The paramedic's face loomed close to mine, 'Karen? How many of these did you take?'

'Two,' I said, 'Well, four today, two this afternoon.'

'Are you sure Karen?' the paramedic bellowed at me.

'I think so. Yes. Is it Saturday or Sunday?' What I meant by this was, could someone clarify the day of the week, not that I didn't know what was going on.

'Not sure that she's oriented. Think we should take her in.'

'Agreed.'

'She doesn't sound like herself, no, I agree,' Archie chipped in, and suddenly they were strapping me into a chair and carrying me downstairs into an ambulance. Archie clambered in once they had attached chest monitors.

'Sounds like you've got a bit of a chest infection there Karen, we'll sit you up a little. I'm Jacob.' He put an oxygen mask over my face.

'The boys?' I said to Archie muffled by the mask.

'They're with Agatha, no need to worry.' Agatha was our nearest neighbour, a retired academic, determined gardener and keeper of multiple obedient sheepdogs. With very little family herself, Agatha happily chatted to the boys in an extremely grown-up but friendly manner, 'Would you like to come in and take a cup of tea?', 'I see you've had a successful visit to the barber,' 'One of the bitches has whelped, would it be of interest to you to see the litter?' I could relax if they were with her.

At the hospital I felt worse. My head felt packed tight, my eyes were burning, and my chest ached. I was given a large mug of liquid black charcoal to drink to absorb the paracetamol. Though I tried to protest I hadn't taken too many, alas, no one was much interested in my opinion. Archie stood outside the flimsy curtain and schmoozed the on-call psychiatric nurse. Yes, I had talked about suicide before, he said; yes, there were concerns about me at work, he could vouch for that because he happened to work with me too; yes, I was struggling as a parent; I had had a miscarriage; I had a difficult relationship with my parents; we lived in a remote area and yet I was too anxious to learn to drive; I relied on him for everything but he couldn't be there the whole time.

'How fucking dare you,' I said, as he came back in looking on top of the world, 'I heard every word of that.'

'Good,' he smiled, 'I hoped you would.' He sat down on the bed next to me and gripped my hand in his. To anyone popping their head around the curtain he would have been the picture of the concerned husband. Oh what lies there are in what we see. 'I don't want you to ever leave me Karen. If you ever consider it, I think, after this little episode, you won't get custody of the boys. You're not exactly stable full-time mother material, are you? At least one suicide attempt under your belt.' At this point he squeezed my hand so hard I could feel the bones grind against each other. I knew better than to cry out.

When the nurse interviewed me later, Archie sat and held my tender hand, sometimes reaching over to stroke my hair. I didn't bother to try to deny anything. They discharged me with antibiotics for the chest infection after a blood test showed normal levels of paracetamol.

Archie tipped the antibiotics down the loo. 'Your immune system will be stronger if your body heals naturally,' he announced.

I said nothing, just walked out of the front door to collect my dear little boys from Agatha, trying not to think about how growing up in this warped household might damage them forever.

7

et us return to my husband's senseless paranoia over Martin. As I have said, his jealousy had no logic. I had to endure hours of questioning, repeating over and over the inane drivel that Martin churned out every break time with the confidence of every man who has never been told to shut up the fuck up and listen to someone else's opinions for a change.

Archie would scroll and check through my phone obsessively (I had to hand it over immediately, sometimes in the middle of texting) and scour my search history. In truth, he would have been well suited to life as a Stasi officer.

No matter how much I refuted any feelings for, or connection with Martin, Archie's suspicions were never allayed.

As Martin's time at Ridge High progressed, I came to rue the day I'd ever met him. His timekeeping was appalling, he was a master of 'threshold' lesson planning, that is he decided what he was going to teach as he stepped over the threshold into the studio. All too often, I would walk in to find the overhead projector on and yet another lower school class watching a film. He made lovely choices for them, *Into The West*, a lyrical odyssey of two Irish traveller boys who find a horse with mythical qualities or *Strictly Ballroom*, the Australian debut of Baz Luhrmann which had several Year 8 boys pounding their chests and trying to Paso Doble up and down the corridors; but these should have been end of term treats not their week in week out drama experience.

At his interview, he'd bullshitted the panel about Boal's Invisible Theatre. Martin clearly had a new meaning. There was to be no real teaching.

Coupled with this were his hangovers, his whining at the bread and butter of teaching such as reports and parents' evenings, plus he delighted in regaling the staff about our time as students, sharing photos of me without my consent which forced me to be a good sport and laugh along or risk further reinforcing what I suspected was the generally held view by the majority that I was stand offish and uptight.

The icing on the cake was Martin's flexible relationship with the truth. This was when I began to suspect that his career trajectory was the result of multiple heads promoting him out of their schools rather than dealing with him head on. Write him a glowing reference (and Martin's were outstanding) and he became someone else's problem.

When Martin and I started teaching, it wasn't seen as child abuse to have a relationship with a sixth form student. In my first teaching post, the second in department in Music, Ginny, had complained about how many rows the head of faculty had had with one of the sixth formers he was sleeping with during the summer concert band tour of Vienna and Salzburg. Far from focusing on the cultural delights on offer, the pair had argued like an old married couple lurching from one spat to another, leaving Ginny to bear the brunt of the entire trip. In my innocence I thought shagging a student would be at least a sackable offence but apparently not. It was common knowledge what was going on. It wasn't until 2001 that the law was passed to make illegal.

Martin had been teaching for seven years by then and enjoying the fruits of his labour.

Okay, I never saw anything directly but, when I observed his lessons he was too familiar with the students, especially the older ones and even encouraged them to call him by his first name. He shared personal details with them and had no sense of personal space, often laying a hand on a shoulder or forearm. I felt uncomfortable watching. I wouldn't have wanted him as my teacher.

When I tried to bring these up with him he accused me of being 'square' and 'conformist'.

'Come on, Karen, we're artists. We're all about expression and feelings. We have to be open and to encourage the same in our students. That's all I'm doing. You know that.' He smiled sadly at me as if I had lost my way, was too bogged down in the bureaucracy of instruction to get the best from my pupils.

Perhaps he was right. Maybe my opinion of the male of the species was being clouded by Archie's behaviour. Maybe I was too suspicious and doubted everyone's motives.

However, I couldn't overlook what a drag Martin was on the department, and how time consuming he had become.

Fielding increasing numbers of complaints from sixth form parents about work not being marked was bad enough but then I saw the 'fun' he was having in his after-school drama club. Frankly, I was amazed that he'd agreed to take it on but he had and it was popular. He had, however, refused to complete even a basic risk assessment, saying they were paper exercises and pointless. Coming into the studio to find several children standing balanced on each other's shoulders without a crash mat in sight, was the icing on the cake. I had no choice but to sit in on every session. 'Sir says he's going to show us how to fight with broad swords!' a glowing Year 9 boy with anger management problems screeched into my face.

Fundamentally, as I have said, Martin was another prick in my life. He did as he chose, showed me no respect and was a truly dreadful teacher.

If my psychotic husband had not been working in the school, I could have approached the deputy head about Martin and dealt with his inadequacies formally. But I knew the way it would go if I raised anything with Angie or Archie. Archie would see any problem as a 'lover's tiff' and me getting back at Martin, or sure fire proof that my affair with Martin had ended and I wanted rid of him. He would never accept the truth because there was never any version of the truth that he could accept apart from the one in his head.

So I took matters into my own hands.

I realised I would have to get rid of Martin myself, I would have to make him want to leave. I was sick of all the time I was having to spend with him, all the dull details of his mother, his dreary social life, holy hell, the man could talk, a never-ending stream of hogwash with him as the centre of the universe, though I suppose it did give me something to tell Archie in his endless interrogations. I don't think Martin ever, over the couple of years we taught together, asked me a personal question, not a single one.

So, I bombarded him with paperwork. More and more pointless demands. Plans for lessons that I then went and observed before demanding written evaluations; I asked him to write up schemes of work from scratch or to adapt those in existence so they were fully differentiated in line with new government guidelines; I requested comment banks for his reports; I asked for written feedback from parents' meetings; I bombarded him with emails with spurious queries and questions and then further emails requesting responses to the emails that he hadn't replied to. And so, it went on. And on and on. Until he got the idea that I would not let up. He even tried to get the union involved but he was fundamentally lazy, and I knew it was easier for him to apply to another school, an evening's work, than see through any kind of formal complaint. Besides I had been logging every single dereliction of duty he had committed from his first day in post.

When I showed him the list, he sighed, 'Fair enough Karen, I'll look for something else.'

'I think that's a good idea Martin,' I replied.

I remembered the battered suitcase; I was ready for him.

In some ways I palmed Martin off. He was a terrible teacher, lazy and ineffective. He became someone else's problem. The question arises why couldn't I work out how to help myself?

8

Tess was an absolute find. Naturally, when we started Uni, we'd hated each other at first and spent the first few weeks of term avoiding contact wherever possible. She thought I was dim, spoilt and far too interested in boys. I decided she was needy, aggressive and too intense. When asked to get into any sort of group, we were magnetic poles positively charged to repel each other no matter what. However, like magnetic poles we were, in fact, the same.

Very late one night, at a dull party in a shabby, gloomy sitting room, we both observed a cheerless boy, cruelly nicknamed Chinless, give tarot card readings on the floor watched by a rapt audience draped on sagging sofas with greasy cushions. Chinless was clearly enjoying the small crowd he had gathered and the tiny queue of participants awaiting to hear his vision of their futures. He kept demanding silence as he shuffled what was, admittedly, an impressive pack of cards. What was less impressive was him thumbing his way back and forwards through what appeared to be a small volume of *An Idiot's Guide to Tarot Cards*. Clearly Chinless had decided he had to come up with something on the hoof to make him a little more charismatic which, to his credit, was currently working.

Chinless was also very much enjoying looking down all the girls' tops or up their skirts, as they sat opposite him and listened to his prophecies. He was not a natural success with the ladies, but he was trying not to leak desperation as he dished out his three card readings in response to their one question and one question alone. Currently, a skinny, coy girl had curled her long, *Olive Oyl* body opposite him on the floor and was sucking a tall, acid yellow drink through a straw. She couldn't take her eyes off him and Chinless was thrilled, though it did make him jumpier and more anxious to impress.

'What's your question, Di?' he tried to sound casual and cool, and he fumbled a dozen cards onto the floor as he attempted to shuffle them.

'I like someone at this party. Should I tell him?' she asked, ignoring his clumsiness and opting for rapid blinking instead. The crowd whooped. Tess however looked across at me, rolled her eyes and pulled a face. I stuck my fingers down my throat and mimed gagging. She stabbed herself in the eye, very fast, blinking like Di. I laughed and so did she.

Chinless had no luck with the first card, it wasn't going to help him bed Miss Sucky Straw. No, no, no. Try as he might he could not make a reversed Death card meaning fear of change, stagnation and decay in any way sexy though, bless him, he did try. Chinless loved saying 'Reversed', which basically meant the card was upside down in the reading; there had been jeering when he'd first used this but now the crowd were fully onboard, and the mocking had largely ceased. A reversed reading was different altogether apparently.

Her second card wasn't much better, also reversed and the Queen of Wands. 'I've got a good feeling about this one,' Chinless said, behaving like a cheap, end of the pier magician, 'I think the Queen is going to take her wand and make some magic happen,' but no, unfortunately the indicators from his little book were for jealousy, selfishness and insecurities.

'I think the cards think you definitely shouldn't tell him,' Tess piped up.

'I agree,' I joined in, 'I mean the Death card can't be the start of anything beautiful or meaningful, can it?'

'No,' Tess added, 'Decay and stagnation aren't the words I'd use to describe great sex.' A few onlookers chuckled but the general mood was disapproval at our heckling.

'Fuck off, you two,' Chinless shouted, 'Let's look at card number three,' he soothed Di who sucked earnestly on her straw. It was the King of Cups. Chinless frantically searched through his book.

'Yes!' he yelled, 'Stay true to your emotions and feelings and do not allow others to steer you off course. That's it! Don't listen to those two, Di, tell him, tell him!'

'Aren't you supposed to take all three cards into consideration?' I shouted.

'Yeah,' shouted Tess, 'Don't listen to the King, my money's on the Queen, she'll know what's coming. He'll be no good for you. All jealousy and mind games.' It was too late though, Chinless and Di were already snogging, and the crowd had started to drift away to the next entertainment, whatever that was going to be.

Tess pushed through a few couples and picked up the cards and the book from the floor. 'Let's do our own reading,' she called to me, and I crossed to join her behind the sofa where she plonked herself down cross-legged and started to shuffle the deck.

'You first,' I said, 'Cut the pack and then I'll deal them.' We made a tiny square of space between us, and Tess cut the pack. 'What's your question?' I asked and, suddenly, I felt like that old cliché, that we were the only people in the room. Her impish face looked into mine and I felt her connect with me too. Tess has a sharp face, it's all angles, a pointed chin, high cheek bones, a bony nose and arched eyebrows. At that time, she was favouring a mop of unruly, curly blonde hair on top of her head; it made her neck look precariously thin.

'I want to know about my future. What's ahead of me? Is that too big?' She leaned closer, rubbing her hands together, her blue eyes almost purple in the darkness of the room.

I shrugged. 'We'll see.' I laid out the cards before her.

They were the Three of Pentacles, the Two of Swords reversed and The Devil reversed.

'Woah,' she said, 'The Devil, that doesn't look good.'

'Not necessarily,' I said, 'Remember Death reversed meant fear of change.' I was flicking through the book, finding the suits. 'Okay, the Three of Pentacles. I think this is good. This card is all about teamwork and collaboration and working with others. I mean, I think that's pretty good for a drama student, isn't it? You're going to be good at working with other people, right?'

'Cool.' Tess grinned. She was enjoying this, 'What's the next one?'

'Okay. Two of Swords reversed. This one I'm not so sure about. This is about confusion, there being no right choice, it says something about the lesser of two evils. Perhaps you're

133

going to have to make a really hard decision at some point and neither outcome is going to be that good?' I didn't know what to make of it, but I knew I didn't want to give Tess bad news.

'I don't like the sound of that, but I did ask about my whole life. I suppose it can't all be plain sailing. Wasn't really wanting a *Sophie's Choice* scenario though. What about the last one?'

'The Devil reversed. Okay, well this one might be related to the Two of Swords. This is about restoring control and freedom. It's a very positive card but can also relate to release from addiction too. Sounds a bit heavy. Not to be too personal but do you have any tendencies that way Tess?'

'Not yet, but I could be persuaded,' she mused, 'I don't think that's a bad future. I'm okay with those, I think. Collaboration, choices, restoration. It sounds like a play structure. Sound. Let's do yours.'

Before she shuffled the cards again, Tess produced a quarter bottle of vodka from her jacket pocket. She swigged then offered the bottle to me. I smiled and pulled out my own. We chinked bottles and drank together, and she shuffled the pack.

I cut the cards.

Tess laid out three and peered down at them.

'The Emperor, reversed,' she said, 'The Hermit, reversed and The Tower.' She sat back up, her cat-like eyes bright with interest. 'All major arcana cards. I wonder if that's significant,' she said.

'Major arcana! You were paying attention,' I said, impressed, 'I couldn't bear his droning voice at the start. Kept thinking about fetching a frying pan from the kitchen and smashing him across the back of the head. He was so boring.'

'Minor are the suits, that's all you need to know. Now let's see what these mean,' and I had another swig of vodka as she found my first card in the book.

'Oh dear. The Emperor reversed signifies tyranny, rigidity and coldness. Not three words I'd associate with you, Karen.'

'Thank you, Tess,' I tipped my bottle at her.

'Just reading on, it could mean you have a boss who's a tyrant or you lose control of your money, or you have a tyrannical partner. Better be on the lookout for all of those.'

134

'Noted,' I said, 'Like you said, it's my whole future. What's the next one?'

'The Hermit, reversed again.' Tess flicked through the pages and cocked her head. 'Oh dear, this doesn't sound great, it's all about loneliness and isolation, no surprise there I suppose, but because it's reversed it's about a loneliness that is forced upon you. Or a time when you're forced to work alone. It doesn't seem to say you have much choice about it, Karen, but it can be a time for reflection or goal setting. Actually, it kind of fits with the Tyrant card, doesn't it? Do you think these things are real or do you think I have some kind of gift?'

'I think the point of the cards is that the power is in the cards, isn't it? That's why people have them. I'm not feeling very encouraged here though to be honest. I've got some crazy dude locking me up in a tower, it looks like. It's a bit *Silence of the Lambs* at the moment. Not sure I'm going to be managing much time for reflection at the hands of some kind of Hannibal Lector.'

'Hang on we haven't looked at The Tower yet,' Tess jumped in, 'At least it's upright not reversed. That's usually more positive. Hang in there, Karen, there's light at the end of the tunnel,' and she slapped my knee chummily and then set to finding the right page.

'Ooh, listen to this,' she said eventually, 'The Tower card depicts a high spire nestled on top of the mountain. A lightning bolt strikes the tower which sets it ablaze. Flames are bursting in the windows and people are jumping out of them as an act of desperation. They want to escape the turmoil and destruction within. The Tower is a symbol for the ambition that is constructed on faulty premises. The destruction of The Tower must happen in order to clear out the old ways and welcome something new. Its revelations can come in a flash of truth or inspiration.'

'So, what does that mean?' I said, confused, 'Is it good or bad?'

'I think it's saying the Tower is fundamentally bad and everything has to be re-built so there is massive change which is positive ... but it comes from disaster ...'

'Great!' I said, 'A serial killer and then a tsunami. Fantastic. Why didn't I get your cards? Mine are fucking apocalyptic.' I drink more vodka.

'What can I say, Karen? At least now we know what's coming. Better to be forewarned, eh?'

'I'd still rather have your cards,' I said sulkily.

'Look,' Tess moved over next to me and linked her lean arm through mine, 'Let's keep the cards and over the years we'll remind ourselves of this night and these predictions, and we'll look out for each other. What do you think? We can change our futures if we want to. What do you say?'

We'd barely been talking for half an hour, but she was everything to me.

'Agreed,' I said gathering up my cards and we set to sorting through the pack looking for her three, 'but you'd better watch out for my serial killer. If I end up in some trundle suitcase at the bottom of a canal, I'm holding you responsible.'

'I promise it won't come to that. And if I change my mind and decide to have kids, you remind me about *Sophie's Choice*. Okay? Really don't need to go through that.'

'You don't want kids?'

'God no.' I was surprised at her conviction.

'Absolutely certain?' It was an unusual point of view for a woman so young.

'Absolutely.' She drank more vodka.

'I want some. But not for years. There's too much to do. Too much to see first.' I drank too.

'Let's go back to my place and drink strong coffee and dance to *The Pixies*,' Tess said and stood up.

'I love strong coffee,' I replied and I took the hand she offered me, 'and you look like a pixie.' I was feeling happily drunk.

'I know,' she smiled and we left holding hands with the tarot cards in our back pockets which foretold our futures.

I still have my three cards.

I'm sure Tess will have hers.

On my wedding day, before I married Archie, she told me he was The Emperor. She told me not to go through with it;

she told me to walk away. I didn't want to listen. It wasn't the last time she tried. She begged me to leave him. Often. And then she stopped. She gave up. I deserved to become The Hermit. That's what I thought for quite a long time.

Archie didn't like Tess. He pretended to. At first. He pretended to like all my friends. He happily socialised with all of them in the early days, trying to fit in, managing it, most of the time. When I think back, there were a few times that the mask slipped. A few times that I caught a glimpse of who he really was, but I refused to really look and see him for what he was. I wanted to be happy. I wanted to convince myself that I had found this perfect guy who said all the right things, showered me with tokens of affection, took me to special places, filled up every minute of every day with more and more of what he wanted me to see.

There were the spitting, snapping remarks to hapless waiters who slopped a little coffee in a saucer or showed us to a table near to the kitchen door or loos; the taking on of an accidental collision coming out of the tube that nearly ended up in a full scale fist fight; and then the appalling unrestrained bellowing at a driver who didn't stop quickly enough, in Archie's opinion, at a pedestrian crossing and more yelling at a young guy who let his perfectly friendly dog jump up at me in the park. All of these were brushed away by Archie as reasonable responses, 'People need taking on/ challenging/shouldn't be allowed to behave like animals/ we are a civilised society/ I won't have you treated like /forgive me for wanting the best,' and so on and so on and so on. And I accepted his version of what had just happened; I accepted his skewed reality.

With my friends, at first, he smiled and charmed and bought drinks and paid the whole tab and over tipped and generally didn't say too much, except to compliment me. He always had an arm around me, a hand on my knee or in my hair or was in some way connected or attached to me. I thought it was affection at the time. Now I know he was marking his territory, showing that I was off-limits, warning off any interlopers.

Once we were married, everything changed. He was suddenly too tired to go out or meet up with my friends and when he did, he was surly and argumentative. He picked fights about anything and everything and when we got home, he pointed out all their faults. 'I just don't think these are the sort of people you should be hanging around with Karen,' 'He's just not that interesting, is he?' 'To be honest I think she fancies me. Did you see how she barely stopped looking at me all evening?' 'I think she's got a drink problem, don't you?' 'What does she ever give to you? She's just take, take, take. I hate to see you used like this, Karen.'

Okay, some of it was nonsense, but then some of it had a grain of truth and it began to niggle away at me and, eventually my friends began to find him difficult, so the dynamics changed.

By the time we moved away I had lost contact one way or another with all but a handful. Or, should I say, Archie had driven them away.

And Tess was one of them.

9

The thorny issue of ways in which to torture Archie has become a bit of a preoccupation. I leave shoes in the hallway between his room and the kitchen and squirt water from my bottle onto the floor to create puddles. I don't know how much of a hindrance these are to his wheelchair, but I'm sure they add to his anxiety.

I stop buying food that he likes, his favourite brands; I buy the opposite. Throughout our marriage I have had a budget unilaterally dictated by him, for the household expenses. It was miserly considering our income. If I tried to scrimp on food by buying cheaper cuts like shoulder of lamb which I slow cooked until it melted in the mouth, Archie would complain with his fists and say he didn't want to be served scraps at his table. The same went for mackerel, 'The rats of the sea,' as far as Archie was concerned. He had expensive tastes and expected me to provide them. Inevitably, that meant I served him a fillet of salmon while the children and I ate fish fingers.

But no more. I am delighting in providing Archie with beans on toast, fish paste sandwiches, spam fritters and chilli con carne with the cheapest of the cheap frozen mince. I tell Ted, who is pitching in with a lot of the cooking, that Archie is feeling nostalgic for his mother's cooking or his student days and, if Archie offers even a hint of a complaint, I whip the plate from under his nose and slide the contents into the bin. He eats what he's given now, like a grateful dog. I don't need to monitor him anymore.

I have learnt from him how to bring your family to heel, you see.

Joe could never tolerate cabbage. He hated the sliminess of the texture in his mouth. He tried to eat it, but it just wasn't for him. I avoided buying it, once I realised he didn't like it but when we moved up here Archie insisted on growing it so there was no escaping it for Joe. Not only would Archie dollop out an over generous portion, but he would demand that it was eaten first before anything else was touched.

I said he didn't touch the children physically, but he had a vice like grip on them emotionally.

Ted and I would watch as Joe's little mouth trembled to accept the cabbage from his fork. Alas, it never could.

So, Archie would take his whole plate and tip it into the bin. There was no shouting or yelling or crashing or slamming. Just cold efficiency as he returned to the table and set the gravy smeared plate in front of Joe who tried hard not to cry.

'Nothing more until breakfast,' Archie would announce as he sliced into his juicy beef or lamb or pork with the satisfaction from a job well done and Ted would take up his knife and fork with a terrible desolation and begin the task of clearing his plate, knowing that if he paused, his food would follow Joe's.

'Nothing more until breakfast,' I say to Archie now if he complains about a single morsel he is presented with and I would, with relish, slowly starve him to death if I could. If he wasn't being visited every day and checked on, that would be my plan.

I have to be careful because I don't want to be found guilty of neglect, I don't want to go to prison, but there have been opportunities which have worked in my favour. He shat himself one morning, so I simply left the house. It was utter joy that the boys were out; my only regret with that was that he managed to shower himself. Ideally, I'd have liked him to sit in his own stinking faeces for the whole day but never mind.

I oversalt any of his food I can intercept, and I make sure I'm creative with the 'use by' dates too. I repackage some things into Tupperware and make him sandwiches with meat that's on the turn in the hopes it'll upset his stomach and cause him a little more suffering.

I buy cordials he likes, but the flavours he doesn't and then he has to drink them because there's nothing else. I never answer my phone when he calls or respond straightaway when he shouts. I send our most annoying neighbours around to visit, over and over again. He's started to read lately so I've taken to carefully removing the last few pages of the books. I also listen out when he's watching a movie on *Netflix* or *Sky*. I let it run to the last ten minutes or so and then disable the wi-fi. Sometimes I can hear him shout in impotent anger when it happens, and that makes me laugh.

I behave like a school bully. I've taken to flicking his ear lobe hard as I walk past him. Or yanking out a few strands of his hair. I rest the teaspoon that I've stirred my hot tea with on the back of his neck and I wait for him to jump. Sometimes I just tap the point of a kitchen knife on the table in front of him, near his hand say. He knows I mean him harm and he knows he can't defend himself. He's definitely getting much more wary around me. And I like it.

I'm considering asking the boys to join in, but I think that might be taking it a bit far.

One day, when the boys were about two and four and we were still in London, we were walking along the pavement, and something landed from above near Ted's buggy. It was a Saturday morning I think, quite busy on the high street near our house. I was pushing the buggy and Joe was holding on like a good boy. Archie was walking next to us, a bag of shopping in his hand. We'd been to the fruit market and the library. As the object fell, I stopped and looked up, then something else, travelling faster, landed at Joe's feet, a crumpled can. Archie and Joe and I all looked at the stationary double decker next to us. On the top floor, the window was open, and a clamour of faces were grinning, laughing and pointing at us. The kids who'd thrown the can thought it was a hoot.

The next moment, Archie's bag of shopping had burst on the floor. As half a dozen oranges, suddenly bright against the flat grey of the pavement, rolled in different directions, Joe pointed at them, and I realised Archie had dropped the bag and was on the bus.

I scrabbled for the oranges and looked up. Seconds had passed but I could see Archie through the scratched glass of the upstairs window bearing down on one young boy. He had him by the collar and was forcing him down into the seat. The other kids backed away up the bus, terrified. Archie was yelling and pointing, his face so close to the poor young lad, jerking him around as if to bring home the message. I clutched Joe thinking surely Archie was going to be arrested, surely someone would intervene, but Archie threw the boy down in the seat, pointed at the other kids, shouting some final abuse and stormed back down the aisle. Another older guy patted Archie's back and applauded him as he disappeared down the stairs.

A moment later Archie was back, standing next to me, eyes shining and grinning like a wolf. He ran his hand through his hair and pulled down his jacket, 'That told them,' he said, standing up tall, 'They could have seriously injured Ted with that missile. I told them they're lucky I'm not pressing charges. They should be grateful I'm a fair man,' and he took the bag of fruit from me. 'Right, where to next, darling?' he breathed, satisfied.

In some ways, I'm surprised Archie didn't empty the fruit out of the plastic bag and take it up and use it as a weapon against the boy. He was good at doing that, improvising a weapon. He'd have done that to me.

I wonder if Joe remembers the bus incident.

The advantage of living somewhere remote is that he's had fewer opportunities to lose his rag with Joe Public; the disadvantage is that he's had to find all those opportunities to vent his spleen at home.

10

We should talk about Georgie. My beautiful girl. An angel of a child, a gift. She basks in the love we all bathe her in.

My plan was once I'd got the boys off to Uni, I'd leave. If they could get away from him, then so could I. I just had to bide my time and avoid being murdered. Joe was working out which courses might suit him; he was Year 12. Ted was knuckling down, really focused on his GCSEs in Year 10 and I thought, 'We're going to be okay; we're going to get away from this hell hole.'

This was around the time Archie became obsessed that I was having an affair with Martin. No matter how many times I explained to him how irritating Martin was, how self-involved he was, how unattractive I found him, Archie would not drop the subject. I remember one weekend, I had had a particularly bad period all week and Joe had a Uni Open Day. I begged Archie to let me stay at home. I was exhausted and still had cramps. My mother had had a relatively early menopause and I wondered, even though I was only forty-one whether this could be the start. However, Archie quite often favoured an efficient body punch aimed squarely at my midriff, so the thought crossed my mind whether he'd at last done some permanent damage.

Anyway, I spent the day sleeping and my bleeding tapered off and by the next day I felt restored. Archie's attitude changed though, and he went through an odd few weeks of being relatively nice to me. I was naturally suspicious.

This coincided with a change in our birth control. I'd been on the pill for years; I wouldn't trust Archie with anything as far as that's concerned. But my doctor told me I'd reached an age where I needed to stop taking the pill and she left me without a prescription but with an appointment to have a coil fitted, six weeks later. 'Just use condoms in the meantime,' she said blithely.

Archie slipped back into his long-lost pattern of gift giving, flowers appeared, chocolates (cheap ones), the odd paperback or two and a bottle of wine midweek. I didn't like it.

He wanted to have sex more. I didn't like that either.

'There's no reason not to. The boys are asleep, I'll get up in the morning, you can have a lie in.' This was unheard of.

I wondered whether he wanted to get through all the condoms he'd bought. It was a big box, and he didn't like waste.

Refusal was never an option you understand.

At the appointment for the coil, the doctor asked when my last period was, and I realised it had been a while. I checked my diary. It had been at least eight weeks, maybe more.

'Let's do a quick pregnancy test just to be sure shall we?' she said.

'I can't be pregnant. I think I'm menopausal,' I'd laughed.

When she told me it was positive, I couldn't speak.

Running through my head was the detail of all the times he'd fucked me. I saw him put the condoms on, but I never once saw him take them off afterwards. He even bought spermicide. 'Sorry about the mess,' he'd said afterwards. Sitting in the bleak of the doctor's room, I realised it wasn't spermicide, it was him, his revolting sperm.

'I'm going to be...' I said and I vomited onto the floor.

For days I didn't tell a soul. I deliberated an abortion. I hoped I would miscarry like before. I tried to antagonise Archie hoping for one of his favoured blows to the belly to make the decision for me. He wasn't biting though.

One night I woke up and felt a familiar slippiness between my legs. In the bathroom, bright red blood and grinding pain confirmed the pregnancy was over. I fetched pants and sanitary towels and waited. Archie appeared. He saw the gash of red on the pad as I sat on the loo and his face fell.

'I thought you were ...' he admitted.

'I was. But not now,' I said my voice strong, my face accusatory.

144

'Shit,' he said and turned and went back to bed.

It was all over by the morning.

When I still hadn't had another period two months later, I went back to the doctors. She did an ultrasound. 'It must have been twins,' she said, 'You miscarried one, but this baby is around nineteen weeks I'd say. Why didn't you come in Karen? You need a check-up after a miscarriage, you know?'

I watched the heartbeat blobbing on the screen, the swollen head and tiny limbs and I thought, 'Well that's that for another eighteen years then.'

Archie hadn't touched me since I'd lost the baby. He'd no idea my breasts were fuller, my belly was rounder. He only paid attention to matters that were of direct concern to him. And anyway, he was blaming me, nursing a hurt.

'You're having this one at home,' was the first thing he said when I told him a few weeks later, 'Hospitals are death traps.'

'Great,' I thought, 'Now I'm going to die in childbirth.'

I did my best to ignore the pregnancy, but Georgie arrived in June the day after Joe's final exam, she was just over two weeks late. Archie refused to call the midwife, said I should manage as long as I could without any intervention, 'Look at the sheep in the field, they cope,' he said. The cunt.

'I begged her to let me phone you,' he explained as the midwife arrived with about ten minutes to go before I delivered Georgie myself, 'But she just wouldn't have it.'

I'm in the garage looking for light bulbs. There's a pair of pliers. I pick them up and toy with pulling off one or more of Archie's fingernails.

11

In 2009, Archie decided he wanted to throw a big Halloween party. 'We've been here for years, and we've never had a party, we'll invite everyone,' he decreed.

This coincided with Tess announcing that she was returning to this country for a few months. If they wanted to get another lot of Arts Council funding, her theatre company had to spend a reasonable amount of time touring in the UK. She'd set up some venues, but I knew she had time at the beginning and was crossing my fingers she could make the party.

We began texting about it and as it got nearer the time everything fell into place. The film *Chicago* had been a huge hit a few years before and we decided to do a double act as zombie Roxy Hart (Tess with her short, blonde hair) and zombie Velma Kelly (me with my then dark bob). I had a couple of twenties costumes in the wardrobe department at school and Tess had always been fantastic at stage make-up. As Halloween approached, I became excessively excited. It was years since I'd seen Tess and it felt like years since I'd actually had any fun.

Halloween fell on the last Saturday of half-term, another good reason to have a party. Joe and Ted and I started decorating the house as soon as breakfast was cleared away. We drooped and draped cobwebs all over the place and fixed ghostly apparitions to the walls. We smeared bloody handprints down the paintwork and attached black paper bats on nylon string to the ceiling. We set plastic spiders marching across the worktops in the kitchen and hung a cardboard skeleton inside the downstairs loo to swing out whenever the door was opened. Our pumpkin lanterns were exceptional, we had gone to town with them filling the boot and spending days hollowing them out and piercing the skin to bring them to life and now they grinned macabrely, lined up along the length of the farmhouse waiting for the candles inside to bring them to life.

As the day wore on, I became jittery with nerves, anxious that Tess might not show, but just after lunch there was excessive car horn tooting in the driveway and I looked out to see her old van lurching to a halt.

'I can't believe I'm actually here,' she said, as we hugged each other tight.

'Come and see the boys,' I said and dragged her inside.

When the boys could hardly speak to Tess, I saw her through their early teenage eyes; tiny, edgy, cool. She was wearing a cropped top and no bra under dungarees with rips all over them, especially a very revealing one just under her arse. Her stomach was taut and tanned and her hair golden from the sun. She'd been in southern Europe for most of the summer; she didn't look British.

'God, it's fucking freezing, innit? Only got off the ferry this morning. Temperature's dropped by about fifteen degrees.' She was rubbing her arms and stamping her feet. To be fair the kitchen was cosy; Tess always liked to drive home a point.

'Joe, go and fetch Tess a blanket from the living room,' I said.

'Really?' Joe answered before he could stop himself. He didn't want to cover this sun-kissed beauty up nor did he want to leave the room. No sir-ee.

'Yes, Joe, a blanket, please. Now, coffee?'

Ted produced cheese and crackers and we huddled round the wood burner, and she told us outrageous stories and we all forgot the time until Archie appeared. He'd been down at the Lakes all day. That summer he'd bought a boat. A small sailing dinghy. Another hobby to drain the family finances. Today was the last day's sailing before the winter proper and he'd been off lovingly packing 'her' away until he could start all over again in the spring. I didn't care. It kept him out of the house. It looked like he'd tagged a run onto the day as he was in his gear and was glistening with sweat. No rush to get back to help with the party obviously.

'I won't come too close Tess, but glad you could make it,' he waved stiffly from the kitchen door like an automaton.

'Hi Archie. Yes, you do look a bit sweaty,' Tess replied, 'The house looks great, doesn't it? I can't wait. They've done a brilliant job.'

'Hmm. Yes. Is everything else done?' He looked at me, sternly, 'Drinks sorted? Food? All in hand?'

'All in hand, yes,' I said, 'Go and have a shower and get changed and then Tess and I can. Your costume's on the bed.' I kept my tone light as if he was joking around.

'Right. Fine.' He hovered but there was nothing for him to say, 'I'll go then.'

Tess raised her eyebrows at me. I smiled warmly back at her.

'You two had better get a move on too,' I said. Joe was gazing at Tess. I'd have to keep an eye on him. 'She's the same age as me you know,' I said to him.

'Mum!' he stood up, embarrassed and cross, 'Come on Ted, let's go.' And he marched off stealing a final look at Tess over his shoulder. We'd agreed the boys could stay up for the party as it was Halloween and half-term. They both had friends coming, friends coming with parents so that meant they were out of my hair too. We'd talked about keeping out of Archie's way and they had games, snacks and drinks set up in their rooms. To say they were excited was an understatement.

'That was a bit unnecessary,' Tess said, 'Let's have some wine.'

As I poured us two big glasses, she said, 'So, how is The Emperor?'

I shrugged my shoulders, 'Let's not talk about that. Tell me about your love life. No, tell me about your life.'

'Let's not talk about *that*? He's not even a person to you anymore. Bloody hell Karen, you have got to leave him.'

'I didn't mean it like that. Stop twisting my words.' I glugged at my glass.

'How did he persuade you to move up here? Where's the nearest theatre? What's the last thing you went to see?' She rapped her knuckles on the worktop.

'Look, it's better for the kids. It's safe. It's quiet.' I hate, hate, hated that I was lying to her.

'Do *you* like it?' She wasn't going to let go that easily.

'It's not about just me anymore Tess, I've got three children. I have to …'

'Oh, spare me the clichés Karen. We can put that on your gravestone. Here lies Karen. She didn't bother to live her own life; she sacrificed it for everyone else. What a fucking idiot.' She looked angry.

'Bloody hell Tess. That's a bit pigging much. You've only been here five minutes. Thank you for your support.' I could hear my voice. I sounded pathetic and I didn't want to.

'Oh dear god,' Tess said.

'Look,' I scrabbled, 'I'm sorry…'

'What are you sorry for?' Tess said, 'I'm the one who's being the fucking bitch. I haven't slept. Jesus. Why don't we get changed then get shit-faced?'

'I'd really love that,' I breathed, relieved.

When she'd finished my make-up, we looked incredible. From our sparkling flapper dresses to our torn fishnet tights to the black kohl round our eyes running down our cheeks to the fake blood dripping from our mouths. We'd backcombed and tangled our hair and we were light and dark, me in black, Tess in silver, we were yin and yang. Two halves of the same interconnecting circle. With the majority of two bottles of wine inside us, we didn't know where one of us started and the other one finished. We were firmly back in the past, luxuriating in the warm, familiar waters of our old friendship.

As we left the bedroom, we connected arms and tap danced our way down the upstairs landing. There were plenty of guests already downstairs and a solid wall of their heat hit us as we turned to face the top of the stairs. 'Shall we?' Tess said, and we proceeded to high kick our way down the stairs in true old Hollywood style, in time to the slow, droning music that Archie favoured. By the time we reached the bottom, all eyes were on us, and applause rang out.

Archie pushed his way out of the dining room. He was dressed as Flash Gordon, who he claimed was a favourite comic book hero of his. When Tess saw him, she shrieked, 'Oh darling,' she laid her hand on his chest, 'You should have come as Emperor Ming,' and we cavorted off laughing towards the kitchen to find more drink.

When I think about that party it is a drunken blur of noise and open mouths laughing and shouting and music played loudly and dancing and so much drink, more drink than I had had for years and years and years. The other point of note is that I have practically no memory of Archie at the party. He must have been there. Just not in the same space I was inhabiting. Which must have been one of the reasons I managed to get so totally legless. Eventually I fell asleep on one of the sofas in the living room, a blanket over me, slipping easily down into unconsciousness.

I had lost sight of Tess what felt like hours before but could have been minutes. I dreamt we were wandering a vast orange desert, climbing an endless sand drift and trying to reach the summit to see what lay beyond. The hot sand shifted beneath our feet and whenever we looked up, the top was further away. It was exhausting.

Then Tess was shaking me awake. She was upset.

'Karen. I'm going. I'm leaving. I'm just letting you know.'

'What? It's the middle of the night ... '

'It's nearly morning. No. Don't get up. I've got my stuff,' but she was still dressed as Roxy Hart, except she looked worse, undone somehow. 'The van's packed. I'm going now.' She bent down and slipped her thin, cold arm down behind me and held me tight, 'I love you, Karen. I'll see you soon.'

'I don't understand. Can't you stay for breakfast?' I struggled to sit up, but a pounding hangover was already pinning me to the couch, 'Wait, please, Tess, what happened?'

'It really doesn't matter,' she said, 'I have to go. I love you.'

'Love you too, Tess,' I said, confused.

She was at the door when she turned back to me, 'Leave your fucking husband, Karen,' and she was gone.

I lay back on the sofa and dread crawled over me like a winter frost. It had to be Archie. What had he said to her? Or worse, what had he done to her? I couldn't ask him. I would have to try and work it out.

Sleep was gone for good, so I pulled the blanket around my shoulders and dragged my sorry body to the kitchen.

Joe was in there. Sitting by the wood burner. Sobbing.

12

What you have to understand about Archie was his complete lack of restraint. If he wanted something he had to have it. He never denied himself anything. I do not hold with blaming mothers for their son's behaviours, except when they are little boys, and, even then, I think a lot of what goes on is genetic, but Archie's parents completely indulged him. He was a longed-for baby and everything he asked for, hell, everything he even pointed at, he was given. So, Archie had an over-developed sense of entitlement, shall we say.

Having said that, once he reached adulthood, any normal person can look at the world around them and make their own choices. Not every man chooses to twist their wife's arm behind her back until her socket is going to pop because the shirt which he has decided on a whim that he wants to wear that day isn't washed. Not every man smashes their cereal bowl onto the floor because one of their children has hiccups and, despite their best efforts, they can't get rid of them. Not every man punches holes through doors inches away from his wife's face because a member of staff didn't laugh at his joke in the right way during lunch at school.

Archie continued to behave like a spoilt, indulged child throughout his adult life in a powerful, aggressive grown man's body.

When Georgie was around five, he surprised all the kids by bringing home a puppy on Christmas Eve. A small, toffee coloured bundle of fur, a Labrador cross. A boy. We'd had cats, mainly to keep the rats and mice at bay in the outbuildings, but never a dog. Joe and Ted had longed for one, but Archie always had spurious reasons against them. I'm not sure what changed his mind, but they heaped him with love and cuddles for this uncharacteristic generosity in producing a charming little chap who we named Otto.

Christmas that year was remarkably calm. Usually, we all waited on tenterhooks for Archie's inevitable meltdown or suffered the steady stream of put downs and complaints that eventually dampened all our spirits so much so that we were often all in bed early on Christmas Day, exhausted and disappointed leaving Archie alone with the telly and a tumbler of whisky. Or, if he was really in the mood for torturing us, we had to endure one of his board games where we had to let him win and belittle us all in the process. That could go on for hours with him drinking more and more, his derision and snide comments ramping up as victory became inevitable and we sat stiffly waiting for the hell to be over.

When Otto arrived, he was the focus for Christmas Day. Much was made of little walks for him and his delight and curiosity at the chickens. He had to have tiny meals and the children even happily dealt with his one or two little accidents. Archie was plied with compliments and genuine affection for such a wonderful gift and thus passed our nicest Christmas Day ever as a family.

The adoration of Otto continued well past the holidays and Joe and Ted, particularly knowing their father, continued to keep thanking him for the dear little pal who trotted after them and was a constant companion.

Otto must have been coming up to about six months when I saw how Archie was looking at him. Joe and Ted had been training him properly and he was receptive and attentive. People say that dogs are intuitive; I think Otto knew that Archie was a monster. He created very little havoc for a puppy. He chewed his own dog toys, not our shoes or slippers even when his little needle teeth were falling out and must have been nipping his gums and the need to bite down must have been irresistible for a little pup. Otto was house-trained almost as soon as he was brought home; he would squeak at the back door and gallop out to the grass and widdle away.

In short, he was a very good dog, but he didn't really like Archie. And Archie didn't like that. He didn't like that the children adored Otto; they laughed and played and cuddled and stroked him and they were happy around him. I saw

Archie watching them and I knew there was going to be trouble.

'This kitchen stinks,' Archie announced one day after school, 'That dog's going to have to live outside.'

'What? Dad!' Georgie started, 'What do you mean? Otto sleeps on my bed. I love it. How can he sleep outside it's too cold.'

'And that's enough of that too. It's unhygienic. We can't have him on the beds anymore,' he slurped from his mug of tea and stood legs apart, looking intractably out of the window. He always took up as much space as he could. Another tactic.

'But the cats sleep on the beds, Dad,' Joe said quietly.

'What did you say?' he turned sharply to stare at Joe.

'Nothing,' Joe went back to the book he was reading.

'After tea, you and Ted can go and clear some space in the barn. He can sleep in there tonight.'

'Archie, it's going to be below freezing tonight, he's going to need a proper shelter. You can't just put him in the barn,' I tried.

'He's got a fur coat, hasn't he? Sort something out, can't you?' he snapped.

Then all three children started simultaneously with reasons why Otto couldn't sleep outside. This kind of mutiny was unheard of, but they were begging their father.

'Oh, for pity's sake, be quiet. Alright. He can stay inside until we sort something else out.' Georgie ran and hugged him and the boys followed until he brushed them off and drank the dregs of his tea. 'I'm off out,' he announced, and the children slipped onto the floor to Otto who was oblivious to what was afoot but was nevertheless very happy to receive the attention.

Later, after we'd eaten, Archie brought Otto's lead into the kitchen. The boys never used it; he was such an obedient dog it was practically obsolete. He clipped it onto Otto.

'What's going on, Dad,' Joe said warily.

'The dog is going to another family,' he said, 'Since you couldn't agree to him being housed in a sanitary way, I have had no choice but to rehome him. I'm taking him there now.'

'Archie, no, for God's sake!' This was a new level of cruelty, 'Have a heart,' I said.

'Daddy, no, please, no,' Georgie was already sobbing and clinging onto Otto.

'Pick her up, Karen,' he said, and I knew the command was a warning.

Joe and Ted said nothing. They just stood and watched knowing that they had no defence against him. Ted's eyes were hard and his cheeks and neck red with fury, but Joe was holding back tears.

I dragged my youngest away from the poor dog who obediently followed Archie out of the house.

Joe collapsed onto the table head on his arms, crying.

'I hate him,' Ted said quietly, 'I hate him.'

Archie didn't come back for ages. Georgie was in bed, asleep, exhausted by her grief, Joe was in there with her. They needed each other to fill the terrible lack. Ted had left too; said he'd be staying at a friend's. I wished I had that option. I had walked through the house gathering Otto's balls and toys, his bowl and basket and stored them away so they would not have to endure them in the morning.

When Archie found me in the living room, he grabbed me and pulled me to my feet pushing me back until I was flat against the wall. He choked me with one hand, it was a favourite move of his, people often remarked on how many lovely scarves I had, and did I always feel a chill? He squeezed my breast painfully with the other hand, his body pushed up hard against me.

'Don't you ever challenge my authority in front of my children again,' he said, 'not ever.'

And he looked into my eyes until I passed out. I wasn't allowed to close them until my body shut down. He'd made that clear in the past. Every time he strangled me, I wondered whether this was going to be it. Would he just keep going? Is this the time I'm going to die? Are my children going to wake up dogless, and motherless?

But no, luckily not this time.

As I lay alone on the living room floor where he'd dropped me, my view was of under the sofa. I could see one of Otto's toys, a chewed-up rabbit. Perhaps Otto had had a lucky escape.

13

I get a text from Tess saying she is coming to see us. It wasn't until August, but she was coming. I hadn't had a word from her for years. Nothing. Not even a Christmas card. It had crossed my mind that she was dead. I had sent a few messages from time to time. Even some pictures but she never replied.

I agonised over how to respond. I was hurt by the fact she had ghosted me but then, when I considered my life now, it contained no one from my past. Archie had seen them all off one way or another. I wanted to tell her about Archie's accident, I wanted to tell her everything was different. Then I thought I don't need to beg for her approval. In the end I just send, 'Fine,' and leave it at that.

Archie's position as Deputy Head was going to be advertised. 'I'd like you to apply again,' Angie had said, 'You're even more experienced now. I'm hoping to keep it to a very short shortlist,' and she had clasped both my hands in hers in an unexpected show of affection. 'It should have been yours all those years ago Karen, and I am so grateful you stayed with us. I want you to know I recognise that loyalty. Any other school could have snapped you up. We're so very lucky you committed to Ridge High.'

I couldn't tell her that I had no choice in my place of work as Archie would never have tolerated me working elsewhere. I could barely go out to buy a pint of milk without his supervision, so thirty hours a week where he couldn't keep constant tabs on me was an absolute no no.

Archie had formally resigned after a bit of a drawn-out process with Occupational Health. In truth, he hadn't the stamina to return to work full-time and he was down to statutory sick pay anyway. A decision had to be made. He had refused to go into school for the site audit to evaluate the possibility of him carrying out his post in a wheelchair which didn't help him consider the reality of the situation. There was talk of offering him a different office and classroom, but I knew, and I'm sure so did he deep down, that Archie's authority as deputy stemmed from his ability to intimidate the kids and how was he going to do that with the Year 11 boys towering over him in his chair?

Nerys, from Occ Health, kindly came to the farmhouse to discuss the final details and we three sat sombrely in the kitchen. Archie sulked his way through the meeting.

'We would do a phased return to work Archie, no one is expecting you to be able to manage everything immediately.' She was a practical woman who had worked with the school for years.

'I'm still on a lot of medication. I need to rest a lot through the day.' Archie rubbed his face. He hated to admit weakness.

'Sure, of course, well we could work around that, and maybe have some of your administrative duties allocated to home working hours?' They really were bending over backwards to help him.

'That's all well and good but what if I need to see a file? I won't be in school, will I?' Archie glared into Nerys' calm face.

'Aren't most files computerised now? And surely everything can be accessed at home anyway?' She was being patient and we all knew he was just making excuses. What he wanted was someone to tell him he couldn't go back to work. He wanted someone else to make the decision for him.

After a long silence he finally said, 'I have difficulty managing my … private needs myself. On my own. I've had problems. Things aren't … stable.' Archie blushed. He was furious at having to admit this to anyone. It was clearly a last resort.

Nerys nodded. 'I see. Look Archie. If you're not physically able to return to work because of your accident, there is no shame. We value you and you've given many good years, but everyone understands that this has been a life-changing event. There are other options. In your case, at your age, we can proceed with early retirement due to ill health if that's a path you're more comfortable with. There will be an effect on your pension if you take it now, you won't receive as much as you would have had you kept working but we can look into it. Your well-being is what is most important here after everything you've been through.

'If you want to return to work, we will do what we can to help you to achieve that, Archie, but, if you're unable to because of the injuries you have suffered, we will work out the best way to bring your career to the easiest conclusion.'

I had to admire Nerys; she had worked out the nuances of the situation and, if it had been anyone else, I would have applauded the outcome. However, Archie was now going to be able to draw his pension at fifty-three and sit around all day doing nothing.

As we watched her car pull away down the drive, I said, 'You can still work from home. There's plenty of jobs you can do. Don't think your pension will be enough for everything you need; the carers alone are a fortune. You'd better find something lucrative and sharpish, if you're not prepared to give Ridge High a chance.'

Secretly, I was relieved though. I didn't want him back there. I loved that I could walk the corridors without the worry that I'd turn the corner and he'd be lurking, ready to pounce, or I'd walk into the studio, and he'd be waiting for me. No, Ridge High was a wonderful place without Archie and now I had the chance to be Deputy Head there as well.

As summer arrives, I feel a new sense of possibility. The weather warms and I get into the routine of locking Archie's window, so his bedroom is stiflingly hot. Sometimes, as I leave for school, I see him wrestling with the bottom sash, desperately trying to push the window up and let some fresh air in. If only he could stand up, he could see the lock on the jamb halfway up.

Joe and Ted are both now working for the first time in their adult lives and Ted is talking about moving out. I'm pretty sure he has a girlfriend, though he's being very cagey about her. It's someone from work is my guess. I'm pleased. I want the boys to be happy. He's away from home a lot more. I like that. I like to think of him functioning in the wider world as a complete person.

It's nearly the end of term and I get another text from Tess. She'll be here at the start of August. There's an arrival time. There is no, 'Hope this is, okay?' It's all just fact. I reply with another, 'Fine.'

I am sitting sunning myself in the garden. For once, there is little wind blowing down from the fells. I am sure I should be doing something else but the heat from the sun on my skin feels wonderful and it is quiet, apart from the chickens squabbling in the distance. Georgie is visiting Agatha; they now have a long running, mutual interest in very difficult jigsaw puzzles. Georgie pops in a couple of times a week and frets over whatever Agatha is working on with her. They consider placing over ten pieces in one session a triumph. I don't have the patience, but Georgie loves it.

Agatha has come to dote on Georgie though she would never use that word. She treats her as an equal and Georgie often brings home great academic tomes that Agatha has lent her. What she makes of them I have no idea; that is between the two of them.

Agatha sometimes visits us though she never used to call round when Archie was at home. Once, she came round and scuppered my chances of making it to widowhood. Archie had insisted on setting off on a fell run in the most ridiculous weather. I didn't care; it was nothing to me. I was hoping he'd never come back. I think I'd encouraged him, in fact. Georgie was a tiny baby and Agatha sometimes used to call to see if I needed help with the boys. She'd turn her attention to their homework, or stoically make them piles of ham and mustard sandwiches and strong coffee or expertly deal cards and teach them poker and betting with matches. Sometimes she'd take Georgie and I'd go and get in the bath, and I could hear her singing surprising low, sexy jazz songs to her as I drifted into hypnogogic reveries in the hot water. She was a very private person. Not prone to idle chatter. She was happy to pass commentary on current affairs, but I knew nothing of her family or friends.

Anyway, that particular Sunday, he'd been gone maybe an hour when she knocked at the back door. When three hours had passed, it was Agatha who insisted we call the Mountain

Rescue. If I'd have been on my own, I'd have sent the boys to bed and waited until morning.

Agatha drove me up to the hospital in her tiny Fiat and rocked Georgie in the waiting room while I went in to see Archie. He was being ridiculously soppy. He grabbed my hand and held it against his cheek. 'I know I can't take chances like this, not now we have the boys and Georgie, it's just thoughtless. Thank God I'm okay. You've no idea, how worried I was up there. Oh Karen,' and he promised he'd be more careful in the future. I just sat there and didn't say a word. The last thing I wanted was him to be more careful, I wanted him to take risks! I loved Agatha but I was sorry she'd come to call that day. If I'd had my way, Archie would have spent the night up on the fell and my problems would have been over.

As I'm lying in the sun, I think I could have had the last nine years as freedom if it weren't for Agatha. Still, she wasn't to know. I then get to wondering about why she doesn't like Archie. What's he done to her? Another enemy on his long, long list.

It's likely Agatha will feed Georgie; she often does. Georgie loves eating with her as there are no rules; Agatha has an 'Eat when you're hungry,' attitude to life, so it can be anything at any time. Sometimes they just have a piece of homemade apple pie and ice cream or hot chocolate and a muffin and that's the meal. Then other times it could be something very grown up like prawns and smoked salmon on sourdough or cucumber soup or something like a pear and a lump of cheese and chilli jam with a few peppery crackers. Because Georgie lives with adults, her tastes are quite sophisticated. Or maybe that's just what she's like? The boys have been popping little bits of adult food into her mouth since she was weened, 'Try this, George,' and in went an olive or an anchovy or a caper or anything else they were eating. And mostly Georgie just chomped away.

So today, I'll do a revolting microwave meal for Archie, and I'll forage in the fridge. I luxuriate in no longer having the tyranny of Archie's culinary demands hanging over me. I have stocked the freezer with budget pap I can nuke in minutes when Joe and Ted are not around. If he wants to make himself something else, that's up to him.

I think I'll just have five more minutes; it can't be that late; I close my eyes.

Archie is bellowing at me from the French doors. I wake with a jolt.

'I'm fucking starving. Are you going to lie there all fucking afternoon? Actually, go ahead. I hope you burn! I hope you get skin cancer, you selfish witch!'

'Jesus Christ, get a grip Archie, you know where the kitchen is.' My heart is thumping though. It's been a long time since he's spoken to me like this and, for a moment, it's hard to remember that I'm the top dog now.

'Yes, I do but there's no fucking food. It's pathetic. You're pathetic. The only stuff is in the freezer, and I can't fucking reach it.'

I stand up and turn and look at him and he's livid. His eyes are wild, and his cheeks are florid from the exertions of the shouting.

'Move out of the way and I'll get you something,' I say as calmly as I can.

'Fine,' he says and reverses his chair back just enough for me to get past.

I'm hot and sleepy and I've no shoes on. I don't feel very together. I step into the darkness of the living room next to him and my eyes are adjusting after the brightness of the sunshine outside. He grabs my arm and pulls me down before I realise what is happening. He has his other arm across my torso, and he smashes me sideways across him. I unbalance, my cheek hits the opposite handle and I'm squashed into his lap. He's pulling me into his body, sort of bundling me up and I'm so shocked I don't react at first. He has one of my arms pinned against him and the other by the wrist and he's holding it tight. So tight. I can't believe how strong he feels. Then he brings his other arm over my face and covers my mouth, and nose.

He always had huge hands Archie. He was proud of them. Great big, manly paws. He's using them to excellent effect now. His hand is clamped over my face, a gag, his thumb pinching my nose closed. I try to thresh my head to escape but I can't move, he has me locked tight.

I kick against his legs, useless, that won't hurt, and then try to get some purchase on the floor. If I can tip the chair, I have a chance. I scrabble, my toes find a hold.

This form of suffocation is worse than the choking, there was no warning, so I didn't manage to take a breath. My lungs are screaming. The blood is roaring in my ears. I think he might actually manage to kill me this time.

I push down hard on the balls of my feet, I have no sense of what is behind us, whether this is futile, but I feel movement. That pinprick of hope is all I need. I push harder and the chair lurches and I feel my other foot hit something solid about six inches off the ground I push hard against that too. As hard as I can, and I know the centre of gravity in the chair has shifted. There is a lurch and, though Archie's hand stays clamped to my face, we topple and crash over and the impact loosens his grip enough to allow me to roll off and crawl out of his reach.

I lie panting and look at him shipwrecked on the floor, half sprawled out of his chair, as far as the belt around his waist will let him.

Rage overwhelms me; I struggle to my feet and run to the kitchen.

On my return, he hasn't moved; now he's sobbing.

I stand over him. He has an arm extended on the floor in dramatic despair. I stand on it just above the wrist pinning it to the floor. Archie tenses and lets out a howl. I look down at the flesh of his exposed wrist. I can see the taut blue veins firm beneath his skin. With a quick movement, I bend down and slice his wrist with the knife I have brought from the kitchen. It is one of our sharpest and the action is surprisingly straightforward. There is resistance, yes, but it's a clean cut, satisfyingly deep but not so bad for the blood to start spurting like some hackneyed old horror movie.

Archie shrieks in pain and then, 'Karen, oh my god, what have you done,' he whimpers.

'You wanted to kill me, Archie. Perhaps I should kill you? How do you like it?' I look down at him as he struggles to push my foot off the arm, but he is, as I thought, in a very weak position and he is still strapped in, caught around his pelvis, and he hasn't worked this out in his panic and he obviously can't feel it.

The blood is pooling on the floor. It looks rather beautiful, and I'm pleased that we have hardwood rather than carpet. I think I may have thought twice if that had been the case.

'Do you know you can bleed to death in about eight minutes? I think you suffocate a bit more quickly though.' I look down at him.

'Karen, please, think of the children,' he begs.

'Were you thinking of the children a moment ago?' I ask, my anger rising again, 'In fact, have you ever fucking thought of the children? Honestly Archie, it's a good job you're not a hostage negotiator. That little remark just made me want to slash your other wrist.'

'Okay, look I'm sorry. You're right, I don't think of them. I just get ... I just ... I don't know ... I see red. I can't help it.' He sounds pathetic.

'You see red? I'm seeing red now. All over the floor. It's got a very distinctive smell blood, hasn't it?' There really is a steady stream coming out and he's beginning to look pale.

'Okay Karen, you've made your point. Can we just stop this now. Please.' He's stopped trying to shift my foot and it occurs to me that the pressure of it must be stopping the bleeding to some extent, so when I release it, it's going to get worse. I make a decision.

I take my phone out of my pocket. The screen is smashed.

'Fucking hell, Archie!' I say, 'Look what you've done.'

'Sorry Karen, I'm really sorry,' he mutters. He really is looking very pale and there's a sheen of sweat across his face. I am enjoying his suffering, but it can't go on forever.

I dial for an ambulance. If they get here in time okay, he's lucky, if not c'est la vie.

Then I phone Agatha. 'Agatha, Archie has slashed his wrist, I tried to get the knife from him and there was a bit of a tussle. I've phoned an ambulance. No, only one wrist. Yes, quite a lot of blood. Thank you. Yes. Will do.'

I crouch down and smear the blood around a little more, with my foot still in place and onto Archie who seems to be drifting into semi-consciousness, so it doesn't look so neat, and finally leave to get some towels. I apply pressure to the wound when I get back. 'Thank you, Karen,' Archie says weakly, and I can hear sirens in the distance.

'I don't want you to die, Archie,' I whisper to him, 'I want you alive. I want you to pay for everything you've put me and the children through. I'm going to make your life hell. Don't think you're getting away with it that easily.' And I slap his face, fairly hard, 'Pay attention while I'm talking to you, Archie.'

He opens his eyes for a moment, and I smile down at him.

Part Three

Joe

1

Mum doesn't know that I have been in touch with Tess for years. I keep trying to work out how to tell her, but I can't find the right moment. Dad is back out of hospital after his suicide attempt, and I don't want her to have anything more to worry about but when she announced Tess was coming to visit I was elated that I was going to see her but also crapping myself because of Mum.

We don't have secrets, Mum and me. In truth, our family is not a normal family, though I don't have many with which to compare apart from those on TV or in the books I've read, but my guess is, we're not average. Most families probably have secrets of some sort, some are probably worse than ours, but the truth is that my father cannot be relied upon, my father is not normal, my father should be in prison, my father is the bogie man.

It's not easy pretending that everything is okay, and, in most cases, I guess most kids would get out as soon as they could, but we can't. We can't leave.

So, no secrets in our house, not from Mum anyway, apart from Tess. And I'm not sure how it happened. No, that's a lie. I know exactly how it happened and I wanted it to.

You have to understand that if your dad is some kind of Nazi deputy head, it's not necessarily straightforward making friends. I had a few. I'm quiet though. Not like Teddy. Dad always liked how chatty Teddy was, how easy it was for him to chat to anyone and everyone. Dad always favoured Teddy to be honest.

When Tess arrived for Halloween, she was something else; she had this massive, crazy, painted hippy van thing and she was all tanned and blonde and what a body. I mean I was a kid, but I knew what a woman was and, my god, I'd never seen anyone like her up close. And Tess is petite, and she was so friendly and interested in me. I know now that's because I'm her best friend's son but back then I thought she liked me. For me. I was often ... overlooked, shall we say.

At school, I received a fair amount of bullying for a number of years from older boys who had been treated to my father's excessive castigations. I don't think he was popular with the staff either because, although I'm bright and hard-working, I wasn't often rewarded or praised for my efforts. Mum would point out those teachers with whom Dad was having particular difficulties (as I said, no secrets) but it didn't make my day-to-day any easier.

So, when Tess arrived at Halloween and wanted to talk about books and films and bands I'd never heard of and didn't care about Dad's opinion and wasn't afraid of him, in fact quite the opposite, I think I fell in love with her a little bit.

In her Roxy Hart costume, she shone out from the rest of the crowd, and I stayed up and watched her dancing, long after my friends had gone home. Tess gave me her number and told me we should keep in touch. She kissed the palm of my hand and pressed it onto her breastbone just below her throat and I thought I would have to marry her.

The party was pretty much over, and I couldn't see where Tess had gone. I'd found Mum asleep in the living room and covered her up with some blankets and thrown a couple of logs on the fire.

I walked through the house but there was no sign of Tess. The sound of raised voices filled my throat with familiar dread. I knew what Dad sounded like. I walked towards the barn in a daze and found them in there.

What you have to understand about my father is that, even though Mum is a brunette and beautiful, Dad likes blondes. All through my life he's been involved with blondes, obsessed with blondes, stalking blondes. He's addicted to them.

He had Tess up against the door of the barn and he was yelling in her face. His forearm had pinioned her chest and he was trying to gag her with his hand, and he was pulling up her dress with his other hand. He looked like a monster against her, hulking and red and powerful and she was a tiny sliver of silver beneath him, a minnow caught on a hook. Part of me wanted to turn and run and fall into my bed and pull the covers over my bed and pretend none of this was happening. It's a pattern from the past. We learnt early on that it's unbearable to be a witness to your parent's atrocities so diversionary action was the order of the day.

But this was new territory.

Dad was attacking another woman. Not Mum. He was attacking Tess. My Tess. I couldn't run and hide.

You also have to understand that I'm not, by any stretch, brave.

There was a long branch lying on the ground, near the door. I made a decision without thinking as the vile shouting of the two adults filled my head. As I ran over, I reached for it, picked it up and swung it at Dad's head.

I had never attacked him before.

For a moment he stopped, like a bear irritated by a fly, dropping Tess who crumpled to the ground. I swung again but he turned and expertly caught the branch which twisted out of my grip.

'Well this is interesting, Joseph,' he snarled turning to me.

'Leave her alone,' I managed but I could feel tears on my cheeks, and I hated myself for them.

'You don't know what you're talking about. Time you were in bed, my lad, rather than playing with the grown-ups. We'll talk about this,' he waggled the stick, 'in the morning.' My stomach turned over with the reality of that threat.

Tess had struggled to her feet and was edging out of the barn towards the house. 'I'm leaving,' she said, 'You're a fucking psycho!' she shouted at Dad. She looked at me, 'Thank you,' she said and ran indoors.

'Stupid bitch,' he said, 'Drunk. And hysterical. As usual,' and he threw down the branch and wandered off down the drive. I watched as he wavered drunkenly from side to side.

I ran into the house and nearly ran into Tess. 'I'm going. Now. I won't be back. I'm sorry,' she said, and she pushed past me. That was it. I headed blindly to the kitchen and sat at the table and broke down full of rage and sorrow.

Mum appeared, cocooned in her blanket, face and voice messy from sleep. 'What's going on? Why has Tess left? Why are you so upset?'

'I don't know, I'm tired. I'm going to bed.' I eventually managed, embarrassed by my sobbing. I couldn't bring myself to say what I had witnessed. And I never told her anything about what I'd seen or gave her any explanation as to why Tess left.

As soon as I got my first mobile, years later, Tess was the first person I text. She replied immediately. And it's been pretty constant ever since.

2

I am a natural worrier. As an eldest child that's probably always going to happen, but what I worry about the most are my genetics. When am I going to turn into my father?

Teddy and I have talked about this. A lot. Part of the problem of growing up with violence is that you're told by society that it's passed down from generation to generation. I feel like a ticking time bomb. How can I have a relationship, with anyone, if it turns me into him? How can I have children and run the risk of producing another Archie?

I accept I will be alone. Always.

I certainly don't want another woman to have to experience what Mum has had to go through.

I did have a girlfriend once, when I was younger. Before I faced up to reality. Her name was Grace. She was funny and smart and when she ate a banana, she split it into three down the middle, top to bottom so she had three skinny long pieces. I thought that was incredibly skilful. We were just twenty. I think I loved her.

It was always difficult for me to get a job because we lived in the middle of nowhere and I couldn't drive. After I realised I could never go to Uni, I got a few local dead end time-fillers and that's how I met Grace.

The other thing about growing up with my father was that we couldn't really invite people round. He always used to go on about his childhood, rampaging around the countryside with a group of friends, but to do that you have to have a certain amount of access into each other's lives. You never knew what sort of mood Dad would be in. If he was playing The Charmer, you were quids in. Everyone would leave thinking you had the best life imaginable. But if he turned. Well, that was always the worry.

So, we kept everything separate from him. Me especially.

When I met Grace, at the beginning of the summer, both of us waiting on in a cramped little tearoom in the village, as soon as we started talking, I was planning for her to never meet him. I was biking into work, so that wasn't a problem, but I knew he'd walk in one day, especially once it was the holidays, and my mind would run and run to all the possible outcomes of his first encounter with her. None of them were good.

'You don't drive?' she had her arms crossed and was frowning at me while I made up more tuna sandwiches while we had a lull. 'I couldn't wait to pass my test. And I grew up in Leeds. How are you managing here?'

Grace had moved into the village at the end of the sixth form. Her younger brother was in Teddy's year. I'd seen her around, but we'd never spoken. She had quickly amassed people around her and I would occasionally glimpse her in the midst of lively, loud groups storming into the local pub or heading to the park as I skulked at the bus stop in the village and then she was gone, off to Uni.

Before the tea shop, we'd barely spoken. She was confident in the way clever, attractive girls can be; fair-haired, greenish eyes with a hint of a sly smirk constantly moving on her mouth. The first time I walked into the shop and saw her wiping down the tables, I sighed wearily. I had the impression that she considered me an idiot, inferior, a nerd. I didn't relish the thought of working with, or rather being pointedly ignored by her, for weeks on end.

As it was, she scooped a pile of crumbs into her palm, looked up and smiled. 'Hi Joe,' she said and that was the start.

'We only have one car. Don't you have anything to do?' I had answered her. Of course, I wanted to drive but there were always reasons, mainly provided by Dad, for me not to.

'I'm enjoying watching you work,' she replied, 'We only have one car. Doesn't mean you can't drive it, does it?'

'It's complicated. Why don't you unload the dishwasher?' I could feel her watching me, properly looking. I didn't want her to do anything else; I wanted her to stay right where she was.

'Why? They're both teachers, right? Your parents. You could take them to school and have the car all day. Yeah? Or is it some kind of sic car? No, they're teachers. Can't be a Lamborghini or anything. I mean, you're twenty, Joe. You should be driving.'

'Should I Grace? Thank you for the information. Anything else?' I sounded grumpy but I liked her talking to me. I loved it.

'Yes. You shouldn't really be living at home. You should be at Uni or something.' I looked at her and she was twisting a tea towel up between her hands, turning it into a rope.

'Right. Okay. Thanks. Any more advice before you do some work?' I kept buttering and cutting. I always wanted our conversation to keep going.

'Why don't you have a girlfriend?' She flicked my bum with the tea towel.

'Ow! That's a bit personal. How do you know I haven't?' I tried hard to concentrate on the sandwiches as this was a departure. Our previous conversations had been hypothetical mainly based on her random questions seemingly plucked out of the air, 'Joe, would you rather have spaghetti hair that regrows ever night or would you rather sweat maple syrup?' she'd asked at the time as she examined the syrup bottle before she put it away.

'I suppose the spaghetti hair would be a constant source of nourishment. Save on the food bills,' I'd replied. I always gave her questions careful consideration.

'A constant source of nourishment! You sound like Alan Bennett,' she giggled. Grace was taking English Lit at Uni. Books were another thing we talked about.

'And I think I'd find maple syrup a bit too sticky under the arms. I'd be loath to get into any warm climates. I mean, would it drip? Like run down my body.' I was wrestling with the milk frother nozzle. It had a habit of clogging.

'Easy tiger,' she sounded mock-shocked. I hadn't meant to be sexy, and I focussed hard on the frother to hide my embarrassment and the fact that I'd said the words, 'my body' to her.

'Would the spaghetti be soft though when it grew? If it's uncooked, that's a whole other matter.' I decided it would be safer to change tack.

She loved that I took all her questions seriously and considered all the angles. 'I think it would have to be soft otherwise it would just break off. You'd never get any length to twirl around your fork. Let's say *al dente* for the purposes of argument.'

'In that case I'm going with the spaghetti, you could just grab a handful and bung it in the microwave with a bit of cheese and that's your tea. I mean, you're cutting down on shopping and water consumption and energy. It's a no-brainer.' A spurt of steam made me jump.

'I agree,' Grace said, 'but I'd like to wipe a pancake over my pits and bite it.' I had looked at her. She was clearly savouring the thought.

'Would you rather have all dogs attack you when they see you, or all birds attack you when they see you.' This time Grace was feeding a cocky herring gull as we sat out on the tiny square of scrubby grass at the end of the jumble of shops which housed the café. We were on our dinner break. It was hot. August. It usually rained a lot in August, or it was cloudy and cool. That year the weather was brilliant, and Grace was tanned and smooth as an animal, her skin not her skin. I had to stop myself from staring at her legs stretched and crossed on the grass next to mine.

We were still friends at this point.

'Dogs can be very vicious, but it might be possible to outrun them whereas birds, most of them are tiny and they might not be able to do much damage but I bet they could easily keep up. I mean, they can fly.' I look at the sky, pale with a veil of high cloud.

'Dogs are fast,' Grace protested, 'You think you're faster than a dog?'

'Okay. Maybe not. You're right and a dog could do a lot more damage with a bite than a bird with a beak.'

'You could kill a bird. Most birds. If you could catch it,' Grace reasoned.

'I wouldn't want to,' I answered.

'It'd be self-defence. You'd have to,' she insisted.

'Fair point,' I said. I rolled over onto my stomach, catching her perfume as I did, vanilla and some sort of berry, maybe raspberry. It was lovely. Grace was always clean. Scrubbed. Fresh.

'It'd be harder to kill a dog,' she said.

'Emotionally and physically,' I said, 'I wouldn't want to do that.' Otto's trusting eyes flashed into my mind and I blinked them away. Grace rolled over to lay down next to me. 'Every single time I went outside, you say?' I clarified.

'Uh huh,' she nodded as she plucked and stripped a piece of grass and sucked on the tender white stem.

'I need to think about this logically,' I said, trying not to think about her mouth. 'The main difference between dogs and birds is that I don't see many birds on leads whereas the opposite is true of dogs.'

'Go on,' she said turning to me. Her pupils were tiny in the sunshine. I could see all the colours in her irises; flecks of jade, emerald and amber outlined with a deep olive-green ring. There were even tiny specks of yellow. Her eyes were beautiful, like looking into a kaleidoscope.

'So, I think I could rely on the humans at the end of the leads to keep the dogs off me. However, nothing would stop the birds.' I was pleased with my reasoning.

'You could never go to a park. Loads of dogs running free. You'd be toast.' She checked her phone for the time.

'Can I choose neither? I don't like the sound of either of them. I think I'd have to stay indoors no matter what. I mean there's a lot of birds, and dogs are a man's best friend. It would render the world pretty much unhabitable for me.'

'Joe. I am shocked. You know the rules. It's one or the other.' She stared at me eyebrows raised and expectant and I wanted to kiss her, but I had never kissed a girl. Or a boy, for that matter.

We waited. Just looking at each other.

'Okay. Fuck it,' I said, 'Birds. I'll just have to kill them. Or carry a big net.'

'Time to go,' Grace stood up and brushed down her legs, 'I knew you'd choose them.'

The tuna sandwiches were almost done, and I didn't want what was going on to end. 'Who'd want me as their boyfriend?' I said fiddling around with the wrappers and the pile I'd made. I instantly regretted it. I sounded weak and pathetic. 'I mean I make a very good sandwich but, like you say, I can't drive.' I tried to rescue the situation.

'I don't think you'd be too bad as boyfriend material,' Grace said, and she moved to stand next to me, facing into the kitchen, arms folded in a purposeful manner, 'Let's go through your good points.'

'Do we have to? There aren't many.' Weak and pathetic again.

'Come on Joe, you've got to think positive. Are you planning to live here alone in the middle of nowhere your whole life making weak coffee and boring sandwiches for pensioners, day in and day out?'

I didn't have the heart to say yes, that was pretty much my plan.

'Let's start with your personality. You're a good listener.'

'Pardon?'

'On the other hand, you have a terrible sense of humour.'

'Bit cheeky.'

'You're clever and you know stuff.'

'It's true. Stuff is one of my top subjects.'

Grace was enjoying this. So was I. 'What else do girls look for in a boyfriend?' I dared to ask, turning away from the sandwiches and leaning against the counter with her.

'You've got to be good looking. For the shallow girls,' she said.

'Oh dear,' I shook my head. 'That's me out then. With the shallow girls. On the other hand, I don't like them. So ... '

'You are good looking though, Joe,' she said. Unbearably her tone was serious and I, to my horror, started to blush. I could feel it on my neck, prickling up and blooming onto my cheeks.

'Fuck off, Grace,' I blurted out. I knew straight away it was the wrong reaction and I panicked. So, like the truly charming Romcom hero that I am, and oh how I cringe to say this, I don't know what possessed me, but I picked up the ketchup bottle and squirted it onto her top.

My plan was just a little dollop, but I squeezed really hard. I don't know why. It was like I lost all control. Of everything. My mind, my muscles and my fine motor skills. I have to point out that this was the kitchen ketchup bottle. It's industrial sized. And it works really well. It's for catering businesses. You get the picture.

In my head, I thought it would be a playful thing to diffuse the situation and stop her looking at my puce face but in reality, the sauce bottle sprayed a solid stream across her chest, up her cheek and onto her hair. All from one squeeze.

There was a terrible silence and I thought in a moment we're going to burst into fits of laughter and end up snogging, but no.

'Fucking hell, Joe. What the fuck?' Grace was furious. She grabbed a cloth and started wiping the sauce and it smeared and spread and her hair caked to her scalp and her make-up ran and I kept saying sorry and she told me I was a fucking idiot and a moron, and she pushed me away, hard, until I had to leave the kitchen because I thought I might cry.

Out in the shop, Jilly, the manager, told me to serve a table but I couldn't remember their order, so Jilly got all narky with me too. I saw Grace talking to Jilly behind the counter and then Grace left. I thought I'd blown it.

When I told Teddy about it that night he laughed. 'She was coming on to you and you soaked her in ketchup. Classic Joey.' He was really enjoying the whole story.

'Okay, okay but how do I fix it? I like her. Like, I really like her.' I was standing in his room, watching him get ready to go out.

'I dunno. Say you're sorry? Tell her?'

I took my bike and pedalled so fast my legs were trembling by the time I got to her house. I knew where she lived but I'd never been there. I hurled my bike to the ground and ran up the path. As I pressed the doorbell, I realised I hadn't changed since work. I hadn't brought her anything. I had no great romantic gesture planned. I had only thought as far as, 'Hello, my name is Joe and I work with Grace. Is she in?'

Grace answered the door, so I was momentarily stuck for words as my opening line was useless.

'It's you,' she sneered, crossing her arms and leaning against the door jamb.

'It is I,' I said sounding like an idiot. I tried to smile but I lost confidence in it. She still looked so cross with me.

'Well?' she said raising her eyebrows as if she had plenty of other much more important stuff to be getting back to.

'I'm sorry, and I like you,' I said. It didn't sound that great out loud.

'Okay,' Grace said, 'What do you mean?'

'I'm sorry for the ketchup and I mean I like you … like you. Like, not just as a friend. I think you're great as a friend, but I'd like us not to be friends.' That didn't sound good either, 'I mean I don't want us not to like each other obviously, I think you're the most interesting person I've ever met and I'd like us to be more than friends. I mean I like you, as a girl. Like a boy likes a girl.'

Grace was just staring at me. It was terrible. I was just burbling on and making no sense and I couldn't tell if I was making a complete tit of myself or if it was in any way worth it.

'So that's what I came to say. So. Sorry again. See you at work.' And I turned and walked away down the path.

'Joe?' Grace called when I was halfway back to my bike at the bottom of the front garden.

I turned and looked back at her. 'Yes?' I said.

'Would you rather time travel plus or minus twenty years every time you fart, or teleport to a different place on earth every time you sneeze?' she said.

I looked at her hard. 'I really wish I had had a cold, or a trump bubbling this afternoon,' I sighed, 'It's a difficult choice though. Every holiday, you'd have a cold or an allergy so that's not great. And on the other hand, you'd have to avoid anything that gave you gas if you were having a sic time and, Grace, I don't know about you, but I'd be plus or minus twenty years about fifty times a day some days. That's gotta be hard to keep a handle on.'

'Do you want to come in and mull it over further?' and she opened the door a little wider.

'Well, I think there's quite a few things to consider, and I am keen on time travel, I'm not gonna lie. Shall I bring my bike up?' I waited where I was.

'Sure,' she nodded, and I set off back down the path to fetch it.

And that was the start of a wonderful time. The happiest time. A very uncomplicated time, at first.

182

We worked together and tried to talk to each other at every opportunity and ignore the customers and the jobs that Jilly gave us. I felt more guilty about this than Grace did, but then she was going back to Uni whereas for me, this job was, kind of, it.

At the end of the day, we went back to Grace's or, if it was fair, we biked or walked up into the hills and lay in the untidy grass and talked and fooled around and I tried not to tell her I loved her but I wanted to all the time. If we went to her house, we went straight up to her bedroom, and I would watch her bum in front of me and put my hands on it and it sort of scared me how strongly I wanted her.

In truth, I was terrified of the strength of my feelings for her and what I could do to her. Like I said, I was waiting to turn into him.

Grace was experienced. Obviously. Sex was no big deal to her. She had a stick thing in her arm for contraception, under her skin. The idea made me feel a bit sick. I'd thought about sex with her as soon as we were talking, as soon as we were friends, but it wasn't straightforward for me. Okay we did it. But as soon as it was over, every time a feeling of shame seeped through me. Grace would lie next to me, happy and pink-cheeked, eyes glinting. Her hair always seemed more golden and glistening after sex, like a Nordic huntress who's caught her prey.

I, on the other hand, could feel myself diminishing, retreating. I'd read loads of books and magazine articles which commented on men rolling over and falling asleep into a deep post-coital blissful sleep and women's frustration over this. I never felt relaxed or blissful. I felt like I had despoiled Grace, like I had revealed a base and savage side of myself which was repulsive. I also, and this is the worst part, blamed her in part for this. Grace wanted me. She encouraged me, she touched and caressed and kissed and stroked until I couldn't do anything else. I couldn't have controlled myself even if I'd wanted to. I didn't like that sensation. I didn't like the force of the feelings. I worried about where they could lead me. I didn't want to see where that path went.

Our first hurdle was her going back to Uni.

I told her I was okay with it. I told her I was okay if she wanted to break up.

I wasn't okay.

We thought we'd try and stay together.

At the end of the summer Cherry Townsend was having a party. She was in my year at my school, but she'd never spoken to me. She liked Grace though, so we were invited. I always find parties difficult but Grace was excited about it so I agreed it would be fun to do something different.

Mum is friends with her Mum, Jan. I find Jan a bit inappropriate. She's been coming round and seeing Dad quite a bit since the accident and they sit and play board games together for hours and I hear them roaring with laughter. Mum says she used to fancy Dad. Maybe she still does? Her husband doesn't seem to be around much.

Their house sits up at the end of a little lane behind the village and it is massive. Apparently, Grace told me, it was the lord of the manor's house at some point. It had been raining earlier and, as we biked up the drive, the trees dripped on us and made Grace shriek in surprise as the cold water hit the bare skin of her warm shoulders and neck. She cackled with laughter and so did I. We'd already had pre-drinks at her house, and I was relaxed, for once. I didn't want to go into the party; I just wanted to keep biking and snickering with her.

Every window, of which there were many, was lit even though it was still light outside. It was a bit like arriving at a movie set. Music was thumping into the cool evening air and Grace gripped my hand as we walked into the cavernous hallway. I'd been to primary school with Cherry too but never been up this lane, never set foot in here. No party invites for me. Not until I was with Grace.

'Grace!' Cherry yelled, pushing through a tight group of serious drinkers in, what I assumed was a living room that seemed excessively big. She stretched out her skinny arms and Grace fell into them releasing me. They danced a little excited dance and squeaked at each other and then Cherry took Grace by the hand and lead her off through the throng down the hallway to the kitchen which felt about the size of our whole farmhouse. It was dazzlingly white and the wall of window doors onto the garden were wide open, and yet more people had spilled out into that and were intensely having fun.

I followed along in a glum fashion feeling out of place and in need of sunglasses and ear defenders. Where had all these people come from? She must have invited most of the county. Or maybe she'd just posted online, and she didn't really know half of them. I felt a sensory overload from the brash, rapid talking all around me, the pulsating music, the toxic layers and layers of perfume and aftershave, the garishly deep-dyed colours of everyone's clothes. And all I could think about was the same air travelling in and out of everyone's lungs. Sucking in and out over and over, used and re-used, mixed with the grey smoke of the cigarettes and the thin steam of the vapes and denser trail from the spliffs and I felt like I was underwater, being held down by the noise and the colour and the oh-so-close proximity of too many people.

I turned and charged back to the front door, burst out onto the drive and ran down the lane veering off to shelter behind a tree where I took in gulps of clean air and the pumping in my eardrums calmed and I beat my chest with my knuckled fist and thought about what a dick I was.

If I think about it, I have had close contact with a handful of people my whole life. Throughout school there were one or two at most who I rubbed along with, but, like I say, I deliberately never let anyone in. At home there were occasional adult visitors, but not many and Dad watched everything. There was no privacy. Living with him was like, I don't know, like being a snail whose shell has been ripped off. When I look back, my shoulders hunch; I want to draw up into myself. We were rarely allowed to retreat, to be alone or to be ourselves. We were scrutinised. And found wanting.

And that kitchen. With so much human contact, pushing and shoving against me; I very much wanted a shell in there.

I realised I couldn't stay under the tree for the rest of the evening staring at my sorry feet. Perhaps I could go and actually talk to some people. Teddy managed it. Why couldn't I?

With a heavy heart, I walked back up the lane but cut around the side of the house instead of walking through it. I figured the garden might be more bearable and that was where Grace and Cherry had been heading.

The alcohol wasn't helping either. I don't really drink. I've seen how it changes Dad. His eyes slide and his mouth tightens, and I know we're in for trouble. I try to avoid it in case it brings out the worst in me too. I need to stay on my guard. That night I felt myself lurching as I followed the cobbled path round the edge of the house. I didn't like the loose sensation in my limbs. I didn't like the warmth in my groin or the fog in my head. I remembered Dad wavering down the path after he had attacked Tess and I wanted to throw up.

A moment later, I was standing on the sandstone terrace with ten million other people and Grace was pushing a red plastic beaker into my hand. 'You'll like this. Cherry says it's her secret recipe. Tastes like bubble gum.' I looked into the cup at the syrupy pink liquid, and I was pretty certain I was not going to like it.

'Thanks,' I smiled, 'Thirst quenching gum, at last,' and had a gulp. The three boys Grace and Cherry were talking to chuckled with mild surprise. I had spoken and it turned out what I had said was acceptable.

Grace turned to the guy next to her, a very tall, grinning wolf with a straggly, dark beard and whiter-than-white fang like teeth. He was standing very close to her. He couldn't stop looking at her.

'I was just asking Barnaby here, would he rather there be a perpetual water balloon war going on in his town or a food fight?' The rest of them laughed at the silliness or the cleverness or the absurdity of the question. I tried to smile but could feel it stuck on my face as a pop of rage burst in my chest. What the hell was Grace doing asking fucking Barnaby one of *my* questions?

'I said water balloon war,' The Wolf announced, 'I'm hoping Grace would be there. Wouldn't mind seeing her in a wet T shirt, eh? Eh? Know what I'm saying?' and he slapped one of the other imbeciles on the shoulder and tapped the tip of Grace's nose. She smiled coyly, then laughed along with the others. 'No offence, Jim,' he said to me.

'Is that all the thought you're giving it?' Grace cut in. I noted she didn't bother correcting him on his error.

'What else is there to think about Gracie? I mean I can't think of anything else now I'm picturing you in that T shirt,' He guffawed again in a filthy way with his mates.

'What about during the winter? Having a continual water balloon war would be freezing. You haven't thought this through, Barnaby.' She crossed her arms and adopted a mock serious tone with him. He pretended to be shamed by her.

'I see your point,' he said, 'Or rather, in the cold, I'd see both your points!' The other two collapsed into snorting giggles in the face of the astounding wit of their friend.

'For goodness' sake!' I said. Of course, they stopped laughing then but only for a few moments.

'Jesus. You sound like my nan,' crowed The Wolf and the others laughed even more, 'Sorr-eeee! Did we offend you, Nanna.' There was more exaggerated laughing and they all clutched at imaginary handbags. I stood, poker faced, trying to breathe normally.

'Are you religious, Joe?' Cherry said pretending to keep a straight face, 'Is that why you don't swear?'

'No. It's because I watched my dad kick my mother down the stairs for saying the word shit when she stubbed her toe,' I answered. Only I didn't. Those words stayed in my head. I knew that any second, I was going to make a run for it.

Then Grace had taken hold of my arm, 'There are thousands of words in the English language, aren't there, chicken?' I felt her looking at me and her hot, soft hand snaking up under my T shirt and across my belly. 'You just try to use all the good ones, don't you? Not the nasty ones. Anyway, he does swear, I've heard him. Once he knows you.' and she leant up and kissed my neck.

The Wolf hadn't look too happy at that.

Okay, Grace was trying to defend me, but it just made me more angry. I didn't want her telling them stuff about me. I sounded like some kind of weirdo. I only swore in front of people I knew. I sounded meek, timid. Some kind of baby.

'How old are you, Jim?' The Wolf grinned.

'My name's Joe. Not Jim. Is that relevant? Do you think I'm underage?' I felt my muscles tensing, I'd lost all the looseness of the booze, now I felt taut and stretched. I wanted to knock his teeth out. They were a big enough target.

'Just asking? Trying to be friendly. Get to know you,' he raised his palms indicating to his loser friends that I was behaving like a nutter.

'Bit of an odd opener for a conversation,' I responded, ''S that what you ask the little boys down at the playpark?'

'Fucking hell, Joe,' Grace thumped my arm, 'that's not funny.'

'I know. I didn't think anything had to be. I thought everything was meant to be offensive. That's all I've heard since I got here,' I answered staring at The Wolf. My mind had split into two; half of it was following the conversation, the other was speculating about what it was going to feel like when The Wolf actually hit me. Would he punch my face? My gut? How much pain was there going to be? Would there be a lot of blood? Was I going to hit back or just take the beating? He looked murderous.

He kept looking straight at me, then his eyes flicked onto Grace and softened. 'He's a bit of a cunt your boyfriend, isn't he? I like him. D'ya wanna go and have a dance? I'm sure Joe won't mind, will you Joe? And on the way, you can ask me another one of those weird questions.'

Grace unfurled herself from me. 'Yeah okay,' she said and stepped towards him.

'You coming, Joe?' he smiled at me cocking his head to one side.

I've never danced in public in my life.

'Just gonna get another drink first,' I said. My voice sounded sulky and young. He had the upper hand.

'Cool,' he said over his shoulder as he shepherded Grace away through the people towards the house.

'Okay,' I heard Grace say, 'Would you rather be handsome and stupid, or intelligent and ugly?' I knew what The Wolf would answer. No surprises there.

I turned back towards Cherry and the two losers, but she was locked in a snog with one of them and the other had already drifted to a group sprawled on the grass, playing some sort of drinking game.

I looked up at the darkening sky and realised that trying to keep things going long distance might be more difficult than I had initially anticipated.

Later, after I'd drunk most of the vodka we'd brought with us, I decided I couldn't stay any longer. Honestly, I don't know how much time had passed but I had sunk further and further into abject misery, shuffling from room to room, observing more and more raucous behaviour. I resisted the urge to pick up half-empty bottles forgotten on Jan's antique furniture, leaching stickiness and staining into the carefully cared for surfaces. I watched the bodies pressing closer together or moving with ever increasing, terrifying abandon; the voices getting louder or softer; the same monotonous driving rhythm of the music which felt like it was smeared inside my skull, pushing into my brain. I put this down to the drink. As I watched, everyone had someone, they were all connected in some way to each other, but I was a solitary shadow on the wall.

I couldn't keep track of Grace. In truth, I didn't want to. For a while I watched her dance with The Wolf, her face tilted up to look at him as she moved in a way that made me think of what she was like in bed. From the look on his face, that was what The Wolf was thinking about too. His hands were all over her.

Why was she letting him touch her? Why was she leading him on? I was her boyfriend, wasn't I? I couldn't stay and watch so I skulked off to another room. I slumped into an empty armchair that was pushed back into the corner. The whole party was like a terrible torture. I'd found this brilliant girl who I now realised, I thought was the answer to all my problems and she was nothing but a slut. I got out the all but empty vodka bottle and sucked out the last dregs. Grace didn't care about me. She had no respect for her body or for what we had. She was just using me, making a fool of me. I thought about how much she wanted to have sex; how she made me feel inadequate without ever saying anything.

Perhaps, Dad was right. Women are trouble. Women need to be put in their place. You can't trust women.

That bubbling rage in my chest burst and I smashed the bottle against the wall. A few people looked over and looked away. Over the music, the noise of the smashing glass barely registered.

Self-pity and shame overwhelmed me and then I felt a warm trickle running up my arm. I looked at my hand and registered a sizable piece of bottle sticking out of my hand. Blood was seeping steadily from it. Not too much but enough.

Like the Action Hero that I am, I passed out.

It was Teddy who rescued me from the party, got me to A and E (his mate had a car and hadn't been drinking) and stopped me from making any more of a fool of myself. I didn't even know he was at the party. 'Of course I was at the party,' he'd laughed.

If I'd known he was there maybe I could have talked to him, hung out with him and his mates. Maybe it wouldn't have been such a wipe out. Maybe Grace and I wouldn't have broken up.

But I keep everything separate from Dad, and Teddy keeps everything separate from all of us. So that wasn't a possibility, I guess.

The nail in the coffin was Dad coming to A and E. I'd been unconscious (the drink I think) so they decided to keep me in for a few hours observation to be on the safe side. No one knew what had actually happened apart from me. Someone had told Teddy there'd been a fight – typical teenage exaggeration. Anyway, Grace came up to the hospital too and she was sitting up on the end of my bed, cross-legged and we were trying not to talk about how hellish the party had been when Dad pulled back the curtain.

His face was like thunder but as soon as he saw Grace, he changed. 'Joseph, Joseph, Joseph. What on earth have you been up to now?' he said with an air of absolute care and patience as if we had weekly trips to the hospital due to my many knockabout mishaps. He didn't wait for me to answer though. 'And who is this lovely, young lady?' he turned his full attention to Grace.

'This is Grace, Dad. My girlfriend,' I answered quietly.

'Hi,' Grace raised a palm in salutation, her voice flat and tired.

'And where have you been hiding this gorgeous thing, eh, Joseph?' He was practically drooling. As I've said, he loves blondes.

'Not a thing, Mr Blackthorne, a person. Not hiding either. I live and work in the village.' Grace answered as if she was his equal. She wasn't intimidated or in awe or impressed. In fact, she sounded a bit bored at having to speak to him.

'Ey up, Joseph. You'll have to watch this one. Brains and beauty. That's a dangerous combination,' he said to me, and I could see he wasn't happy with her reply. He turned back to Grace, 'Did you go to Ridge High, Grace? I don't usually forget past pupils.'

'No, we moved the summer I finished my A levels. My brother's there though. Aaron. Aaron Flint?' She got out her phone and began to scroll through it.

'Oh, Aaron, yes, I know him. He's a bright spark too, isn't he?' He turned back to me, clearly annoyed that his charm was having no effect on Grace.

'So, they're saying another couple of hours here Joseph, that right? How does it feel?' His face had tightened. There would be repercussions for getting him up in the early hours of the morning.

'It's fine Dad. They had to numb it to stitch it so I can't feel anything at the moment. You needn't stay. Grace is here and we'll wait it out and get the bus in the morning. It's up to you though. If you want to stay, you're more than welcome.' I tried to sound casual. You have to tread a fine line with Dad. If you tell him to do something, he will do the opposite.

'Well, it would give me a chance to get to know the elusive Grace. You've yet to bring her over to the farmhouse,' and he flashed a smile at her. Grace didn't even look up from her phone.

'Perhaps you're right,' he said clearly annoyed by her rebuttal, 'No point in all of us hanging around here just for a little cut on the hand.'

'I can call if there's anything that comes up,' I said, 'but I'm sure nothing's going to happen. They're just being cautious.'

'Bit of a waste of NHS resources if you ask me,' he said, digging his hands into his pockets and rocking back onto his heels.

'Thanks for coming anyway, Dad,' I said.

'No choice. They phoned me,' he barked a laugh and looked at Grace who remained fixed to her screen.

That was the decider. He scruffed the top of my hair, something he never does, 'Okay, see you when you get home,' and he made to go, 'Bye Grace. Nice to finally meet you,' and she raised her palm again without looking up at him.

He looked at me and then back at Grace and raised an eyebrow of disapproval, then disappeared through the curtain and I breathed.

Too soon though.

The curtain whipped back, and Dad stretched across and flipped Grace's phone out of her hand and onto the floor where there was an unmistakeable sound of the screen cracking.

'You're a very fucking rude young lady, Grace,' he whispered in her face, 'Shame about the phone. Hope you have insurance,' and he tugged the curtain back and I heard him marching away.

'What the actual fuck?' Grace said looking at her empty hand and the phone on the floor, 'What just happened?' She clambered off the bed and showed me the shattered face.

'Grace, I'm so sorry. I'll pay for it. Really. I'm so sorry.' I stammered out.

'Fucking hell! Look at my phone! Is he some kind of psycho?' She was so mad. 'I'd heard stuff about him, but this is next level. This is my property. Fucking twat.'

'I know, look, he's … you're right, he's mental. I'm sorry. I never wanted you to meet him. I'm sorry.' I thought I was going to be sick. She was so angry.

'And you. Are you a fucking nutter too? Smashing a bottle into your hand? What was that all about?' She was looking at me like I was some kind of hideous creature, something repellent, nauseating.

'I don't know. I just, I just got upset about you and Barnaby, you and Barnaby … dancing. And him groping you and you letting him. And you hardly talked to me, and I should never have gone. I'm no good at parties. I told you that.'

'Are you joking? I'm having to fight off that neanderthal and you take offence? Barnaby's a fucking jerk but we can't all be perfect Joe, all the time. We went to the party to have fun. To get pissed and dance and have a laugh with our friends. And you react by smashing a bottle in your hand because I'm dancing with a chump. Shitting hell, you are your father,' and she slumped down on the end of the bed.

I grabbed the bedpan next to me and threw up.

When she said it like that I felt like an idiot.

But I also had to admit to myself, I didn't know if I had the control to behave any other way.

When I'd finished throwing up, I said, 'I'd understand if you want to break up with me.'

'Of course, I want to break up with you,' she hissed, 'I've just got to wait for the buses to start.'

'Okay,' I said, and I lay down and tried and failed not to cry.

'And you're still paying for my phone,' she said over my pathetic snivelling.

3

When they told Dad he was paralysed he went mental. I kind of hoped, with the drugs he was on, he wouldn't be able to do much, but he just exploded, started ranting and raging and calling them all sorts of names and swearing. There was so much swearing. Teddy was trying to calm him down. Teddy can do that sometimes, but this time, it wasn't working. 'I run fucking marathons!' was what he ended up yelling over and over and his neck was pulled taut, tight chords straining from chin to collar bone and his eyes were wild. One of the younger doctors, she wasn't much older than we were, steered us out and into the corridor.

'They'll sedate him,' she said calmly, 'It's a lot to process. It must be a shock to your dad but news like this does strange things to people. Try to remember what he was like before,' and she smiled and nodded at us. 'Why don't you go and get yourselves a coffee and have a bit of a break.'

'If only she knew,' Teddy said, as he funnelled a third strip of sugar into his cup. He leaned back in his chair and smashed and rubbed his face with the palms of his hands. 'Christ, I'm sick of this, Joey. I really am. He's a fucking nightmare.'

'Yep,' I answered glumly, 'I think he hit Jude when he threw that book. We'd better buy her some biscuits or something.' Jude was one of the older nurses. Brisk and efficient but with a dry sense of humour who checked on us as much as she checked on Dad.

'We've spent all our lives apologising or trying to cover up for his bad behaviour,' Teddy sighed.

'I know.' I looked at my weak coffee.

And then Teddy blurted out, 'I wish he'd died,' and, to my horror, he burst into noisy, jagged sobs. You have to realise Teddy never cries. Through all Dad's gruelling punishments and tests and trials and everything we've seen and heard, it's me who's blubbed even though I was supposed to be the eldest and Teddy was the baby for years. Teddy took it all and never shed a single tear.

I just sat there, watching him cry, frozen. We were in a hospital cafeteria, and I guess this sort of thing happens all the time so no one really noticed.

It only lasted a minute or two. Teddy grabbed a shiny napkin and smeared it across his cheeks, ineffectively wiping his tears and blowing his nose.

'I do too,' I said. I thought I'd feel guilty when I said it, but I didn't. It was just the honest truth. The most peace I'd felt my whole life was when he was in the coma. When he was lying there, hooked up and unconscious and he couldn't meddle or grab or strike into our lives. I know I should have been praying for a recovery, but even though he's my dad, I wanted those eyes to stay shut. Forever.

I reached across the table and gripped Teddy's hand, and he hung his head and sighed a deep, shuddering sigh.

I'm woken up by Dad's piercing scream from the baby monitor. It's my turn to have it in my room. It's been my turn for days.

I half fall out of bed and hurtle down the stairs. The screams are getting louder. I slam through the door and switch on the light.

The screaming stops. Dad is bolt upright in bed, one hand clutching onto the hoist, the other pulling the covers up to his neck. His face is white. I know it is impossible, but it looks like his hair is standing on end.

'There's a ...' and he gulps and looks towards the fireplace.

'What? There's a what?' I say. He appears genuinely terrified. In my head I run through his medications. He's on hardly anything now. Is he having some kind of hallucination or a breakdown?

'It was … It was … I woke up and it was in my bed.' He's beginning to freak me out.

'What was, Dad?' I say gently, but I stay by the door, my eyes flicking from his stricken face to the fireplace and back again.

'A rat,' he manages.

'What?' I say in disbelief. We've never had rats in the house. The cats are too good at keeping them at bay and we're careful with the chicken feed and not providing anything that would make a home for them.

My eye jumps to a flicker of movement and I see it. Its grey-brown body scuttles and slinks along the wall and stops under the table near me. It's huge.

'Teddy!' I bellow, 'Teddy! Come down here, now!' and I wish I had my phone. My eyes are fixed on the skirting below the table. 'It's okay, Dad. It's over here now. It's nowhere near you.'

Dad hates rats. He never admitted it, but you could tell. It was the only thing he didn't like about living in the country. He would set traps, put down poison, anything to make sure we were rat free. Even if there was a rat on the TV, he'd change channel. He could manage spiders and mice even, but rats, he totally lost his shit.

'Mum! Georgie! ANYONE! I need help now.' I have to admit, I have no idea what to do. I can hear Dad panting though. His face is clammy and greyish. If he has a heart attack, I'm stuffed. I don't want to leave the room because I want to keep an eye on the rat. How the hell did it get in here?

'It's okay, Dad,' I say again with less conviction and Teddy bounds down the stairs.

'There's a rat. Under the table. I've seen it. It's real. It was in Dad's bed.' I say to Teddy's creased from sleep face.

'Are you alright to go in and lift Dad out? Take him to the living room? I'll deal with Roland?' Teddy's eyes are steady. I want to hug him. For I hate rats too. I'm a coward on all fronts.

Of course, to get to Dad, I have to step into the room. I don't fancy that much. Teddy stretches in and picks up a blanket slung across the back of the chair. 'If it makes a run for it, I'll throw this over it,' he assures me.

I edge in sticking close to the wall getting to Dad as quickly as I can. I fling back his sheets, 'We're getting out of here,' I say and, with his help from the hoist, I scoop him up and carry him like a child out and through into the living room. I lie him on the sofa and cover him with a blanket. 'We'll have it sorted in no time,' I say confidently. He looks back up at me but his eyes are still glassy with fear.

As I walk back through to the bedroom, I hope Teddy has caught the creature and dispatched it to the garden.

He's half-way through the job. The blanket is spread on the floor and a small mound is slithering frantically back and forth beneath it. Teddy is stopping it from reaching the edges by pushing and bunching the blanket and stamping his feet, chasing it closer and closer to the centre.

'Good job, Teddo,' I say, relieved I'm not going to have to look the rat in the eye.

'Help me,' says Teddy and he drops to his knees and grabs one of Dad's shoes to herd the rat more efficiently. I do as I'm told, falling to the floor as well, and we gather the blanket towards it. 'Keep the blanket close to the ground, we don't want it to get out. They can squeeze through the smallest gaps,' my brother orders.

Sensing its impending doom, the rat begins to attack the blanket and we can see the outline of its snout as it nudges and gnaws at the cloth trying to escape. There's scrabbling and clawing and in moments a minute hole appears, and I catch sight of a long, greenish tooth. My stomach lurches.

'Oh God, Teddy, quick, we've got to act now. It's going to get out.'

'Righty-ho,' says Teddy cheerfully, and he leans back, lifts Dad's shoe high above his head and wallops it down with tremendous force on top of the rat. There is a terrible silence as Teddy raises the shoe speculatively and the thin blanket settles and blood blooms across the weave of the fabric.

'I didn't mean kill it!' I splutter out, letting go of the fistfuls of material I was clutching and sinking back onto my heels.

'It's only a rat, Joey,' Teddy says, calmly, 'There's plenty more of them on the planet.'

'I know, it's just that that was a bit brutal, is all,' I manage. I am trying not to picture what is under the blanket.

'Sorry, mate. I didn't mean to freak you out. You go and check on Dad and I'll clean this up,' and he gives my shoulder a squeeze and that's all I need to get me out of there.

I take Dad's chair and wheel him into the kitchen and make him tea and toast. He's looking a better colour now but is still shaken.

He can't manage to talk about it much. 'It crawled up under my arm. I felt it between my ribs. I was fast asleep. I thought it was one of the cats. Thought how could one of them have squeezed in there? And so, I reached over and turned on the light and it was up on my chest. Oh Christ, Joseph I've never had such a fright in my life. It ran though, once I shouted. Jumped off onto the floor.'

'Let's get you back to bed, Dad.' Teddy has finished disinfecting the lino and there's no sign of the untimely visitor. We get Dad round to the hoist and are about to lift him in when Teddy says, 'I think we should change the bedding.'

I go to the cupboard to get fresh sheets and Teddy strips the bed. 'Joey, look at this,' he says.

There's blood on the sheets at the bottom of the bed. We lift Dad's pyjama trousers. He's been scratched and bitten quite badly on one leg.

We ring 111 who advise us to dress and clean the wounds and get Dad down to the surgery for antibiotics first thing. Given the lateness of the hour, this will be as speedy as a long wait in A and E and easier on Dad. Once Dad is finally settled again, Teddy and I sit in the kitchen, exhausted; it's almost dawn.

'I have to tell you something Joey,' Teddy says.

'Okay,' I reply.

'Dad's bed,' he says, 'The way it was made. Everything was, well, tight, like, too tight, too ... tucked in. Not like it normally is.'

'What are you saying, Teddy?' I say carefully.

'I think Mum put the rat in the bed,' he whispers.

'So do I,' I nod.

4

We realised she was opting out of everything when he was in the rehab unit. No, I'm exaggerating. Not everything. Just Dad. She still went to work and was raising Georgie, but she did not want to talk about him. At all.

Once she'd sold Farrah and had the work done on the house so that he could 'manage', it was like she'd dusted him off her hands. He wasn't her responsibility anymore.

So, it fell to Teddy and I.

We'd more or less expected it, after she barely visited him in hospital. It was a bit of a shock though.

'He can go and live in a care facility or one of those Independent Living places if he wants to,' she said when Teddy said his room was a bit bleak. She was rock hard about it. Not that I can blame her.

I can't quite place when I first noticed the darker side of our new set-up. Teddy and I had hashed out a makeshift arrangement to cook and spend time with him so his life wasn't completely meaningless. We included Georgie too and we were trundling along and managing to pretend that it was completely normal for Mum to never sit down and eat with us or watch a film, or even join in any part of a conversation that involved Dad.

We spoke to her about divorce early on; this was her chance, we said, but, oddly, she refused. She wasn't going to abandon him, she said.

I often thought that when the inevitable newspaper report was written, following the murder of someone in my house, the first thing the reporter would write was that very few people came to visit. My father certainly didn't have friends. And before the accident, neither did Mum. I knew our life was odd; two adult sons still living at home, neither of them ever having had proper jobs, neither of them able to drive; no family friends; no relatives. The only constant has been Agatha, my surrogate granny who cannot express any overt feelings but who looks out for us all.

Agatha used to intercept me on my way home from school. If Dad had a meeting after school, we were allowed to get the bus and Agatha would contrive to be in the front garden or standing by her window and she'd nip to the door and give me a shout. Just me, not Teddy. Now I'm older, I realise she knew that I was the one who needed her. Teddy, with his easy-going manner and bright smile was always going to be alright.

'I've been reading a paper about Asian hornets. I think you'll find it interesting,' she'd say. Or 'I know you've got chemistry homework tonight. Let's go over it together.' There were no 'hellos' or 'how are yous', she was all business. She'd push aside her piles of newspapers, notebooks and textbooks from her large, round dining room table and I'd unpack my bag and we'd work and chat. She was inspiring; she was the reason I wanted to do chemistry at Uni.

Only once did she refer to what went on in our house. There had been a terrible row the night before. It had been in the kitchen. Dad had Mum trapped in there and it sounded like he'd thrown every pan we owned at her. He'd finally succeeded in breaking one of the windows. None of us had got much sleep but we'd dragged ourselves into school. Mum and Dad had Year 7 parents' evening and Teddy had got off a stop earlier with one of his mates. As I walked up the lane, I felt blank with the misery and loneliness of my life. I pictured Dad glad-handing all those parents who would automatically transfer respect to him, assuming because of his status in the school, he must be a good person, he had to have earned his position, he couldn't be capable of punching his wife in the kidneys for spilling a splash of tea on the carpet.

Agatha appeared at her door as I reached her gate. 'I've been experimenting with flax seed as a binding agent. I've made a hearty fruit cake. Come and taste it and I'll note down your findings.'

The cake was good, cinnamon spiced and moist and held together very well, which was the point of the flax seed.

Agatha cleared the plates and we moved onto my homework. I was never in any hurry to leave.

At some point, Agatha had put her hand over mine on the table. I looked at it, then at her. 'If you ever need help Joe, you or Teddy or Georgie, you just come here. Day or night. There's a key under the green pot by the front door. The green pot. Remember. Just let yourselves in. No need to knock.'

'Okay,' I said quietly, 'Thank you.'

'You know your father's a wicked man, don't you? A wicked, wicked man. But luckily, you're nothing like him and neither's Teddy. Don't forget that.'

'Okay,' I said, and I blushed; someone outside the family acknowledging the horror that was my father was toe-curling.

'The green pot,' she said, 'Now let's get back to these covalent bonds.'

I have never used the green pot but it's nice to know we have somewhere to go if we need it

I digress.

So, since the accident, there have definitely been more people in our lives. More people than just Agatha. Mum goes out. A lot. Sometimes people come back to stay. Not often. She has friends now. I don't think they're close yet; at least, she's not the same with them as she is with Tess from what I can see.

And then there are all the carers in and out of the house. It's a good job the carers come.

Plus, Teddy's life has really taken off. His job for a start, and he has a proper social life now, not one that's hidden from Dad. When we were growing up Teddy had to be careful. There were rules, of course, about when he was allowed to see his friends. Mum and I helped Teddy as much as we could, but it was complicated for all of us.

Teddy doesn't bring his friends back to the house. Neither of us are out of the habit of keeping people away from Dad really, even if he has calmed down quite a lot.

That's another thing, since his suicide attempt – which was completely out of the blue by the way – he's changed. Just the day before it, he was in a great mood. He'd had a good workout in the garage, and he was talking about getting an adaptable car so he could drive. He'd completed another level on his on-line course too and been in touch with a recruitment company. It was a good day.

I came back from my shift at the café to find an ambulance parked up. They were just loading Dad in, and Mum was standing on the drive with a cup of tea. 'What's going on?' I yelled and hurled my bike against the garage wall and sprinted the dozen steps over to her.

'He's slashed his wrists, son,' she said, watching as they carefully backed him into the ambulance.

'What? How? When?' He had his eyes closed. He was a terrible colour.

'I found him in the living room. He wouldn't give me the knife. We had a bit of a battle. Lucky I didn't get stabbed.' She was relaxed though, blasé even.

'Are you going to hospital with him?' I asked but I knew the answer.

'No.' She didn't look at me, kept her eyes on the ambulance. 'They'll need to stitch the wound. It's quite deep apparently. But he's in no danger. I can pick him up later.'

'I'll go with him,' I said trying to keep the exasperation out of my voice, 'We can get a cab back.'

'Okay, love. That suits me,' and she turned back into the house, and I heard her feet drumming up the stairs.

I grabbed some supplies for him and climbed in the back of the ambulance, texting Teddy on the way.

When we got back, Mum had gone out. Dad's blood was still in the living room, cracked and dark. I was surprised she hadn't cleaned it up; she liked that room to be pristine.

I fetched a bucket and cloth and took it through. Teddy padded softly down the stairs. He perched on the sofa as I knelt down on the floor.

'How is he?' he said

'Shaken,' I replied, 'They've made an appointment for him to see the mental health team. I was reassured when they said that this sort of thing is not unusual in cases like Dad's and that emotions can rollercoaster during the first few months, even years.'

'He was top notch yesterday.' Teddy sprawled back, yawning.

'I know,' I said, 'It doesn't make sense,' and I set to on the blood. 'And why did he come in here? He hardly ever comes in here. He much prefers the kitchen or his own room.'

'True dat,' said Teddy, 'It's effort, isn't it, to leave the bedroom, go to the kitchen and get the knife and then come all the way back here? Why didn't he just do it in the kitchen?'

'Maybe he wanted a better final view,' I said briskly, 'Looks like Mum's already had a go at clearing this up. I can see where's she's wiped through it with something.' I sat back on my heels.

'No, I don't think so,' Teddy said, 'She went out not long after you'd gone. I got back just after the ambulance went, she said.'

'Huh,' I said, peering more closely at the curving track marks in the blood, 'Maybe she did it while she was waiting for it then. Whatever she did, she's not done a very good job.'

The day after though, there was a noticeable shift. Dad looked at Mum in a new way. He shrank when she walked past and, whereas before, he would try from time to time to engage her in conversation or tempt her to sit and eat with us, all that stopped. He avoided all contact with her. Now he was scared of her.

That's the only way to describe it.

He looks at her sometimes and I see fear in his eyes, the way I used to see fear in hers.

5

It's been a quiet day in the café and I'm considering taking some brownies home for Georgie when Grace pushes open the door. I've seen her from time to time over the years; we haven't spoken but we've crawled our way back to polite smiles.

'Have I time for a quick coffee? Not too hot?' she smiles.

'Hey,' I say offering a hand to all the empty tables, 'I'm the manager now and I'm locking up. You can make it a slow coffee if you want to.'

'Thanks, Joe,' she says and slings a bag over a chair in the window. 'I'll have some crisps too, please.'

'Barbeque?' I say.

'What else,' she says and gets out her phone. We had a long running to and fro about her disgusting love of barbeque crisps and coffee.

I take over the coffee and she smiles at me. 'Enjoy,' I say and turn away.

'Joe,' she says, 'Sit and shoot the breeze with me,' and she pushes out the chair next to her with her plimsoled toe.

I sit down a little warily. 'I always think that's a bit of an odd phrase,' I say, 'Quite a hard job to shoot something you can't see.'

Grace looks at me quizzically. Her eyes are crystal clear, brilliant with colour. 'You're right. Except I think it means shoot your words *into* the breeze rather than fire an actual gun, doesn't it?'

'That would certainly make more sense,' I say.

She sips her coffee and says, 'I imagine those old timers sitting on their porches, you know those long ones that wrap all around the houses, on rocking chairs, just chewin' the fat.' She smiles and opens her crisps. 'Catching up, gossiping, that's shooting the breeze.' She pops a whole crisp into her perfectly formed mouth and crunches down. 'Yummy,' she says, raising her eyebrows. She knows I hate barbeque crisps.

'Okay,' I say, 'So catching up and gossip it is then. You go first.'

'I'm eating,' she says through a mouthful of crisps.

'Right, sure,' I nod, 'Well, I have risen to a management post, as I told you, in this fine establishment and am now the proud holder of my own set of keys, plus I have the heady responsibility of updating the specials menu with my own chalk pen. I am still living at home, and I still cannot drive though I have had a couple of lessons. And, newsflash, I didn't much like it.'

'Okay, well that's me caught up!' Grace smiles again, 'I'm very impressed Joe, particularly about the chalk pen. Dizzying heights indeed.' She eats more crisps.

'What about you, Grace?' I ask but I don't really want to hear the answer. I don't want to hear about a buff boyfriend or a flourishing career or even amazing holidays she's been on. I don't want to hear how her world has expanded since we broke up whilst mine has shrunk and shrivelled.

'I too, am living at home,' she says and takes a slurp of coffee, 'I really want to move out, but I just don't know how I can at the moment. And I'm working on stuff which I consider a full-time job, but my mum disagrees and we're fighting. A lot.'

'Are you writing?' I say. I'm genuinely thrilled and intrigued. 'Working on stuff,' is a fantastic answer. The best answer.

'Nope.' She's looking at me speculatively. 'Are you doing anything now? Like, when you shut up here?'

'Grace,' I look shocked, 'Obviously, I've got a canapé party, then a small soirée with the local literati before my weekly late night high roller poker game.'

'So, nothing then?' she says.

'Not a damn thing,' I confirm.

'Do you want to come back to mine?' she finishes the coffee and screws up the crisp bag.

'Absolutely,' I say.

'Good,' she says and pushes her chair back, 'When do you close?'

'Now,' I answer.

We walk up to her house, me pushing my bike which I leave leaning against the wall. After a brief hello to her mum, I follow her upstairs. Instead of going into her bedroom though we keep going up the steep narrow stairs to the attic room.

'I've set my studio up in here,' she tells me as we climb the stairs, 'Chucked out a load of stuff and sold some bits and put some in the garage. Aaron wanted to turn it into his gaming room once he saw it was clear, but I told him to fuck off. He's barely home now. Final year at Uni. He's planning to work in the City. Wants to be a stockbroker.' I'm only half listening as I am ashamed to say I'm mesmerised again by her perfect bum.

It's a relief to get into the attic.

She's pulls on a cord and the room lights up and she sets about turning on other lights. There's a large central island come workbench set up and a run of worktop along one side. This is covered in tools and scraps and jars and bottles, and underneath is crammed with bags and boxes and there is a lot of stuff.

At one end of the island, a camera is set up on tripod and there's a ring light to one side. There's another light with shutters above, suspended from the beams. And then another, and another. I look down onto the island and as I step closer, I realise I'm viewing what looks like a tiny TV or film set.

It's a scale model, or rather several scale models of rooms made with pinpoint accuracy. One is a sixties kitchen in bright oranges and lime green. It has a window with tiny curtains and even a cat curled in a basket. Another looks like a library with hundreds, maybe thousands of books lining the walls. Then there's a more modern living room with miniature, upholstered sofas and a glass coffee table. The detail is extraordinary.

'What is this, Grace?' I say.

'I'm filmmaking for *TikTok*,' she says. She puts her hands into one of the sets and adjusts one of the pieces. 'I'm making teeny real-life rooms and then interacting with them, and manufacturers have started sending me their products and I make a tiny version of it and put it in my film.

I look across at the worktop and see a row of tiny cupcakes. They are so realistic. So detailed.

'How are you making them all?' I say.

'I seem to get through a lot of sand, a lot of paper and a lot of paint,' she says.

'Are you making money?' I ask. I know that's a little rude, but I have to know. How had she thought of the idea? How much was she making?

'Yes,' she says, 'I am. Some of the videos are getting a lot of hits. I mean loads Joe. And that's when you start getting money. People want you to promote their stuff. And I'm starting an on-line store but it's teeny at the moment. I'm just trying to get my head around it.'

I'm looking through the miniscule props on the workbench. There are a perfectly rendered pair of trainers. 'These are fantastic Grace,' I say, 'Can I pick them up?'

'Sure,' she laughs, 'It's all pretty robust.'

In my hand, I hardly feel like I'm holding them. 'How did you make the laces?' I say.

'They're a little chunky, aren't they?' her tone is irritable, 'It's floss, for your teeth.'

'I think they're perfect. That's ingenious.'

'Do you recognise the brand,' she says.

'Of course, I do. Anyone would,' I say carefully laying them back down.

'I thought if I got a got a lot of hits with them, it could lead somewhere big,' she sighs, 'nothing yet though.'

She gets out her phone. 'Have a look at a few of them. I'm on *Insta* too. They're a bit longer. Less rushed. I like that. And I'm building my website too, Li'l Grace,' she smiles, 'There's a lot to do.'

I watch as a tiny world unfolds on the screen. A tiny little model Grace delicately flickers around wrapping a teeny present in stop start animation and she takes the microscopic present to a friend's party, and they use it for a twenties game of pass the parcel and the beautiful wrapping paper flies away like butterflies. At the end real Grace leafs through sheets of real wrapping paper and there's a link where you can buy it.

Or Li'l Grace is lacing up the trainer in a tiny cool sports boutique and other weeny trainers start a crazy dance like a modern Sorcerer's Apprentice. Or she's grooming an impossibly long-haired cat with a hair dryer and straighteners and the cat goes out on the tiles and wows a load of other cats with his fancy hair. And then she's using all sorts of garden equipment, hedge trimmers, robo mowers, strimmers. The hedge cutters cut the hedge so low that Li'l Grace sees into her neighbour's garden and there's a groovy party going on and they all merge into a tiny colourful wonderland. Li'l Grace puts on make-up from miniature pots with needle thin brushes, I can hardly see. In the films, the camera focusses on the logos though and there's some kind of meta moment where Li'l Grace is filming herself making a post for *Insta* with a teeny ring light in front of her mirror using some kind of bronzer slash lip stick. It's a little surreal.

I don't really want to stop watching but I have so many questions. I can already see the number of views some of them have. It's hundreds of thousands.

'Grace, this is insane,' I say, 'How does it work? How are you making money? How long is it taking you to make the films?'

She laughs. 'It's quite intense. Let me show you my room,' and we head back down the stairs. 'I'm getting pretty quick, and I've bought a really good quality printer for the product logos and that's cut out quite a lot of time though sometimes I like to recreate them, you know, make them look like they're from my minute handmade world. And I've got a whole stock of 'mini-me's to adapt and I keep switching up my sets as and when. It's quite a high turnover and that's the key. Lots of new content all the time. It's exhausting but it's better than a real job, eh?'

She pushes open her bedroom door and her once roomy space is now full of cardboard packages of every shape and size. There's space to squeeze to her bed but that's about it. 'Welcome to my warehouse,' she sighs.

'What the ...' I say shaking my head, 'Did you offer to represent all these different ...?'

'Nope,' she interrupts, 'New stuff arrives every day. Mum's sick of it. I make the film and then it's ours. Weird huh?'

I spot some very high-end brands. 'What's in the boxes?' I say.

'No idea,' she says leaning on the door frame, 'No time to open anything now. I just do it when I've got the chance. You should see the garage.'

'There's more?' I'm amazed, 'How long have you been doing this? How long did it take to get going? Do you get money as well?'

'Yep. About a year and yep.'

'I'm so impressed Grace. This is brilliant. Your mind always was so brilliant. So … I don't know … quirky and this is just a great way to express it.'

'Yeah and make a load of money.' But she doesn't sound that happy.

We go back up to the attic. I sit on the floor, and she has a bit of a sift through some of the bags. 'How are things at home?' she says.

'You heard about Dad, I guess?' I say.

'Yeah. Couldn't have happened to a nicer bloke,' she says coldly, 'Sorry. I didn't mean that,' and she looks at me.

'It's okay,' I say, 'I know he's a dick. I've lived with him all my life. You're right.'

'Why're you still at home, Joe?' She stops rummaging and stares at me.

'I'm scared to leave,' I say and that is the honest truth.

'The world's not that bad,' she says, and she reaches out and her instantly familiar, small, soft hand covers mine and my heart speeds up.

'It's not the outside world I'm scared of, that's never been a problem, it's the inside one,' I say, ruefully.

'What do you mean?' she says, and she scoots over a bit closer to me. I want to talk to her. I always want to talk to her, I've never lost that feeling but even when we were together, I was never, well, completely honest. I'm not honest with anyone, not really.

I look at her and she's so beautiful. I would do anything to be with her but in my heart, I know I will always be on my own because of my parents. I feel a shift; it's not seismic, just a shudder. What if I take a chance and tell her what's going on?

'I can't leave them alone together. My mum and dad. We can't. Teddy and me. We've never been able to.' I look at my hands. It seems stupid when you say it out loud. Like it's not real.

'They're adults, Joe. You can't waste your life worrying about them.'

'It's not just a question of worrying, Grace,' My voice is harder, impatient, 'They're different. He's ... different. You don't know what it was like growing up there. And now he's in the chair, well, Mum's ... different. It's confusing. I can't leave. I don't want someone... I don't want them to ...' I run out of words.

'You don't want them to what, get divorced? Have affairs? What? You can't control their feelings, Joe.'

'I know I can't. I just don't want them to kill each other,' I say quietly.

'That's a bit melodramatic, isn't it?' she laughs

I look at her. 'Think about when he broke your phone,' I say.

She's quiet, and then she says, 'Oh fucking hell, Joe.'

'Yes, Grace,' I say, 'Fucking hell.'

She sits back on her heels, and I can see her mind making connections, sifting through our relationship, through every scrap of information she's heard about my father, through old interactions with Mum, she's piecing it all together. 'That's why we never went round to your house?' she says.

'Yea,' I say.

'And why I never met him before the hospital?'

'Absolutely. I couldn't rely on him to ... behave. I've never been able to rely on him.' I sound a bit pathetic.

'Did he hit you? You and Ted?' She sounds ready to get angry now; I can feel her energy building like a storm brewing. When we were going out, I'd sometimes get a headache from her relentless outrage in the face of some injustice or other – the plight of the asylum seekers, the reaction to another high school shooting, the deforestation of the Amazon – she would suddenly launch into an impassioned and extremely well-informed monologue about whatever issue had grasped her attention and she couldn't stop. It gripped her, clamped to her emotionally like some giant octopus wrapping around her sucking out all her emotional energy. It was exhausting to watch.

'No, no,' I reacted quickly, 'he just … controlled us. But he was violent. To Mum. A lot. And we had to … protect her. I mean that sounds like she couldn't do it herself, she could have left, I know, but he had something over her, I don't know what. She told us, when we were older, she couldn't leave, we couldn't leave or we, the children would have to stay with him. She'd never have allowed that. She couldn't have left us. Not with him. He's not fit. He's not fit to be a father.'

'You had to protect her? How did you do that? You didn't fight him, did you?' The energy is still there, fizzing amber behind her eyes.

'God, no! I mean we were … a diversion. We worked as a team. I don't know. He had to be … managed. There were lots of routines that we followed to keep him in check. To keep the peace. To keep Mum safe. It didn't work all the time. Once we were adults, it was harder for him. We stepped in. Together. He didn't want to take us on. So, we decided we had to stay. To protect her.' I want Grace to understand. I want her to know that I'm not just a complete loser managing a poxy coffee shop that has barely any customers in the back of beyond.

'So, Uni?' her voice trails off. She looks like she might cry.

'Not a chance,' I shrug, remembering the bitter set of Agatha's mouth when I broke the news to her that I was declining my place.

'And for Teddy too?' Grace's forehead furrows and she looks so young as so many do when sorrow overwhelms them. I nod.

'Loads of people don't go to Uni,' I say, trying to sound brighter, 'It's not that big of a deal.'

'It is,' she says, 'It's where you find out who you are. It's where the world opens up.'

'Maybe,' I say, 'Maybe you're right.'

'Maybe you can go now?' she says eagerly.

'I don't think so,' I reply, and I look up at the sky out of the attic roof light. It's a dark, woolly grey; they'll be rain soon.

'Why not? You're not that old!' she prods my leg and tries to sound a little more playful which I appreciate.

'I still can't go, Grace,' I shake my head.

'Why not Joe? Your dad can't expect you to stay at home and look after him your whole life and, let's face it, he can't be much of a threat anymore. Not now? Not after his accident.' She picks harshly at her trousers, flicking non-existent fluff onto the floorboards.

'It's not him I'm worried about Grace. It's her.' She looks up from her trousers confused.

'She's got a job, she's got Georgie. She'll be fine. I don't understand.' There's exasperation in her voice.

'I know that. It's not that,' I sigh heavily, 'She's changed. I'm worried that … I think she might have … I don't want her to … hurt him.'

'Wait, what? So, you're saying, the tables have turned and now she's … Hang on Joe. Are you sure?' I wish I'd never started this. I feel exhausted by the whole thing.

'No. No, I'm not sure. It's just a feeling I have. The way Dad is around her. And the way she is around him. I don't know what I'm saying really. Look forget it,' and I stand up. 'I should be getting back. It looks like it's going to rain, and I didn't tell anyone I was going to be late so …'

I head towards the stairs.

'Joe, wait. Stay. Don't go. I thought we could go and get a drink. Maybe something to eat? There's loads more to catch up on, isn't there?' Grace is standing too, and she pulls her froth of hair back from her face and knots it behind her head as she speaks. Her glorious sharp elbows jab and dive as she does it and her T shirt pulls tight across her breasts. I feel a snarl of desire for her building in the pit of my stomach.

'Sorry Grace, gotta go,' I say, and I duck down under the beam and escape back through the house and out to the safety of my bike. As I pedal home, I smack the side of my head with my palm. Rather than leaving me feeling unburdened and relieved, my confession has left a sickly taste in my mouth; I am a newly hatched featherless bird, all thin skin and hollow bone, vulnerable and unable to take flight from a useless nest. Another person knows my secrets and I gave them up too freely in a moment of rash nostalgia for a failed relationship. What was I hoping for anyway? Why would

215

she have any answers? I never even asked Grace not to tell anyone, not to do anything. I pedal faster as the inevitable rain batters downs onto me, quickly saturating my inadequate T shirt.

Part Four

Karen

1

I love the sunshine but the heatwave is beginning to get on my tits. I'm rolling and kneading an elastic dough in preparation for Tess's arrival and, even with all the windows open and the back blinds down, the kitchen feels tropical and it's barely mid-morning. Sweat prickles on my neck and I wipe the flour from my hands and scoop my hair up into the elastic band that was round a bunch of wilting asparagus. Nothing can hold its own against this oppressive heat. Georgie has already devoured three ice pops for breakfast and is lying on her tummy in front of a fan in the living room, sleepily watching a comforting film. 'It's too hot to do anything, Mummy,' she said miserably as she started on her third frozen chemical concoction. I've promised I'll put the sprinkler on the lawn later for her but if Joe catches me there'll be trouble. We are weeks into a hose pipe ban. He will hurl statistics about water wastage and cast words like irresponsibility and climate crisis in my face, but my little girl will dance through the spray, slick with water and joy and I know I will not be able to resist stripping to my bra and knickers and joining my baby to frolic on the sodden grass in the icy water, despite the protestations of my sensible, eldest boy.

Tess has promised she will arrive by six, seven at the latest and I can't quite believe she will be here at last. There are hearty salads chopped too early, wine is already chilling, and an over-priced quiche or two and expensive smoked salmon await her arrival. I am making ciabattas and walnut bread. I imagine sitting outside on the terrace by the garden room, eating and drinking long into the night. I cannot imagine us going to sleep. There will be so much for us to say to each other; so many years to catch up on.

The dough goes in for a second prove and I flop down at the table with a glass of iced water. The front of the house faces north so no need for this blind to be down. The weeds in the drive are shrivelled brown from lack of rain and with one crunch underfoot, they crumble to dust. Even though it's only August, some of the leaves are turning on the trees, an indication of no water deep in the soil. The chickens are sulkily pecking around in the shade offered by the tenting I have constructed across their whole pen. We've barely had any eggs for weeks. My poultry aren't accustomed to this weather either. I consider again moving them lock, stock and barrel into the barn. There is at least a breath of air coming down from the fells most days so I'm holding off and surely the weather will break soon.

He's been shouting on and off for an hour or so.

Georgie has been in and filled up his water jug. I think he must be bored. I'm doing my best to ignore him but, as Joe is over at Grace's and Ted is working, I suppose I will have to see what he wants.

He's panting and lying in bed when I check on him.

'What's wrong?' I say.

'I'm not well, Karen,' he says, 'I think I need a doctor. I can't seem to get my breath properly and I'm sure I've got a fever.'

'It's nearly 30 degrees outside. Everyone thinks they've got a fever, Archie.' He has a couple of pink splotches on his cheeks though; he doesn't look particularly pukka.

'I know. I know it's hot. It doesn't feel like that. I don't feel normal. I haven't felt normal since I had that cold.' His voice is strained and weak and I think I can hear a wheeze when he speaks.

'You're the only person in the country with a cold, Archie. Everyone else is baking and sunbathing and basking in this glorious weather and you've been stuck in here feeling sorry for yourself nursing a few sniffles. It's about time you bucked up.' I'd like to go but the dining room always was the coolest room in the house, in fact the only time we ever came in here was when there was a heat wave. I move in and sit at the table, crossing my legs and looking out of the window. There's a lovely view of the crab apple from here; I can't remember the last time I looked out at it.

'You might be right Karen, perhaps I just need to make more of an effort,' he sounds dejected, 'I just don't feel myself. I think I could be sick. Actually vomit. And there's a pain in my chest when I cough. I honestly don't think I'm imagining it.'

I look at him. He does look pathetic, collapsed back against the crumpled pillows, grey faced and sunken eyed. A definite prison pallor about him. He's aged a lot in the last year. 'Let's see how you feel later on? You'll have missed all the morning appointments now, anyway, won't you?'

His breathing is shallow, laboured. 'Thank you, Karen. I appreciate your concern,' and he meets my eye.

'I suppose you might have a chest infection,' I muse.

'Yes,' he says, 'That's what I was thinking. A chest infection,' and he sounds genuinely pleased that I am onboard with his predicament.

I lean forward on my chair towards him and tilt my head sympathetically. 'Do you remember when I had that chest infection when the boys were young, Archie?' My tone is innocent and light.

'I don't know,' he is wary, hesitant, 'Maybe.'

'I'm sure you must,' I cajole, 'I was given antibiotics, a long course, I seem to remember, and you, with your many years of medical training, flushed them down the loo. Coming back to you now, Archie?'

His panting is quickening. His eyes dart around the room.

'You said to me something like 'your immune system will be stronger if your body heals naturally.' Do you remember that, Archie? Do you remember how none of us were ever allowed to be ill? Never allowed to have a day off school or work? Never allowed to show weakness? Never allowed to be human?'

'Look, Karen, I know what that must have looked like ...' he starts.

'It's not what that looked like, Archie, it's what that was. It was cruel. It was torture. It was needless, and it was abusive. Abusive to me and to my children.' I stand up. 'Now I'm pretty sure your symptoms sound like, what with the wheezing and the chest pain and the nausea, at best, a chest infection, at worst, perhaps, pneumonia. But luckily for you, your immune system will be stronger if you fight it naturally.' I smile into his horrified face. 'I'd try and get some rest if I were you, something we were never allowed to do under your regime. Best chance you've got for recovery.'

I stand up and head for the door.

'But Karen …' he implores.

'Yes Archie?' I turn back and look at him.

'Never mind,' he gives in and turns his head away from me.

His lunchtime mush goes untouched and, when Joe and Grace appear much later for Tess's arrival, I tell them he's resting. Though I'm pretty sure the carer will insist on calling the doctor, at least I've delayed any intervention for a good twelve hours and, hopefully, added some discomfort to his day. I make sure I have a large glass of wine at lunchtime so I can't be called upon to drive him to the walk-in centre. A GP will have to come out if they think he needs to be seen.

My excitement over Tess has reached fever pitch by the time Georgie's friend, Millie calls round to pick her up for a two-night sleepover. The girls giggling chatter entwines and overlaps as they plot to spend the whole of the next three days in the new plunge pool that has arrived at Millie's house. Georgie repacks to include all her swimsuits and barely anything else as well as anything inflatable she can lay her hands on, while Millie's Dad and I moan in a tedious manner about the heat and the sun buckling the roads and railway tracks until the girls twitter their way into his car and they disappear, and I have a second glass of wine and try to stop looking at my watch.

My head's in the red-hot oven checking the ciabatta when I hear Tess's van. The toot sounds rhythmically familiar but more weary than last time. I slam the door shut and race up the hall.

Joe has beaten me to her and has Tess in his arms and is swinging her around. I'm a little taken aback by such a fulsome greeting. When at last she puts him down, Tess cups his face, 'Your beard's gone Jelly Bean, and I like it,' she says and she turns to Grace who is standing behind Joe, 'And you must be the very talented Grace. I love your *Insta*. So creative. Whole new way of advertising. Not totally on board with the whole consumer vibe but if that's your jam who am I to judge.'

They hug warmly and Grace says, 'I've heard so much about you, it's like we've met already,' and she laughs.

'I know, right?' and Tess laughs too.

I walk down the ramp saying, 'Heard so much from one party when Joe was, what? Thirteen? Fourteen?' They all turn and look at me and their smiles coagulate on their faces.

'Karen, come here and give me a snog,' and Tess runs over, and the moment is broken.

So, my son has had much more contact with my best friend than I have had over the last decade and I am being swallowed alive with jealousy.

As they sit and chat and cross reference Tess's meanders around the globe with Joe's reading history, I feel like I have been living in a different universe. It transpires Joe has been texting Tess for years and, whilst I thought she wasn't that responsive to texting, that perhaps she disapproved of technology or was off grid for chunks of time, it appears she just didn't want to talk to me.

For Joe, she had all the time in the world.

I escape to the kitchen to open more wine and get out the food. Joe appears. 'I wanted to tell you, Mum. I really did. I just couldn't find the right time or the right words.' He peels the foils from the salads and folds it carefully for reuse later.

'And did Tess know I didn't know?' I ask, not looking at him, 'Of course she did,' I answer my own question, 'otherwise she would have said something to me about the way things were going for you, your life choices, such as they've been, Uni, the business with Grace, I don't know. She'd have said something. So, you agreed, between the two of you, to deceive me.'

'That's a bit strong, Mum.'

'Is it? It feels like a deception. How often were you in touch with her? Eh? How often?'

'I don't know. It depends. It depends what's going on. Sometimes every day. Sometimes not for a week or so. I don't know?' He has picked up the Greek salad ready to take outside.

'I see. Well, how lovely.'

'Excuse me. Mrs Blackthorne? Can I have a word?' Amber the carer is standing at the door.

'Sure, Amber. What is it? How are you? Everything okay?' Joe puts his head down and disappears out the door with the salad.

'Oh, yes, I'm fine. Except for this heat. Could do without that. Especially in this uniform. Feel like I'm going to spontaneously combust! No. What it was, was, Archie's not feeling so good. A bit breathless. Bit of a sore chest and I'm wondering if a call to 111 might be an idea?' She's having a good look at everything on the table, especially the salmon.

'I see,' I say, 'He has had a cold for a few days. Do you think that could be the problem?'

'Yes, I saw that,' Amber says, 'I think it's a bit worse than that. I mean, I'm only a carer, not a trained medical person but his chest doesn't sound good to me and when I got him changed for bed, I'm pretty sure he's running a temperature.'

'Did you listen to his chest with a stethoscope?' I say.

'Oh no,' she says, 'but...'

'And did you take his temperature with a thermometer?' I interrupt.

'No, it was just how he felt, to the touch, you know,'

'So, it's just a hunch you have, no medical basis?' I say.

Amber begins to look flustered. 'Well, I've a lot of experience, Mrs Blackthorne,'

'What you have to understand about Archie is that he always was a terrible hypochondriac and a dreadful whiner. Shall we see how he is in the morning?'

'It's just that with his mobility issues something like a severe chest infection could be...'

'Let's see how he is in the morning. Thank you for your concern, Amber. We really appreciate everything you do.' I stare at her hard until she has no choice but to leave the kitchen. I turn away from her disgruntled and departing back.

Joe is standing by the door.

'I'm calling 111,' he says tightly.

I pick up the breadbasket and the salmon and walk over to him. 'I don't know why you're telling me. Apparently, you can call whoever you like,' I say and step out into the evening sunlight.

Irritatingly, we have to stay relatively sober as we wait for the on-call doctor to arrive. I stay outside for the consultation, but pneumonia is confirmed and antibiotics are prescribed. The doctor says the surgery will want to see Archie in 48 hours to check he's improving and doesn't need IV antibiotics and a hospital admission. After the doctor has left, Joe tries to tempt him with morsels of bread dipped in olive oil and the delicious quiche, but he won't take anything. The fleeting party atmosphere has dissipated so Grace heads home and Joe decides to sit in with Archie to keep an eye on him.

Tess and I walk back across the lawn, barefoot, to the garden room with large glasses of cool wine and sink onto the lawn chairs as the sun is deepening to an extravagant pinkish orange.

'Sorry about all this bullshit,' I say to her, 'This was not the way I wanted us to spend your first evening here.'

'No worries,' she breathes out. She hasn't been in to see Archie yet. I'm not sure if she will. 'It's just good to see you all. I know things aren't straightforward.'

'You can say that again,' I say and drink.

Tess lounges back in the chair and stretches. There are flecks of grey in her blonde hair and I think her skin is a little crinklier than mine around her eyes; she looks alive though. Vigorous and sinewy and supple and strong as a young tree whipped by the wind.

'Is that a bed in there?' she's peering into the garden room.

'Yes,' I say.

'Who sleeps out here?' she keeps looking.

'I do. Quite a lot actually. If Georgie's not here. Or sometimes if she is and one of the boys is home.' I look up at the sky. It is darkening, broad brushstrokes of crimson tinged with gold sweep across the horizon, so another blistering day tomorrow.

'Why? When you've got a perfectly good house to sleep in?' she turns to look at me, genuinely puzzled.

'I spend a lot of time out here,' I say, 'I had it built especially as a retreat from the house.'

Tess looks back at the newly built solidly pleasing structure beside her.

'How much time?' she asks.

'I dunno,' I say, 'I quite often eat my meals in here, there's a radio and, you see that shelf? That folds down into a desk so I can do work out here too.'

'Right,' she says but I think she has more to say. 'Isn't it a bit cold? I mean it's okay when the weather's like this but we are in the north of England, Karen.'

'Look in the corner. There's a little wood burner. When you go into the house, you can see the chimney in the back corner. It's cosy. Snug. Perfect.' I have an answer for every one of her objections.

'So,' she says sitting up and swivelling round to face me, 'it sounds like you spend most of your time out here, in fact.'

I think about this for a moment. 'Yes, I suppose I do. You know what they say, 'In space no one can hear you scream'.'

'You come out here to scream?' she sounds confused.

'No, silly, I come out here to get away.'

'From the kids?'

'No, from him.'

'Oh. I see,' she says, and she lies back down.

We are quiet for a moment. I look at up again at the stars beginning to blink through the pale sapphire of the night sky. It is still wonderfully warm.

'I thought you'd be on board,' I say, 'I mean you sleep *al fresco* every night more or less.'

Tess snorts. 'Yes, but not my choice, Karen. Bloody hell I'm in my fifties and I still haven't figured out what to do with my life.'

'What are you talking about?' I say amazed.

'I mean, if I had a beautiful five-bedroom farmhouse I wouldn't be building a shed in the garden and sleeping in that.'

'It's not a bloody shed,' I say, offended, 'It's a garden room.'

'It's a glorified shed, Karen, and you have a perfectly good house which you have apparently vacated.' Reaching for the wine bottle, she tops up her glass. 'He's still controlling your life.'

'What do you mean?' I sit up now too. I don't want to argue but I can see where we are heading.

'How much did it cost?' she says swigging from her glass.

'How much did what cost? I say.

'Your garden room,' she sneers.

'Not that much,' I evade her.

'Liar,' she says, 'So you spent, what twenty grand or more to get away from The Emperor when you could have just divorced him. You're crazy, Karen. Like I say he's still controlling you.'

'He is not!' I say, 'I'm controlling him. I'm in charge now. I decide everything now. I can do whatever I like, and I do whatever I want. I can do whatever I want to him. You're wrong, Tess, he doesn't control me. Not anymore.'

'He's still in your life though, isn't he? And you're all still here after all this time. Christ, he can't walk but you're all still dancing to his tune. I'm back here, first time in ten years or more and he still makes the whole evening about him. My God, we're even arguing about him. He'd love that.' She drinks again.

'I don't want to argue,' I say, and I mean this, I don't want to argue with this dear, dear friend who I have barely seen because of my despicable husband. 'Honestly, Tess. I know what I'm doing. I could have ... let him go. We talked about it. Me and the boys. But then ... but then he would have got away with it.'

Tess looks up from her wine glass. 'Got away with it? What do you mean?' she says quietly.

'Got away with everything he did to us. To me. I couldn't let that happen. This way I have him here. I can ... make him pay.'

I haven't admitted this before and when I see Tess's face, I'm not sure I should have. I thought she of all people would have understood.

She just shakes her head. 'You're not making him pay, you're just punishing yourself. There's a whole world out there and you're here hiding in a shed justifying this half-life, this distortion as some kind of justice for what he put you through.'

She stands up. 'I'm going to bed. I'm going to enjoy sleeping in your wonderful spare room in a proper bed with a plumbed in bathroom rather than my customary tin can. Know what you have, Karen.'

I watch her walk across the grass. It's still early. I won't be able to sleep for hours. I reach for the wine bottle.

2

Joe is telling Tess about Grace's latest exhibition over breakfast the next morning and is giving her much more detail than I've been privy to thus far. I resolve not to make any barbed comments but get on with replenishing the mango and pineapple I'd prepared yesterday and warming more croissants. I top up their coffee and neither acknowledge me. Joe looks tired as he's slept on the chair in Archie's room, but he has reported he thinks that the antibiotics are working as Archie doesn't seem so feverish this morning. He has managed some tea and a croissant and for that we are supposed to be thankful.

'I said that there was more to Grace than just *TikTok*, didn't I?' Tess is saying as she forks more fruit into her bowl.

'I know,' Joe says through a mouth of croissant, 'I think we're lucky to have found such good contacts but the *TikTok* following has helped, no doubt. Her followers want to come and see Li'l Grace in the flesh. What's cool is that she's able to break away from the overtly commercial, and she's managing to express some of her own ideology now.'

'Yes, yes, I can see that,' Tess nods enthusiastically, '*TikTok* is astonishingly powerful. You can see why China banned it.'

'Absolutely,' Joe says, 'We're trying to move away from the whole Influencer side of things now and focus on Grace as a serious artist and activist. She's promoting still but just carefully selected products and our goal is to ultimately link the two so the one helps the other; the proceeds help the cause.'

'You've got to be so careful with all of that, haven't you? So many companies are green washing now, so unscrupulous.' Tess shakes her head and pops a piece of juicy pineapple from Brazil into her mouth. I raise my eyebrow and lean against the kitchen counter.

'I know,' Joe is earnest, 'That's largely my role. Grace is creativity and I'm research and negotiation. So, I went to this gallery initially and did all the legwork and scrutiny before I brought Grace in.'

'So, you're her manager?' I say.

'God no, Mum,' Joe sounds appalled, 'Grace does *not* need a manager. In fact, we are both ethically offended by any form of hierarchical terminology. I respect Grace's talent and genius far too much to impose my patriarchal will onto her creativity. We are working as a mini collective, but Grace's work and the furthering of her message is at the core. Ideally, we'd like to add to the group in the future.' He furiously tears another croissant, refusing to look towards me.

'Then what's in it for you? What about *your* creativity?' I say. I'm hungover and grumpy. I don't particularly trust Grace with my delicate son.

'There's plenty in it for me,' he retorts, 'Grace has given me the chance to be part of something that matters. Part of something that could make a difference or change people's minds. Bloody hell, it's a million times better than working in that shitty café.'

'Yes, but it's not exactly permanent, is it? Look how things worked out last time.' I can hear how I sound and Tess lets out a heavy sigh to show her disapproval.

'I'm not interested in having this conversation, Mum.' He looks at me with a rigid hostility. 'Okay?' He turns back to Tess. 'You could come to the gallery? The show's just about ready. The opening isn't until next week, but they'll let us in for sure. What do you think?' It's like he's chatting to one of his mates.

'Cool,' Tess says, nodding.

'The lighting is sic. Mini spots on each of the different exhibits and the rest of the space is dark. It's like little pools of light and you're walking through this mini world; it's kind of magical. And the exhibition room is this rich, midnight blue so all the colours of Grace's work just pop out too. It's like an immersive experience.'

'Sounds really cool,' says Tess again.

Joe pushes his chair back and finishes the dregs in his coffee cup. 'Okay, I'm going to check on Dad. I'll catch up with you later Tess, yeah?'

'Sure Joe, yeah,' she says smiling up at him. And then he strides out of the kitchen without another word to me.

I clear his plate and mug.

'So much for not imposing his patriarchal will,' I say as I stack them in the dishwasher and turn smiling to Tess. She doesn't return the smile.

I sit down opposite her.

'Oh, fucking hell, Tess,' I say, 'If you're going to be so po-faced and judgemental, we might as well call it a day now. I can't be bothered with all this.'

'I didn't sleep very well last night, Karen,' she says and she's staring at me.

'Well, boohoo for you. You should have bunked with me in the garden room. It was delightful.' I pick up a chunk of mango and eat it, sucking the juice from my fingers noisily. I feel like a petulant child who's about to get into trouble.

'It was what you said. What you were saying,' she says, 'Last night. It just kept going round in my head.'

'I can't remember what I said,' I say blithely, 'I'd had too much wine and what with all the drama with Archie. Ignore what I was saying Tess.' I reach my hand across the table. I want us to be friends.

She frowns and there's a moment where I don't know what is going to happen next. She could stand up and walk out and I'll never see her again or she will take my hand and we can move on. I hold my breath.

'There's a storm coming. I heard it on the radio,' she says, and she pats my hand and stands up and starts to clear the breakfast table.

As Tess and I lie on the lawn chairs and gaze up at the cloudless sky, it's hard to believe a storm is brewing but it's all over the news. There are already flash floods wreaking havoc further south and the air feels fat and full. There's not a breath of wind and we are listless and lazy, basking in the heat, still as stones, waiting for what is to come.

Joe comes out from time to time to report on Archie who is mainly sleeping now his cough is easing. I make no comment, but Tess makes the appropriate responses.

'He's mad that you weren't going to get The Emperor help,' she says as I watch him plod back dutifully into the house. He has directed all his remarks to Tess.

'I know,' I say, 'But you don't have the whole story,' and I leave it at that.

It's too hot to eat any lunch and we are beaten indoors by the heat to the relative cool of the living room. We play poker and start on the wine lying on our stomachs on the tiled floor constantly shifting positions to find a colder spot.

Our poker hands are appalling, nothing much better than the occasional two pairs but we are betting excessively and recklessly so the time is passing, helped by a second bottle of wine.

At some point, in between hands, I say to Tess, 'Have you still got the tarot cards?'

It takes her a moment. 'My future laid out? Yes, of course. Have you?'

'Sure. Where do you keep them?' I ask.

'Right here,' and she scoots across the floor on her belly and pulls over her little rucksack. She rummages inside and produces the three rubbed and familiar cards. Giving them a reverential kiss, she crawls back over then lays them down on the tiles between us.

The Three of Pentacles, the Two of Swords reversed and the Devil reversed. We both stare at the creased and faded pictures.

'How did they work out for you?' I say.

'They're the story of my life,' she says and gently lays the tips of her fingers onto all three.

'Tell me,' I say.

'Well, you said the Three of Pentacles was about collaboration and teamwork, didn't you? And that's what I've done. All these years, all over the place. Working with so many different souls, so many different people in so many different places. Finding ways to communicate and to work together. It's been fucking magical,' and she laughs.

'You see,' I say, 'You have got your life together. You've done what you were meant to do. You've travelled and performed and collaborated and made a difference.'

'Maybe,' she says, 'maybe.'

'What about the next card?' I say.

'The Two of Swords reversed,' she says and raises her glass to toast it. Our glasses clink. 'This card, if you remember rightly, Miss Karen, is my *Sophie's Choice* card. The card about confusion and one choice being the lesser of two evils.'

'Oh, I do remember this card,' I say, 'But you never had children so what was your choice?'

'You were,' she says.

'Me?' I say, 'How so?'

'Once you were with The Emperor, I made the choice. I couldn't watch you and him together, so I left you.' Her voice cracks.

'Tess,' I start but I don't know what to say.

'Twice,' she adds.

'What?' I say.

'After the Halloween party. I should never have come back. I just missed you so much. I had to go through it all again. Losing you all over again.' She's crying. The drink is making this much worse.

'You didn't need to. I mean, we could have kept in touch. Lots of people have difficult husbands and still keep their friends. Don't they? Don't they Tess?' I am gripping her hands, begging her. Her tears fall onto the cards.

She looks up. 'I don't know, Karen, do they? Not with a man like him. No, Karen. I don't think so. Not with The Emperor.'

'What about the last card? The Devil reversed?' I say. My hands are shaking, and I feel the loss of the last two decades wash through me, a loss I need never have suffered if I had not stayed with Archie.

Tess wipes away her tears. 'Yes, the card that foresees restoring control and freedom. I hope this is his accident. I hope this is your way out. I want this to be a way for us to be together again.'

I sit back. 'But Tess, these are your cards. How can Archie's accident be in your cards? You've been hundreds of miles from us for all these years. What about your relationships? Your loves, your losses? What about those?'

She shrugs. 'They just never seemed to matter to me as much as you did. No one has ever mattered to me as much as you have. I think that's why he's in my cards.'

'If I matter to you so much, why have you punished me? Why are you punishing me? Why have you been in touch with Joe all this time and not a word to me? I don't get it. It's not logical.' I think she's talking out of her arse. It's the drink. She's just saying all of this to make me leave Archie. She's playing with me.

'Joe came to me. He text me. I like him. I love him. He's just like you. He was a connection to you without having to connect with you. Does that make sense? I am sorry though; I didn't want to hurt you. Truly I didn't,' and she leans over and cups my face laying her hand, cool from the stone floor, against my hot cheek.

'Okay,' I say.

'What about you?' she says, 'Did you keep your cards?'

'Of course,' I say, 'We promised each other we would.'

'Where are they?' she says.

'Upstairs,' I say.

'Let's go and look for them,' she says, and she stands up, takes me by the hand and leads me to my bedroom.

3

'**M**um! Mum!' I am startled out of sleep by Ted's urgent whispering and soft knocking. He is outside the bedroom door. I kick back the covers and, pulling on a dressing gown, go over and open the door a crack.

'The weather's turning. I've shut the chickens up and closed all the windows. It's really windy outside. Sorry to wake you. Joe's heading over to Grace's. Dad's asleep. See you in the morning,' he smiles. His tie is slackened at the neck, sleeves rolled up, jacket hooked on his finger over his shoulder. Hard to believe he even bothered to take it into the office in these temperatures.

'Thanks, love,' I say, and he walks away and I turn back to Tess sprawled and naked on my bed. The room is surprisingly chilly and, as I shut the windows, I take in the solid, purple clouds pushing and rolling over the fells. 'Rain at last,' I think but I'm sleepy and my body feels loose and lazy and I can't stay awake to marvel at the lightning. I notice our six tarot cards intermingled on my dressing table. The Emperor is obscured and so is The Hermit but The Tower is on the top of the pile. I always thought of this card as a kind of Rapunzel prophecy rather than an indicator of cataclysmic change; I suppose because I felt I had been locked up metaphorically for so long. In reality I suppose Archie's fall must be the meaning of The Tower; it had certainly been a paradigm shift. Though I have to admit I feel a little galled that Archie is so much the focus of my cards. I hear the words I had spoken to Tess earlier, why was I so central to her cards? Why was Archie so central to mine? I wanted to be the main character in my life, the driving force, the protagonist. I also hadn't been able to stop thinking about what she'd said about the garden room; what was I doing? Was he still controlling my life without me realising it. I resolve to give this proper thought in the morning.

As I pull the sheet over my shoulders, Tess mumbles something in her sleep. It sounds like, 'Sleep tight, Jelly Bean,' but the words lack endings, and she snuffles back into gentle snoring rather than adding any more. I sigh and shut my eyes against her naked presence. I'll think about all of that in the morning. I drift into dreamless sleep.

A crack of thunder breaks overhead and we both jump awake. It is explosive, terrifying and wonderful. I wait for the deluge to hit the roof and start battering the windows but there's nothing. The bedroom swings open and Ted stands before us, face split with elation, 'Did you hear that?' he yells, and I realise the wind outside is cacophonous.

In my memory, it's hard to work out what happens next. I recall an ear-splitting crack and a dazzling flash outside as if blinding white sunlight has burst through the window for a fraction of a second. In that same moment, Ted is suddenly smacked against the bed, like he's flown across the room, pushed or shoved by some giant invisible hand. A creaking or groaning on a massive scale follows but it sounds like its underwater. I shake my head and look across at Tess who's out of bed and dragging on a T shirt and shorts. Seconds have passed. I smack my ear, hoping the ringing that's filling my head will stop, and crawl over the bed to Ted. He's lying on the floor, dazed. I can't see anything visibly wrong.

'Are you okay?' I say, but the words sound like they're in my head and not leaving my mouth.

He looks at me, 'What's going on?' I lip read.

In the hall beyond there's a flickering, rosy glow against one of the walls. It's a little mesmerising, coupled with the ringing in my ears.

Tess shakes my shoulder and I jiggle my head again as my senses begin to rebalance. 'The house. I think it's been,' and there's another tremendous crack of thunder as if the cloud is splitting metres above the roof. We all instinctively flinch.

Dragging Ted to his feet, Tess makes for the hall but then steps back into the bedroom and shuts the door firmly.

'There's a fire. It's in the corridor. Up here. We'll have to go out the window,' she shouts against the noise.

With the door shut, I realise the screeching in my ears is partly the smoke alarm. Reaching for my phone, I dial 999. The calls fail. There's nothing. No signal.

'No time. Take it with you,' says Tess. She's knotting a sheet to a blanket. Ted is looking on, dazed and glassy-eyed.

'Joe, Georgie?' I say.

'Not here,' Ted says, and this seems to rouse him and he opens the window and helps Tess tie the sheet around the foot of the bed and throw the sheet out. 'You go out first, Tess. Then Mum, you're both lighter than me and I can hold the sheet too and take some of the weight. You'll have to drop the last bit, looks like. Hard to tell, there's no light. Power's out.'

'Okay,' we agree, and they bundle out the duvet and pillows to soften the fall. I grip my hands together to stop them shaking. I believe I can smell smoke in the room already, but I don't know if this is real, or panic induced.

I watch Tess clamber out onto the windowsill and my stomach lurches as I recall the sound of Archie falling from the roof. I rush forward to help and hold onto her bony arms as long as I can, but she has to make her own way down alone. With horror, I realise the fire to our left is now lighting up her progress, her curly blonde hair is a halo of reddish gold, and the garden is alive in its glow which can only means it's spreading fast.

Her slender body hits the ground with a surprisingly loud thud but she's on her feet in seconds. 'Come on, quickly!' she shouts and, after kissing my boy who urges me to leave, I slither out and down the makeshift rope, praying the knot will hold and I can make it to the ground.

'Where is the bloody rain?' I think as I see tongues of flames licking up through a gaping hole in the roof and curling up out of Georgie's bedroom window. Storm rain would at least slow it down.

The strained blanket runs out too quickly and my legs kick and flail, trying to find the ground. It's like the horror of being in too deep water. 'Jump Karen. Now! Ted needs to get out!' and that's all I need to hear.

I don't think the duvet or pillows make much of a difference but it's not a bad fall and I roll onto the grass, and I'm not hurt as I'm on my feet and bellowing to Ted in moments. 'Stand back Karen, slates are coming off the roof. It's not safe,' Tess yells and I head further up the garden towards her, and we huddle against the wind.

I look up and Ted's at the window and out onto the rope and it all seems so hopeful but, just past the blanket, the knot stretches, slips, unravels and gives up and, as we run with outstretched arms, I watch him fall. It's a terrible moment.

As we reach him, he's smiling, the tough little bugger, 'Don't look at my ankle,' he says, 'I think that's gonna be bad,' and then he briefly faints.

At that moment, it begins to pour; fat, freezing rain driving down. We drag him on the duvet to the garden room, the rain pelting onto us, attacking and relentless. Once under shelter, we assess and Ted is right, the ankle is undoubtedly broken but it will heal. We are out of the house. I try my phone again, still no signal.

'Dad,' Ted says simply.

Tess and I look at each other and run back across the soaking grass as the rain thunders onto the baked ground.

As we career around the side of the house away from the fire, we stumble a little out of the glow of the flames but the front has the light of a medieval banquet, rich and golden and pinkly red. It is hard to believe that such devastation is occurring. I lay my hand on the front door, but I can't tell if it's warm or not. Tess is peering in through Archie's window.

'I think the strike was above the stairs,' I say, 'It must have been the bloody weathervane. I told Archie years ago it needed a lightning conductor when he restored it. But he never listened to me. The stairs are wooden and varnished – it could be outside his door by now. Hell, there's so much bloody wood in the house.'

'Does he sleep with the door open?' She's already trying to get the window open teetering on an upturned plant pot.

'No, closed. He's afraid of the bogey man,' I reply peering in too. I can't see anything. I try to help. It won't budge. It's locked.

I step back. 'You die pretty quickly from smoke inhalation,' I say calmly.

I take out my phone. I have a signal.

I dial. As I summon help, I watch Tess go to the garage and fetch a hefty shovel.

'It's hard to break a double-glazed window,' she shouts, as she marches towards me, 'Stand clear.'

I have to admire her strength and determination. It takes several blows to crack the outer skin. I am standing clear.

As the shovel crashes through the inner pane, I am calculating how long I think it will be before the fire engines get here? Will Tess and I be able to get him out? Should we even re-enter the building?

Tess has run back to the garage and comes back with arms full of thick dustsheets. 'We'll lay these over the frames, cover the sharp edges,' she bellows as she picks out the larger jagged pieces jutting from the wood.

I grip her arm. 'Is it safe to go back in?' I say.

'Fucking hell, Karen,' she says, 'It's not up to you.'

'What isn't?' I say.

'To decide.' She continues to prepare the window, working quickly. 'Archie? Archie? Are you awake?'

'To decide what?' I say.

'Whether another human being lives or dies, whoever or whatever they've done. That's not up to you. It's not up to anybody. You should know that.' She hops up onto the windowsill, 'You do know that!' she yells above the roar of the fire and the wind and the rain, and in one movement, she disappears into the room.

I blink.

I turn on the torch on my phone and shine it through the window.

Tess is by the bed. 'Is he awake?' I shout.

'Yes!' she calls back, 'Drowsy, from the drugs I think.'

You can hear the fire crackling inside the house, a dull moaning and popping, not the right noises our home usually makes. I lean back out of the window. Joe's bedroom is above Archie's. The glow of flames lights the window. Judging by the amount of smoke belching up and out and still managing to form its own impressive cloud formation above the farmhouse despite the wind, I think the roof must be all but gone. The air around me is filled with a hazy miasma of delicate particles, an acrid gauze of our past lives disintegrating around me. In movies, timbers and joists fall on people in burning buildings. How long before the farmhouse is completely compromised? The walls are stone, thick, solid. That's what I always thought. I don't understand what is burning so quickly and efficiently.

'Hurry up Tess, it's got a hold above. It's bad!' I shout. They've managed between them to get Archie out of bed and into the chair. Archie mouths something at me but I don't know what it is. He looks terrified.

Tess hurtles him over to the window and his hand goes to grip the ledge. 'Careful!' she barks, 'There's glass everywhere.' This doesn't help Archie's confidence and he looks at me with little boy's eyes unsure what to do next.

'It'll be okay,' I say briskly, 'We can patch you up afterwards. Let's get you out. That's the important thing.' He smiles faintly and Tess snatches another blanket from his bed and lays that over the ledge and up around the frame too.

If he could walk, he would be able to stand and lever himself out of the window, wouldn't he? There's no hoist. Nothing to properly grip on to. He leans forward using his arms and shoulders, with me pulling him and Tess pushing but it's the dead weight of his bottom half dragging down which is too much. His centre of gravity is just too low, and Tess hasn't got the strength to manhandle him any higher. We're not making any progress.

He flops back into his chair exhausted, fingers still uselessly gripping the vandalised window.

'You need to get in here too,' Tess shouts, 'I can't do it on my own. The ledge is too high. There's smoke coming in Karen. A lot of smoke.'

At that moment, Joe's window bursts above me. I shriek, crouch down and shelter against the wall as glass and debris shower down around me and a flash of heat briefly surges as the fire claims another room completely.

There is a settling, though the roar from the fire above is now an additional startling menacing presence. I stand up again, trying not to cower. It's like having flaming helicopter blades whipping round above me; I know they can't reach me, but I want to shrink from them. Archie looks at me, recognising the enormity of what is happening and how the situation is unravelling around us. 'Get out, Tess,' he shouts, his eyes locked with mine, 'It's okay. Just get out.' There's a monstrous groaning and creaking inside the room. The fire is systematically gnawing and chewing through the stability of this structure that has stood for hundreds of years. Archie knows the fire is winning and that his body has let him down. His face is apologetic and resigned but also accepting. He smiles at me. It is the first time I have had a truthful connection with him in years. Perhaps, it is the only time. It really is okay with him.

Tess looks at me, her eyes wide and desperate, and there is another groan from above as if we have a fiery slumbering giant above who has just woken and is slowly turning in drowsy half-sleep. Any moment he will crash through the ceiling and wreak a horrifying havoc.

I climb up and squeeze past Archie into the room which feels much thicker with smoke than outside, and this panics me. I swallow back the urge to cough. Tess and I lever Archie up from his haunches. This time, we get him further through the window and he manages to get a solid grip onto a handful of honeysuckle vine that grows up around the front door and along the front of the house. They used honeysuckle ropes to drag the stones to Stonehenge; it's strong stuff.

The creaking gets worse and as we concertina his spindly legs higher, I shout, 'We're going to tip you now, Archie,' hoping he's got a hand to the ground, and he can roll to safety.

Gravity takes over and his weight slips away from us and suddenly our hands are empty as he tumbles out of the window. We stick our heads through and he's lying in a heap on his back like an upturned turtle squished into the flower border. He's panting. Looking stunned. A splitting and ripping behind us make us turn together and we watch a crack zigzagging across the ceiling. Plaster dust and chunks fall away, and I grab Tess and push her up and into the window as a beam gives way and crashes into the room. I'm right behind her and she turns and is pulling me out. We grab Archie between us and haul and drag his sack of potatoes body back around the house to the safety of the garden room and my beautiful Ted.

Once we get our breath back, Tess sets to lighting the stove while I boil the kettle and make everyone sugary tea. 'Mum, you're bleeding,' Ted says pointing to my arm, as I hand him his mug and some paracetamol I have found. There is a deep gash, neatly sliced, on the fleshy part of my upper arm. I can't believe I haven't felt it. Tess wraps it tightly with a scarf.

We watch the house light up the night sky and wait for the fire fighters. It smells like bonfire night.

Part Five

Archie

There isn't quite the view of a street I had wanted, one that is bustling with people trotting to and fro on their way to diverse activities that I could imagine based on their attitudes or even their apparel. I foresaw passing the time people watching rather than resenting the bleak desolation of the farmhouse. In reality, I see mostly cars, occasional pedestrians, more when school comes out, but my flat isn't in the heart of town so there's no constant footfall trudging past my door, more's the pity.

'Where do you want your magazines?' Joseph shouts from the bedroom. Very little survived the fire. I had a crate of old car mags in the garage, and they have moved with me. They've been sitting in a box since I got here though. It's a job Joseph has found for himself today. There's always something; I think he prefers to be busy rather than sit down and talk to me.

'I don't care,' I shout back. I don't.

I dip a biscuit in my tea, eat it, turn my head back to the window and wait. There's a lot of waiting now. I can see rooftops, a church spire, no, two church spires, there's another one even further away, and rows of Victorian terraces. I'm in the older part of town. In one of the few newer buildings. It's nice not to be looking at my building which is fairly dull. No, it's very dull. Architectural mediocrity at best. Joseph says I can consider myself to be like Guy de Maupassant who hated the Eiffel Tower so much he ate in the Tower restaurant every evening, so he didn't have to look at it. In the distance are the treetops from the park. That's about it for nature but that's fine. I've had enough of nature for the time being.

There is definitely more of interest to see than there was at the farmhouse.

Eventually, Joseph comes out of the bedroom, smiling. 'They're all stashed away now. I've left a few on your bedside table but I can rotate them as and when, though you can always reach them yourself.'

I haven't the heart to tell him that I have no interest in classic cars anymore. Though I may be able to drive again at some point in an adapted car, it will never be a classic. What's the point of looking at all those beauties? I can't aspire to own one again. No Sir-ee.

It's a strange thing being stripped of everything. I have lost my legs, my house, my possessions, my wife. My life is wholly different. Two terrible events, nobody's fault, both freak accidents, a fall and a storm, have completely overturned my previously perfect existence. If I was a religious man, I might think that some higher power had it in for me. Ha! The boys are still visiting when they can, Joseph more than Edward as his career has taken off so I can't blame him for prioritising that over his cripple for a dad. Joseph is still in thrall to that nightmare of a girl, Hope or Faith or some such name. Or maybe, it's Beth. She is rude anyway, and dresses poorly for someone who is supposed to be worth a mint. As far as I can see she treats Joseph like some sort of lacky. What she says, goes. It's demeaning. Emasculating. He needs to show her who wears the trousers, in my humble opinion, but then he always was the soft one of my two boys. I can't ever see Edward stomaching that kind of behaviour.

I always knew Edward would go places. He was always much more like me; Joseph takes after his mother. Whereas Edward was sporty. Got on well with people. He's funny. Personable. And now he's landed on his feet in this job and it's a meteoric rise, as they say. Yes, he's definitely a chip off the old block. Just needs to find himself a good woman now. Put a stop to this funny business he sprang on us last time we saw him. Yes, a sexy woman with a killer body who does what she's told that would be the ticket. And not some bolshy feminist like Beth, or whatever her name is, that Joseph traipses around after.

I think it might rain. Feels like we've had nothing but rain for weeks. After such a long hot summer, I suppose I can't complain and, now I haven't really got much outside space it doesn't matter that much to me what the weather does. There's a little balcony here. Joseph waxed lyrical about it when I moved in, like it was bloody Kew Gardens, saying I could grow herbs and have pot of tomatoes on it as it faces south. I can easily get my chair out onto it though, no raised sill. The flats are purpose built; it's not a retro fit. I quite often take a cup of coffee out in the morning. It's covered and sheltered too. Far easier than getting out onto the terrace at the farmhouse. I don't let on to Joseph how much I use it though. If he thinks I'm having too good a time, he might stop visiting.

Since Karen and Georgie have moved back down to London, I honestly don't know how often I'm going to see my little princess. I tried to stop her, Karen that is, from going but she wasn't having it. She's moved back in with her parents. I don't know why; she's hardly had anything to do with them over the years. And she'll find a teacher's salary won't go far down there. Mark my words, she'll be back up here, with her tail between her legs before Georgie's had a chance to get a grip of the local lingo.

'Do you want another cuppa, Dad, before I go?' Joseph is wiping down the worktops.

'No thanks, son,' I try to sound cheery. This is independent living after all, and I can easily make my own tea when I want to, what with the lowered worktops and the pull-out drawers instead of cupboards. A sheltered facility. Multiple small dwellings with a live in warden. There's a large lounge downstairs with social events I could participate in if I wanted to. Chess, bingo, a book club, Warhammer amongst others and some rowdy drinking sessions. I saw the young guy from the rehab centre here last week in the lobby. He remembered my name; I couldn't recall his. Think he was in a car crash or bike accident or something. Cried himself to sleep. Seems pretty cheerful now anyway. He had a snazzy chair. One of those lightweight, aerodynamic ones. He'd bulked up a lot too. Obviously managing the gym. There's one here. Don't know if I'll be using it. Might get myself one of those chairs though.

I can't say I've taken to the warden. He could do with a haircut and he's overly friendly with everyone. One of those helpful busybody sorts. Yes, I think I'll be keeping my distance from him.

I might just stay up here and watch a film once Joseph's gone. I would phone Edward but we're not quite seeing eye to eye at the moment. He'll come round to my way of thinking soon enough. There's always the internet too. I've got quite involved in some fascinating conspiracy websites. It's amazing what's been kept from us over the years. I never had time to look into current affairs properly before when I was working, but now my eyes have been opened as to what's been kept from me. Kept from all of us. There's a lot of evidence that is just hidden but believe me, it's out there if you've got the brains to know where to look and are in touch with the best people to point you in the right direction.

I suppose I should think about getting a job but I'm sure I'm suffering from PTSD so I'm claiming benefits at the moment, and I've got my share of the insurance money squirrelled away out of sight of the authorities, for any little luxuries I fancy. I figure I'm entitled to my benefits, after all I paid my taxes for years and I've hardly seen any return on them, have I? So why shouldn't I get something back for a change. Yes, it was a good pay out in the end for the house. Especially when you added up the contents as well. Almost worth the horror of the fire. We'd never have sold it for that much. Jan told me as much, and she should know, the amount of property she owns. She'll be over soon no doubt. Can't keep her away. I've ordered a few little treats for her online. She's been full of stories of how neglectful her husband is. Never pays her any attention, never really has done according to her. I figure if I can shower her with gifts I could be in there. Okay, I'm not fully functional but what she wants is a sounding board more than anything. Roger, or Rupert, or whatever his name is, is hardly at home and she's lonely. I might not be able to provide everything in the bedroom department, but I can listen to her blether on, especially if it means getting out of this place. I might even be prepared to let her win at *Monopoly* from time to time if she plays her cards right. Yes, she's definitely worth cultivating. Reckon I could do a lot worse for myself than old Jan.

'I'll see you the week after next, Dad. Grace has an exhibition opening next week. Remember I told you?' Joseph is putting on his coat.

Grace! Yes, that's the little bitch's name. I do remember about the exhibition. It's all he bloody talks about. 'No,' I say, 'Can't you manage to pop by at all? I mean it's going to be unbearable with no one coming over for two weeks!' I squeeze my eyes shut pretending to cry.

I feel Joseph's hand on my shoulder, 'I'll see if Teddy has time to call in, shall I? We're down in London so I can't come back up. You're going to have to try to get to know some of your neighbours, Dad. I'm sure you could make some friends here.'

'London!' I say, 'What if there's an emergency? What if I need you?' I grip his hand. I know there won't be an emergency, I'm messing with him. I don't really care that I won't see him next week. He's getting fussy. I half expect him to put on a pinny and produce a feather duster. I know it's not genetically possible, but he reminds me a little of my mother.

'If there's an emergency, I'll come straight back,' he says smiling at me.

'Promise?' I say with an anxious look on my face, gripping his hand even tighter.

'Promise,' he says, and he pulls his hand away and places mine back in my lap, 'Now I've got to go. There's still a ton of stuff to do before next week. I'll send you photos and ring you when I can.'

'Okay. Thanks Joseph. Have a good time. I'm sure it'll be brilliant.'

And I smile and wave as he leaves, and I start to plan which emergency I will fabricate next week to call him away because he has promised to come straight back to me and he is a man of his word.

Part Six

Karen

1

Georgie is tugging on wellies ready for another trip to the park. My memory of living in London is that the weather is better but since we moved here, there's been non-stop rain. I worried she would miss the country, the space, swapping the rambling garden for Mum and Dad's smaller back yard. I needn't have given it a thought. Turns out Georgie is at heart a city kid. She strides the pavements, chin up and face open, taking in everything around her. The park around the corner is a favourite; swings, a slide and loads of kids who she manages to chat to and where she can find a playmate with surprising ease. We've been to the Natural History Museum, (I laughed out loud as she gawped at the blue whale) and the V and A where she loved the theatre section, and that is my greatest delight. We are gorging ourselves on plays and musicals, taking advantage of last-minute cheap seats up in the gods and seeing anything and everything that is remotely suitable. I watch her face rapt and shadowed by the glow from the stage and I know she is my child and I kick myself for all the time I have wasted, focused on Archie and not realising what was under my nose.

It is as if my ears are unplugged and my eyes are finally open; I have surfaced from a long, slow swim across a chillingly cold channel of oppressive, unfriendly water. We are finally in the sunlight, together, basking on the sand, allowed to play and free from all tyrannies.

'What on earth are you doing here?' were Mum's first words to me when we appeared on the doorstep. I admit neither of my parents were entirely friendly, but you have to understand that I have been forced to exclude them from my life, all of our lives. Archie made every visit so unpleasant for all concerned it was easier, and kinder, to push them away. Kinder to them obviously; heart-breaking for me.

Georgie showed her granny her myriad of swimsuits with pride, as she unpacked her solitary suitcase into the drawer Mum had cleared in one of the spare rooms. My heart squeezed as I watched Georgie trying to eke this out as long as possible when she realised how much Mum was enjoying the careful explanation which accompanied each one, 'This one is a favourite,' Georgie said, holding up a sliver of slippery scarlet polka dot for Mum to admire, 'I love red and so does Mummy. Really, it's too small but I packed it anyway. The last time Mummy was sorting out clothes for charity, I hid it so she couldn't take it. I also love spots, so this is a win-win. I'm just not ready to say goodbye to it. Thank goodness I took it to Millie's, or else it would have gone with everything else.' They share a rueful sigh.

Remarkably, Georgie was straightforward and practical after the fire. Her main concern was the animals, who were thankfully all unharmed. Archie had always been ruthless with possessions so all three children had learned early not to form attachments. If you showed too much favour towards anything it would likely end up stamped on or ripped in two to prove a point or hurled into the stove or onto the fire in one of his rages. As we found with Otto, even the animals weren't excluded from the cruelty of his jealousy and desire to reign supreme. So, Georgie had few real physical objects she truly mourned.

'I don't like what it smells like,' she said as we stood before the charred skeleton of the house. 'It's like it's gone bad.' She was right. The combination of fire damage, torrential rain and water to put the fire out had resulted in an unpleasant, rotting odour. I'd brought her back only briefly; my thinking was that I wanted her to know I was telling the truth. In her future as an adult, I didn't want our exodus morphing into some kind of tall tale I'd hatched to extricate her from a sentimentalised life in some kind of pastoral idyll.

I hauled a few boxes from the garage, the garden room packed up, and stuffed them into the back of the car. 'We're going down to London. We're going to see Granny and Grandad. You'll love it.'

It wasn't until we were most of the way down the M40 that I realised she hadn't even mentioned Archie. I figured Joe or Ted must have told her about his plans. Or maybe she just knew I didn't want to talk about him; that he wasn't part of our life anymore.

Joe was taken in by Grace, instantly and happily. They're talking about buying somewhere, with a bigger studio space but we'll see. Ted has moved in with Sohaib.

It was quite a shock when I found out Ted was gay. When you see programmes on TV, the mothers are all there saying, 'I always knew, he was always special.' I had no clue. Somehow, Ted managed to lead a more ordinary life than Joe and me until the blessed day that Archie fell off the roof. He kept up a couple of team games once he was old enough to negotiate the lifts to and from games and practices; Archie would never take him. He managed friendship groups. But when I think back, neither boys ever brought anyone home.

Not that I blame them. I didn't either.

I assumed there were girls. For Ted, I mean. I just assumed; he was easy going and good looking in an open, golden, warm as a freshly picked apricot sort of way and that there would be girls.

I did not assume this for Joe. He was awkward and geeky and blushed easily. He was spiky, resistant and I saw how he flinched in the corridors at the barked interactions between his peers. I thought he would find girls and girlfriends more difficult to negotiate. When he quietly told me about Grace, it was hard to hide both my amazement and joy. It was also not surprising how he cleaved to her. I had seen her marching through the village, strong and capable; Joe was ivy to her oak tree, steadily coiling and curling around her, shallow suckers clinging on. It had all looked so secure for a while, but he was easily discarded. A firm grip and he was ripped from her life with little effort. I hated her for that. He never told me what happened. Private too I suppose, like Ted. He never told me a thing.

Ted arranged to meet us all in one of the nicer restaurants in town a few days after the fire. 'My treat,' he said. Archie was in emergency accommodation, but we knew he was going into the flat. I had been 'camping' in the garden room but had moved Georgie and I into a fancy hotel once the insurance cleared it. It was exciting for us all to be going out. Georgie and I lazily luxuriated in the deep hotel bath for hours, singing and giggling, then enjoying our new clothes bought for the meal out. We had all been used to seeing each other more or less every day and suddenly we were separated, far flung, dispersed, scattered and strewn by our recent tragedy. Only Georgie and I had managed to stick together. I was loving it. My grown-up sons were safe, secure and, though I couldn't get the image of Archie's puppy dog eyes at his window with his bedroom black behind him out of my head, as far as I was concerned he was no longer my concern. One of the boys would pick him up. I would tolerate him tonight, but I knew my contact with him in the future was going to be minimal. Preferably non-existent.

'I'd like to get my ears pierced, Mummy,' Georgie had said as she studied her reflection in the mirror.

'Sure,' I said, 'Why don't you get your tongue done too?'

'Ew, Mum, gross.' Georgie squirmed and tucked a notepad and pencil into her backpack.

'Okay, just a suggestion,' I said, 'They're both fleshy and in or on your head, but it's up to you. Let's get going.'

We'd splashed out on matching umbrellas, pardon the pun, a necessity now the weather had broken. It was hard to imagine the weeks of relentless heat as we marched briskly up to the high street navigating the pavements shining and slick with rainwater, trying to avoid the deeper puddles and steering around other miserable pedestrians, heads down, hunched against the filthy weather. Ted was already at the table, face bright with a smile and I tried not to show my surprise that Sohaib was next to him. As Ted hugged and kissed me, Georgie shrieked, 'JoJo!' and I turned to see Joe pushing Archie towards us.

After a good deal of fussing to get Archie settled by the boys and the waiter, Ted ordered champagne and fancy plates of small bites of lovely savoury things arrived and Georgie and I tucked in and Sohaib laughed and said, 'Hungry girls, we'd better order quickly.'

Georgie replied, 'Yes, I'm starving! It's days since we had lunch.'

'Georgie! Don't speak with your mouth full please,' Archie snapped and there was a brief moment where the boys stilled, drew in, tensed, alert.

'Sorry!' Georgie sang out and stuffed two more of the little crudités into her mouth in a far from lady-like fashion, 'I'm just so famished, Dad,' she added through a mouth full of pastry.

In the past, that would have been it. Archie would have blown up. This would have been tantamount to full blown insurrection. The dinner would have been over before it had started. Not that we ever went out, no, that was far too risky, we couldn't let Archie loose on the general public.

Instead, Sohaib picked up a couple of little tarts, popped them in his mouth and said, 'Me too!' and winked at Georgie.

Ted followed suit, 'And me!' spluttering a little and laughing and leaning into Sohaib as he did so.

Joe grabbed at the plate and crammed too many for his words to be audible making Georgie hoot with laughter. He then offered the delicate pastries to Archie who was not looking amused. He primly took a single tiny tartlet, examined it closely and then flicked it across the table at Georgie, resulting in surprised and delighted laughter from all of them.

'Okay, that's enough everyone. People are starting to stare. We don't want to get kicked out. I really want to eat!' I said and they quietened a little, relieved the crisis had been averted and drank their champagne and everyone looked happy.

The waiter came and took our orders and Archie asked Ted about work. 'It must be going well if you're bringing your boss out to a family meal, Edward,' he gloated.

'We're pretty much equals now, Eddie has just had another promotion. I can't lord it over him now like I used to. We're both in charge of different sectors,' Sohaib said with unmistakable pride in his voice.

'Yes, work is fine, Dad,' Ted said, 'But that's not the reason that I invited you all here. I wanted to make an announcement. Hence the champagne. I want to tell you something.'

'This is exciting,' said Joe, 'If it's not work, what can it be? Are you buying a house?'

'I don't want to play guessing games, so I'm just going to tell you. We're getting married. We're engaged.' Ted beamed at Sohaib and then at the rest of us.

'Bloody hell!' said Archie, 'That's fantastic!' And he took a gulp of champagne, 'So who's the lucky girl? When do we get to meet her? By Christ, you're a dark horse. Not a sniff of a woman about the place and then you're getting married! I hope she's not up the duff. Mind you, so what if she is? It's the twenty-first century, after all. What do you think about being grandparents, eh, Karen? Fine with me. Bet she's a bloody cracker, isn't she, son? Sonab here going to be your best man, eh? Have a bloody riot of a stag do, eh? Go to a strip club and ...'

'Dad!' Ted had cut in as quickly as he could, but Archie was just rambling on one of his rants, 'Dad. There is no girl.' He was furious, hurt, embarrassed.

'What?' Archie looked non-plussed.

'It's *Sohaib*,' he said his name to make Archie hear it, '*Sohaib* is who I'm marrying. *Sohaib* is who I'm in love with. *Sohaib* is the love of my life. When he asked me to marry him, of course I said yes.' And he leant towards Sohaib and tenderly kissed him.

At that moment, everything made sense and I felt so happy for them. 'Congratulations, darling,' I said and stood up to hug him and Sohaib, and Joe was on his feet too, shaking their hands and clasping his brother tightly to him.

Joe took his brother's face in his hands, 'I think you're a bit young to be tying the knot, but I'll let it slide,' and they laughed.

'I hope there's going to be bridesmaids,' Georgie said and insisted on sitting in between Ted and Sohaib and getting a full picture of Sohaib's family. She got her notebook out and began to sketch her dress for the wedding; Sohaib very sweetly indulged her, agreeing that bells would be a nice addition to any bridesmaid's dress.

Archie had said nothing.

Not a word of congratulations, not a word of apology for his assumptions and the offence he had caused. Nothing.

Both boys ignored him.

The food arrived and we ate heartily as if we had all been starving. Except Archie. He barely touched his.

Georgie ordered an excessive, mountainous ice-cream sundae and managed to spill much of it down her front. Ted and Sohaib went to help her get cleaned up in the trendy unisex bathrooms.

'Is this all some kind of joke?' Archie said.

'What do you mean, Dad?' Joe said patiently.

'Edward isn't gay. That man has tricked him. Brain-washed him in some way.' He was livid.

'Teddy has always been gay,' Joe said gently.

'No, he fucking has not,' Archie replied, quietly furious.

'Dad, he's had lots of boyfriends. It's just that ... well you've never met them because he thought you wouldn't approve.'

'Damn right, I wouldn't approve,' he was breathing hard but casting around the table, a sure-fire sign that he wanted to throw something.

'Archie,' I said, 'What difference does it make to you, to your life? Eh? None. None at all. You should be happy that he's found someone to be happy with. That's the important thing. That he's happy.'

'Shut up Karen,' he glares at me, 'I suppose you knew all about this and kept it from me. Didn't you?'

Now here was a dilemma. Pretend I knew all along and add to Archie's suffering or tell the truth.

'I was just as much in the dark as you, Archie,' I replied, 'To be honest I feel a bit stupid that I didn't realise. That I didn't know something so basic about my own son, but he must have had his reasons for keeping it from me. His joy is the most important thing though and that should be your concern too.'

'Don't fucking lecture me, you sanctimonious bitch,' he spat out.

'Not lecturing, just trying to make you see reason, but I should know after all these years that there's sod all point in trying to do that with someone as limited as you. Please yourself Archie. Lose another person. It's not my problem.'

I saw Georgie heading back over to the table. 'Are you tired, my chicken?' I said as she squidged onto my knee rather than back into her seat, 'Where are the boys?'

'Paying the bill and, no, I'm not tired. Not one bit,' but she yawned deeply and cuddled down onto my shoulder.

Ted and Sohaib slid back into their seats. 'Bill's all taken care of,' Ted said, smiling.

'Would have been nice to have been asked,' Archie piped up huffily.

'Dad,' Joe remonstrated.

'Leave it,' Ted said easily and exchanged a look with Sohaib.

'It's getting late, Joseph,' Archie announced tightly.

'Sure, let's get going,' and he pulled the chair back from the table.

Ted and Sohaib stood as Georgie went over to kiss her dad goodnight.

'It was good to meet you, Mr Blackthorne,' Sohaib said, offering his hand.

Archie looked at Sohaib but kept his hands tightly clasped in his lap. 'Time to go, Joseph. Night, Georgie.'

Joe shrugged and Ted put his arm around Sohaib as they watched them leave.

I stepped forward. 'It was lovely to meet you, Sohaib. I hope you'll find time to come and visit Georgie and me in London. Mum and Dad have lots of room. And Mum loves to talk weddings,' I turned to Ted, 'I'm not going to apologise for your father because that's not my job anymore but I'm sorry for you that he's an idiot.'

'It's what I was expecting, Mum,' Ted said, wrapping his arms around me, 'but stupidly I hoped it might turn out better.'

He pulled back and looked at me. 'You're not surprised, are you?'

'A bit surprised that you're getting married,' I said, dodging the question. Had I been so self-absorbed not to notice something so fundamental about my son or had life with Archie just skewed everything. He was some kind of toxic sun around which we were all forced to revolve and, therefore, could never give each other the proper focus we should have.

'We'll definitely come down soon,' Sohaib said.

'Great,' I said, and I meant it. I wanted to be part of their lives. I wanted to know who Sohaib was and to make sure he was good enough for Ted.

Georgie insisted on splashing through the puddles on the way back to the hotel as she knew her socks would be off soon. I didn't care. I was tired and full, and I loved the feeling of her stretching my arm as she swung and leapt, gripping my hand tightly as she splattered her way to our temporary home.

2

Dad and I are sitting reading the Sunday papers. I delight in the fact that they still get them delivered. Mum and Georgie have gone to the park. Again. We each have a different section. There is a fresh pot of coffee. Dad has made Sunday lunch, a small leg of lamb he has slavishly basted and perfect raspberries with a sprinkle of vanilla sugar for pudding. and now we are just relaxing. I cannot remember when I have felt so peaceful or so rested.

'When do you think, you might start dating again?' Dad says.

'What?!' I say. This is very far from what I was expecting. Normally, I would expect Dad to pass comment on Putin's progress in the Ukraine or the passage of some piece of thorny legislation through the House of Commons or even the decline of some breed of bird or mammal, but I have never known him comment on my love life much less use the word 'dating'.

'Just wondering when you were thinking you might see yourself as back in the game again.' He doesn't even look up from the paper.

'Dad!' I hardly know how to respond. 'I really don't know what 'the game' is anymore, let alone whether I want to be in it.'

'I think you should think about it. After all, you're not getting any younger.'

'What's that got to do with it?' I put down my paper and consider my father. He lowers his too, and peers over his glasses at me, hazel eyes now dull with age, but an unmistakable flicker of genuine interest. 'Actually Dad, I don't think I want to get involved with anyone again. I've had enough of men. I want to be on my own. Live my life the way I want to live it. Just with Georgie.'

'Not every man's like him, Karen,' Dad says, 'I'm not.'

'I know,' I agree, 'but my experience is that they're not that great. You may be an exception to the rule.'

Dad sighs and returns to his paper. 'Honey, don't go shootin' all the dogs cos one of them's got fleas,' he says in an American drawl.

'I'm sorry?' I say.

'It's from *Hud*,' he says, 'One of my favourite films, an old sixties Western, Paul Newman.' The paper goes down again, and he leans across to refill his coffee cup, then stares up at the ceiling, obviously puzzling over his advice. 'Come to think of it, he plays an absolute rotter though. Uses that line to try to convince Patricia Neal to sleep with him. On reflection, he's definitely a dog with fleas.' He sips the coffee, 'What a disappointment. Never realised that in my youth. Ah, well.'

'Well, there you have it Dad, another con man, a trickster. I've known too many, and Archie was the ultimate. I need to steer clear. And frankly, my dear, I don't need a man.'

He smiles at me. 'You're right of course. I was just checking. I would far rather you stayed on your own if you're happy enough that way,' He pauses for a moment, 'I can't tell you what a blessing it is for us to have you and Georgie ...' and he swallows the words, and his eyes fill with tears.

The doorbell saves us both from any further discomfort. We have never been an openly demonstrative family. It must have been hard for him to even raise the subject as a matter for concern.

Burrowing in his pocket for a hankie, he rises to make for the front door. 'Probably Jehovah's Witnesses as it's a Sunday,' he grumbles, 'I'll head them off at the pass,' and he adopts a John Wayne swagger and totters out of the dining room, bandy legged on imaginary cowboy boots.

I return to the paper. I'm on the theatre page scouring for something for Georgie and me to see over the next week or two.

'Surprise!' Tess yells and she's hoisted me out of the chair and into her arms before I can take in that she's here.

'You're supposed to be in Bucharest,' I say as we twirl around the room like silly, giddy children.

'I know, but I'm not. Isn't it wonderful?' and she plants a big kiss on my cheek.

The last I had heard she was back with Isla, and they were going on tour again through Europe. The rain had facilitated a hasty exit from the UK; Tess really was a fair-weather friend. She craved the warmth. 'I'm part reptile. I can't help it,' she justified on her last phone call to me just after the fire.

'What are you doing here? It doesn't make sense,' I slowed her down from her furious hugging and dancing.

'Had a bit of bad news. Isla's brother. Not so good. She had to come back. So, I'm here. She's back up in Scotland and I thought I'd pop in. Just for a wee while. Wanted to see how you were doing.' She looks fantastic, of course, tanned, fresh, and she smells so good, I want to bite her.

'I've brought you something,' she grins and disappears into the hall. She returns with what is obviously a picture. A large one, wrapped in brown paper and string and looking curiously old-fashioned because of it.

She thrusts it at me. 'Open it,' she demands and plops down onto the sofa.

I obey. Her wish has always been my command.

As I peel back the paper I see a gilt frame, a matt navy mounting board. It takes me a while to work it out. Tess has had our tarot cards framed. Beautifully framed. They are unrecognisable behind the gleaming glass.

'I don't understand,' I say, 'The fire?'

'I snatched them from your dressing table and stuffed them into my shorts pocket before I went out the window. I couldn't leave them behind. They've been everywhere with me. It felt like bad luck to let them burn.'

I snort. 'I'm not sure what followed was good luck,' I say carefully.

'We survived,' she says, 'We all survived.'

I look at the cards. Hers lined up at the top and mine at the bottom. The navy background makes the faded colours sing, restores them to their past vibrancy. Their edges are fat and worn but they look so special, so perfectly placed, so elevated in this lovely frame. 'I still don't get it,' I say, 'Why are you giving them to me now? You've had them with you for years. What's changed?'

Tess is on her feet and by my side and looking at the cards. 'It's over Karen. You're safe. Whatever the tarot told us, we don't have to worry about it anymore. That part of our life is finished. Look at the card,' and she points at the final card on the bottom row. The Tower.

If someone had asked me to describe the card, I don't know what I would have said. A tower that looks like the chess piece. Many of the details I had missed though. I stare closely at the medieval building. There are flames coming from the upper windows and two figures are plummeting, headfirst, from the roof. Most shocking of all, there is a bolt of lightning.

'Oh Tess,' I say, 'that's creepy.'

'We were looking for interpretations but that's what happened in real life. Your life. My life. A bolt of lightning. A terrible storm and your house burnt more or less to the ground.' She has her arms around my waist, her head on my shoulder looking at the cards.

'And two people fell from the roof,' I say. The dull thud of Archie hitting the ground replays in my head, the knot uncoiling above Ted's hands is as vivid as if it were a moment ago.

'Yep,' she says.

'I don't know if I like this,' I say.

'Don't worry about it,' she says, her voice light, 'We had the cards, or they found us, but,' and she turns around to face me, 'what if nothing we did mattered?'

'What?' I say.

'What if it was all decided already and the cards were just a window into the future?' She's smiling still.

'I don't understand,' I reply

'We did nothing to change our futures because there was nothing we could do. Everything that was going to happen was destined to happen. The cards just told us about it. And now it's over.' She smiles back at the frame.

'Then what's the point? What's the point of knowing what's ahead?' I say.

'Beats me,' she says happily, 'All I know is everything's cool now. There's nothing after The Tower.'

I lean the frame against the sofa as Dad comes in with a tray of tea. 'Thought you might want a cuppa,' he says cheerfully.

'Love one,' Tess says moving towards the plate of biscuits he's offering but I can't take my eyes from the picture.

Tess stays the rest of the day, playing with Georgie, chatting to Mum and Dad, and pilfering some of their old clothes for costume for her next show. We say nothing more about the cards.

Georgie insists Tess reads her a long bedtime story and Mum and Dad retire to bed early. I am alone downstairs and, with the house quiet at last, I search online for more information about The Tower card.

The more I read, the more unsettled I feel. Apparently, The Tower itself is a solid structure but, because it's built on shaky foundations, it only takes one bolt of lightning to bring it down. This would appear to have been true of my entire adult life, my marriage and, indeed the farmhouse, which is now a ruin, beyond repair and awaiting demolition.

The lightning is also symbolic and represents a sudden surge of energy and insight that leads to a breakthrough or revelation. That word, revelation, keeps coming up. As I read, I picture Archie at the window over and over again. I hear Tess's voice telling me that it is not up to me who gets to live and die. As I sit in the safety of my childhood home, it is abhorrent to me that I was seriously considering letting him die. No, it was more than this. His window was locked; my doing. If Tess had not been there, I know in my heart I would have left him to perish. And I would have relished it. I would have allowed that twisted inner voice of mine to tell me that he deserved that. As Tess and I stood at the front of the house, barred by the flames from getting in, I was reliving every punch and kick and slap he rained down on me and there were so many to call upon. As she ran to the garage to find a way to free him, I was running through my life with him, all the insults and tears and hurts he had meted out on our children because I was willing myself to become his executioner. I cannot tell you how, even amongst the warmth and light of what was the exultant and joyful blaze engulfing my home, I was subsumed with such darkness, such cold, and such steely detachment from the man inside the building.

I look at everything that is so familiar around me, the clock on the mantel steadily clicking as it did throughout my childhood, the pleasant and unremarkable watercolour Dad bought Mum decades ago on a trip to the Vendee, even the hydrangea blooming at the window as it always does, year in year out, reliable and overlooked precisely because of its familiarity. I had risked the loss of everything that night. The loss of the every day. The loss of normality. Let's face it, I had lost my grip on reality. Who was I? What had I allowed myself to become in the pursuit of revenge?

I stop the rabbit warren of my thoughts, my self flagellation for my actions and read on. There is a particularly vivid interpretation. 'The Tower represents a scene of turmoil and destruction. On an ink black night, a chaotic scene unfolds. Lightning has struck a stone tower, sending its dwellers into free fall. The building begins to be swallowed by the flames as the storm rages. The lightning suggests an act of God is responsible for this natural disaster. As there will be little, if anything, left of the old structure after the dust has settled, it will be up to those remaining to rebuild. Lightning is a fitting karmic payback for the guilt of those whose fortunes come from the exploitation or abuse of others. A flash of lightning topples the hierarchy of the old order, after which everyone can have a fresh start on a more equal footing. The lightning is a flash of truth illuminating shocking revelations and paradigm shifts.'

I sit back from my laptop.

Yes, we have a chance to rebuild but can we? As a family we have lost everything because Archie has behaved so horrifically for so many years. The lightning certainly had allowed us all a new beginning, a fresh start. I look at the frame again and my eyes are drawn again to the two figures tumbling from the tower, pitching headfirst, possibly to escape the flames.

A thought strikes me. It was Archie falling off the roof that started this. Not the fire. The fire has concluded everything.

And can God or Karma, or whatever higher power there is, have decided everything all those years ago? Or is it as Tess said, that our destinies are mapped out and the tarot just gave us a view of what was already in store.

What I do know is that Tess told me that Archie was The Emperor. I also know my mother told me to wait a while to marry him and she knew nothing of the tarot.

I am exhausted. I climb upstairs to Georgie's room. Tess, as small as a girl, is sleeping next to her, the book, *Pollyanna*, open and discarded on the covers. I sit on the floor next to Georgie and lay my head on the bed next to her, taking her soft, relaxed hand in mine and I smell the sweet smell of freshly bathed child and I question why she was born into this family. Why did she have to have Archie as a father? Why did she have to suffer because of my choices?

And there we have it. We have choices and I made the wrong ones. So many times. The right one was listening to Tess. 'It's not up to you to decide. You should know that. You do know that.' I have wasted too much energy believing that the opposite was true.

I lay my head on Georgie's hand and close my eyes. It is quiet. I can hear an owl far, far away in the distance above the low gentle pulse of the city traffic. Soon the foxes will start their next campaign to breach the dustbin.

I breathe in deeply, filling my lungs and I breathe out. A long, long sigh; a letting go of all that has been before... I hold my daughter's hand and I know that I don't believe in the cards. We have escaped and we are free of him and that is what matters I believe in us, and I believe in our future, and tomorrow I will take the cards out of the frame and burn them too.

I don't want any reminders of the past; I intend to look forward.

No looking back.

Acknowledgements

Thanks to Graeme for your continued help with listening and reading and re-reading and talking through my ideas throughout the birth of this book. You are my love.

Thanks to Mum and my brother, Rory for your excellent proof-reading skills and to Rory for your valuable classic car knowledge. Much appreciated.

Thank you also to Sheila; an early reader, top-notch friend and all round cheerleader; you're terrific.

A Rust of the Heart

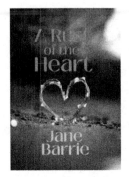

Meet Jen, eldest child, undervalued and overlooked, sharp-witted and sharp-tongued. Her desire to be the centre of attention never leaves her. Follow her story through engaging and often amusing windows into her world, decades apart over fifty years. She is not afraid to say what others often think as she navigates through a life filled with envy and dissatisfaction. Watch as Jen tries to escape her dysfunctional family; a failed actor father and reluctant mother intent on turning a ruined castle into a B and B plus her magnificent, younger sister who is the apple of everybody's eye, much to Jen's annoyance. Will she ever find happiness? Or fulfilment?

Sharply evoked characters and clarity of language plus a story with unexpected twists and turns make for a lively, page-turning read in this debut novel by Jane Barrie.

Reviews for **A Rust of the Heart**

'Highly immersive and disturbingly relatable. With rich characterisation and a plot that will keep you guessing. A definite 5 out of 5 read.'

'Intriguing plot, with well-drawn characters. Explores a family dynamic through the eyes of a seemingly unsympathetic protagonist, full of local Cumbrian colour. Highly recommended.'

'Brilliant debut novel from Jane Barrie. Really enjoyed trying to work out what the main character would do next. All the characters were very well described, the family dynamics were spot on.
Definitely a page turner, can't wait for Jane's next book!'

'At the centre of the story - exactly where she'd want to be - is Jen. Deliciously spiteful, furiously intolerant, it's difficult sometimes to dislike her as much as she deserves. Amidst the tragedy and heartbreak, the writing is laugh out loud funny; Barrie handles her minor characters superbly, setting them each like jewels within a well-crafted vignette. This book is recommended - and I'm interested to see what this new writer does next!'

'To be honest, I'm still not entirely sure what to make of this book, but there are a few aspects of which I can be certain. First, it's compelling and addictive. The characters get under your skin, and you have to keep going to find out what will happen to Jen and her family (I won't say friends, don't think she has any) in the ensuing decades. Second, it's very well written. Third, for a first novel, it's really impressive. Fourth, don't start it when you are busy elsewhere. You need to clear the decks and be able to keep going. I can't wait to see what Jane produces next.'

Find more reviews on Amazon and order your copy of <u>A Rust of the Heart</u> there.

A final word …

If you enjoyed **The Emperor Reversed,** please do leave a review on **Amazon** or **Goodreads.com**. This makes all the difference in reaching a wider audience.

Follow Jane on Facebook @ **Jane Barrie Writer,** or on Instagram **@janebarrie,** or check out her website **janebarrie.wordpress.com** to read her blog and to keep up with news of her next novel coming out Summer 2024

Printed in Great Britain
by Amazon

44766953R00155